CORNISH MI

PEBBLES & S1

CW00738881

First Printed in United Kingdom 2020

ISBN – 978-1-9996559-21

Email –davidlenderyoubooks@gmail.com

Author – Publisher

David Lenderyou

Cornish Mist Trilogy

Cornish Mist (1) – Pebbles & Stones
Cornish Mist (2) – Butterfly & Nettles
Cornish Mist (3) –Robins & Hawks

AUTHOR

David Lenderyou direct lineage dates back to the year 1318 from the Lynderiowe family in Mylor Village near Falmouth. Many of his descendants were Yeoman, Tin Miners, Pikemen, Paupers and Butchers. David was raised in Cornwall with his Father being from Falmouth and his Mum from Palmers Green, bless her, who met one another in Trafalgar Square just after the War. David laughs at the time he had to dance in the Hal an Tow on Floral day, 8th May 1971 in Helston, and having to wear his Mums tights with his mate Denis Bagnall. Life has many ups and downs and so keeping that Cornish spirit will help you on the path.

PREFACE

CORNISH MIST (1) PEBBLES & STONES

In the year 1705, the rich and arrogant Philip de Albret, has dared to plant sleepers deep into a Cornish village. Once accepted and trusted by the locals they can then get on with their plans and, once achieved, get out and get paid. Their aim is deadly and will devastate the local community of hard working and innocent families but, gain much notoriety and wealth for the proud Albret .Joshua and Rebecca, inexperienced and unbeknown to each other are brought together into a secretive world to find and expose them, aided by hushed means.

....

BRISTOL

Joshua, who lives and works in Bristol, got the job vacancy through his ability to think straight and analyse things clearly from different angles. His military career of ten years in the royal marines also helped.

However, sitting in the pub and drinking yet another tankard of ale, he felt lonely. Yes, people were around him laughing and joking, but Joshua liked to sit on his own and think life through. At thirty five years of age he was thinking where it all went wrong, why was he alone once more. Even when he was married to his beautiful wife he still felt alone.

Maybe it was the brutality of the ten years of service as a marine between the years 1693 and 1703. Also, he never quite knew whether he was a soldier or sailor, as being a marine you served both. Either way, front line action in nasty bloody wars cannot be seen as living a normal life in a civilised world.

It was then that a man approached him and asked if he was ready. Joshua picked up his tankard and in one long slurp finished off the ale. He then wiped his mouth with his sleeve and said, ''I am.'' Joshua got up and walked quietly towards the back of the Inn.

Joshua had a soft side, he knew it. When his lovely wife was pregnant with their first child she could wrap him round her little finger. He chuckled to himself at the thought but then she was a woman, they are delicate and lovely.

In front of him now was a man who thinks he owns the place. They are both alone in the filthy outhouse where people urinate and loosen their bowels.

The man has been spouting his mouth off that he rules all the men in the munitions factory at the Bristol Docks. And so, it was now down to Joshua to right this wrong. Joshua is prepared but doesn't say a word and keeps still and quiet, waiting for the man to make his move. Sometimes Joshua will attack first but this time his inner feeling is to wait. Then, as quick a flash and without thought, the man made his move. Joshua, standing only a few feet away, remains still and doesn't move an inch but raises his inner tenses to almost breaking point, like a praying mantis ready to jump. Then, a split second later, Joshua tacks his body forward slightly off centre and in one flowing movement drops to the floor. While doing so, he whips his legs to the side taking the man's feet clear off the floor. Brutal as it is only one person is going to walk out. It's the rules.

The man being taken completely by surprise and totally off balance, crashed to the ground. Like an agile wasp, Joshua needs no further thought as what to do next. He immediately goes for the head and when it is done, it is done. When the man enters the state of total surrender, whether conscious or unconscious, Joshua backs off.

Leaving the beaten man on the toilet floor Joshua walks out. On entering back into the bar area, he notices the deadly silence and so without fuss or ado walks straight out of the Inn. Then with his head down, Joshua walks quietly away heading for his little cottage alone.

Once he was inside his small home, Joshua picks up the brandy bottle and then sitting down in front of the fire, feels nothing but shame. Taking another large gulp, he looks into the flames and thinks why, why does he do it, there must be something out there better than this or, is this it.

He misses his wife and his lovely Mum and the warmth of the Cornish family. His Father is also working away and hasn't contacted him in years. Joshua tells himself again that there is only one person who can change the situation and that is you Joshua. 'You have a good brain and a good heart.'

After polishing off the brandy, Joshua fumbles his way up the stairs to his bedroom. Then falling on the bed he tries to undress himself but this proves impossible as he cannot coordinate his mind with his body. After two or three minutes of this chaotic disorder, Joshua just gives up and lays outstretched fully clothed. When three or minutes of total quiet had passed, peace and rest finally enters his body through sleep.

When the morning comes Joshua is suddenly woken up by a continual knocking on the front door. Thinking it may be a reprisal from last night, he starts to make plans of escape. But then, even with a heavy head from the intake of last night's brandy, changed his mind and gets up and moves quietly to the window. Keeping his body back from being seen, he peers out through the side curtain and sees a young lad. Joshua did not feel any fear from this young man and so walked down to open the door.

"Excuse me Sir, are you Mr Pendragon?" "Yes that is I," Joshua replied. "My master has asked me to ask you if you could come to our offices this morning as he would like to talk with you." "And who are you?" "Oh sorry Sir, my name is Clive, and my master is Mr Bray of Bray and Butler Solicitors in the high street." "Is it about last night?" "I don't know Sir, I only know to give you the message." "Fine, then tell Mr Bray, your master, I will be there within the hour."

Joshua didn't know whether he should go or not. If he did it could be a trap and if he didn't he would never know what it was all about. So, he decided to freshen up and go to this Solicitor but with a fully loaded pistol as support.

Being an early Saturday morning the streets were not as busy which Joshua appreciated. He wasn't feeling great but was sprite enough to be curious as to what these people wanted with him. On his arrival he was ushered into Mr Bray's office where a middle aged man got up and said, "Mr Pendragon, thank you for coming please take a seat." "Is this about last night?" Joshua asked. "I don't think so, why what happened last night?" "Sorry, I think I have my lines crossed, may I ask what you want of me?"

"Please, I have been told to inform you that your Father has died whilst away abroad and that Mr Trevean at Trevean and Trevean Solicitors in Helston has asked that you visit them this Wednesday morning to go over his will. Everything has been arranged for your carriage to Helston from the Queens Head this Monday morning. Overnight accommodation has also been arranged and all has been paid in advance. I am also this day to give you a purse of ten shillings."

Joshua looked in disbelief and was quietly letting the loving thoughts of his Father subside before he said anything. Then when the reality had set in said, ''Yes of course I will go as asked.'' Mr Bray had done as asked with nothing really more to add. And so, with matters concluded Joshua slowly walked home in deep thought. His mother, his wife, his still born daughter and now his Father, all have gone. How life goes on with hurt and pain and still the world turns. He will get himself ready.

Joshua didn't venture out after the news of his Father. He stayed by the fire with brandy and pipe reminiscing over his family and the laughs and love he got from them all. But something somewhere had changed and so he made himself some hot food, tidied the house and washed some clothes, something he hadn't done in ages. On the Sunday and Monday he even shaved. Although money doesn't do it for Joshua, having the cash of ten shillings gave him the confidence to forget about work for a while. It also gave him some peace to stop trying to make ends meet every day and also take the pressure off in trying to save a little, no matter how small.

Joshua looked at the instructions on the ticket given to him by Mr Bray. He was to stay in Exeter the first night and then the Blue Anchor in Helston the night after. Joshua felt good about going home to Cornwall.

The travel to Cornwall proved long and tiresome but somehow made Joshua feel alive, but then sad when he thought of his Fathers passing away. However on the Wednesday he arrived in Helston on time at the said Solicitors and escorted to Mr Trevean's office.

"Joshua, thank you for coming and please let me say how sorry we are to hear of your Father's death, he was a good man." "Thank you," Joshua replied.

Once Joshua was seated the Mr Trevean did not waste any time saying, "Well let's get down to things shall we Joshua, I have your Father's Last Will & Testament." "Before you start, where is my Father?" "We do not know exactly where he is but believe he drowned abroad in Spain and his body lost. A memorial service is to be held in the Church at Gunwalloe Cove this Sunday coming." Joshua never really knew what his Father did and so the drowning and loss of his body didn't surprise him at all. Mr Trevean went on to discuss the will and testament.

"Joshua, your late Father John last will and testament is very specific in that everything is to be passed to you including his cottage at Gunwalloe. However, there is one proviso in that you live there directly receiving a stipend of twenty pounds paid out of his, and now your Pension fund, every month by the executor solicitors Trevean & Trevean in Helston."

Joshua sat quietly throughout and listened intently to what was being said and when Mr Trevean had finished asked, "and what if I decide not to live in the cottage?" "Then the will would not have been met as your Father had wished and you will get nothing." "And where will the cottage go?" "It will go to our good Queens Estate." Joshua loved the Queen that much is true but not that much. "And I receive Twenty pounds per month also for doing nothing?" "That is correct." "Where's the catch?" "Mr Pendragon, your Father was a good man and had worked hard, there are no catches. Now please could you answer whether you accept or not?"

Joshua looked up to the ceiling trying to find some kind of help from his Father. He looked back at Mr Trevean and realised that this is the opening for a better life and why not take up his Father's wishes. It just felt strange that he need not have to toil for money anymore.

He would also have to leave Bristol where memories of his wife and daughter lay and that in its self would be hard. Leaving the Munitions Factory would be a joy. Joshua silently thanked his Father and then with a calm voice said, "You are right Mr Trevean, the answer is Yes, I accept and feel proud that I had a hard working Father as you described."

With that Mr Trevean asked Joshua to sign in several places. "By the way Joshua, there is a small footnote at the end of the Testament which I have been asked to read to you." "Please do." "It reads, should you meet a person who asks you to help a colleague, trust them."

PLYMOUTH

"The peas are lovely Rebecca but I think you may have over cooked the swede." She looked up across the table in dismay but just smiled politely and said nothing. However, inside she thought there must be more to life than peas and swede. She really just wanted to throw a saucepan in the air or jump up on the table and wiggle her bottom at him.

For three years Rebecca had lived with Simon who was a respectable clerk at Samuels Ship Builders in Plymouth. Three years and they hadn't had sex for two of them. She looked across the table at him while he was in full concentration on cutting a roast potato on his plate to the exact size before putting it into his mouth. Rebecca sat without word but her mind started to drift back. Simon was a really nice man at heart and in his late fifties when they met. Rebecca was twenty eight. She had been hurt badly by her previous partner who had gone astray and so with that inner pain of loss decided to be on her own. After two years of isolation and saying no thank you to many advancing men, she decided to hitch up with Simon who was very decent and see where things go.

She didn't love him as she had loved her previous man Cuthbert. But then Simon in truthful reality just wanted company and someone who could cook. Rebecca could do both and agreed to move into his small cottage.

She knew Simon had been married for twenty years and that his wife had passed away. She also knew that he had loved his wife very much. But, in this relationship there was no love, just living and eating under the same roof.

11

They had tried sex but Simon preferred not to and so Rebecca obliges every night by saying nicely, "Good night Simon." And the same respectable response comes back, "Good night My Dear."

Cuthbert, her previous love, would have had none of this and would have kissed and squeezed her to death but then Cuthbert was rebellious and liked his drink. They had been together for four years during which time she had miscarried twice. She shouldn't really think about him as it upsets her but one thing she knows, she cannot stay here and waste her life away in the kitchen of a man she doesn't love just for the sake of it. She was only thirty-one years old, shapely and full of spirit in the knowledge that surely there must be more out there. But one thing about Rebecca is her honesty and not letting people down. She also knew that if one day she did indeed leave him, he would be alright and was sure he would understand.

"Are you alright my dear?" Rebecca realised she was day dreaming and hadn't eaten hardly anything. "Yes thank you, I was just thinking," she replied. She then continued, "I think tomorrow I will get up early and go into town to buy a new bonnet." "You know I have a lie in on Saturdays my dear," Simon replied. "Yes I know you do, I will not disturb your sleep and will go on my own. I think I need some fresh air and it will also give Lilly some needed exercise. I will put some breakfast out for you."

After both had finished their food and Rebecca had done the washing up, she went outside to the back yard to see her lovely horse Lilly. Then, while gently brushing her down she quietly talked to her as if she were a human being. Rebecca spoke about her emptiness with Simon and of her missing her Father who died when she was young. She also talked of her Mother, Jeanne, who she had not seen or spoken to for many years and who was working abroad somewhere.

Come next morning Rebecca was already up and getting herself dressed for the run into town when she heard a continual knocking on the front door. Not wanting the noise to wake Simon she quickly rushed down the stairs and opened the door.

"Excuse Madam, are you Ms Pendarve?" "Yes that is I," she replied. "My master has asked me to ask you if you could come to our offices this morning as he would like to talk with you." "And who are you?" "Oh sorry, my name is Ben and my master is Mr Johnson of Johnsons Solicitors in Kings Street." "What is it about?" "I don't know my lady, only to give you the message." "Fine, tell him I will be there within the hour." Rebecca closed the door and quickly finished off getting dressed and while doing so made the decision not to tell Simon.

On arriving at the Solicitors premises she was ushered into Mr Johnson's office where a middle aged man got up and said, "Ms Pendarve, thank you for coming please take a seat." "Excuse me," she replied, "before I do anything, please tell me what you want of me?" "Please, I'm sorry, I have been told to inform you that your Mother Jeanne has died whilst abroad and that Mr Trevean at Trevean and Trevean Solicitors in Helston has asked that you visit them this Tuesday morning to go over her last will and testament. Everything has been arranged for your carriage from the Kings Arms this Monday morning including overnight accommodation and, all has been paid in advance. I am also to give you a purse of ten shillings this day." Rebecca looked on in disbelief and was quietly letting the thoughts of her Mother subside before she said anything. "Yes of course I will go as requested." After a few more minutes of discussion and matters concluded, Rebecca went out to Lilly and rode home while in deep thought of her Father, and now her Mother gone. She must be strong and get herself ready.

When she entered the cottage Simon was already up and seeing nothing in her hands said, "Where is your new bonnet?". "Oh, I couldn't find the right one," she replied and then quietly turned around and let herself out again to be with Lilly. Something inside her would not let her tell Simon anything about her visit to the Solicitors and what she had been told.

The weekend carried on at the same slow pace and Rebecca tried to act normal but kept reminiscing over her Parents and the laughs and love she got from them. But, she kept her spirit up and Simon didn't notice a thing. However, she had to think of something to tell Simon. She didn't want to lie to him and so decided to write him a letter. She would say, she has gone to Cornwall to speak to her Mother about urgent matters of Family and would be back when she could and he need not worry.

Rebecca looked at the instructions on the ticket given to her by Mr Johnson. She was to stay the night at an Inn called the Blue Anchor in Helston ready for the meeting with the Solicitors Tuesday morning. Rebecca felt good about going home to Cornwall and the ten shilling purse was a blessing to ease things for a while.

The Monday morning came and so getting up very early and without murmur from Simon, Rebecca quietly got her things together. Leaving the message for Simon on the mantel piece she quietly went out to see Lilly. Then, after giving her horse a loving kiss, she left the cottage.

The trip down to Cornwall with the overnight stay at the Blue Anchor went well and as planned. And so, the Tuesday morning came and after an early breakfast she walked out of the Inn to head for the Solicitors to meet Mr Trevean.

''Rebecca, thank you for coming and please let me say how sorry we are to hear of your Mothers passing, she was a good lady.'' ''Thank you Mr Trevean,'' Rebecca replied. ''Well, let's get down to business, as they say, I have your Mother's Last Will & Testament.'' ''Before you start, what exactly happened and where is my Mother?'' ''We don't know the exact details but we believe that she drowned somewhere abroad in Spain and her body was lost. A memorial service is being held in the Church at Marazion this Sunday coming.'' Rebecca never really knew what her Mother did and although emotionally upset, the drowning and the loss of her body didn't surprise her at all. Then, staying quiet, Mr Trevean carried on discussing further the will and testament.

''Rebecca, your Mother Jeanne, last will and testament is very specific, everything is to be passed to you including her cottage at Marazion. However, there is one proviso in that you live there directly receiving a stipend of twenty pounds paid out of her, and now your Pension fund, every month by the executor solicitors Trevean & Trevean in Helston.''

15

Rebecca sat quietly throughout and listened intently to what was being said and when Mr Trevean had finished asked, "and what if I decide not to live in the cottage?" "Then the will is incomplete as your Mother wished and you get nothing." "And where will the cottage go?" "It will go to our good Queens Estate."

Rebecca hesitated and was silent as she needed to think clearly. Mr Trevean understood and in respect waited without word for her response, but then only after a short while interrupted Rebecca's thoughts by saying, "Ms Pendarve, I am sorry for your loss but we do need a clear yes or no to proceed?" She looked back at Mr Trevean and realised that this could well be a blessing in disguise for a better life she had been wishing for.

She would need to leave Plymouth behind but there was nothing there anyway. "Sorry Mr Trevean, the answer is yes but I have my horse Lilly who is dear to me at my address in Plymouth and a person named Simon whom I live with, what am I to do with them?"

"Is it your wish that this person Simon lives with you at Marazion?" Rebecca went silent and knew deep down she did not and this would be the end of their so called relationship. It would also be a turning point in her life. "The answer to that Mr Trevean is no, I do not wish that but I do not wish for him to be left in limbo not knowing if I will come back." "Very well Ms Pendarve then we on your Mothers behalf will sort these things out for you and be rest assured it will be done with discretion and respect."

With that Mr Trevean asked Ms Pendarve to sign in several places. "By the way Ms Pendarve there is a small footnote at the end of the Testament which I have been asked to read to you?" "Please do." "It reads, should you, my beautiful Daughter, meet a person who asks you to help a colleague, trust them."

FRANCE

Pierre Bouchier and his team of three were sitting round the table by the fire in the Morlaix Tavern, South West France. "So what are we having to drink," Pierre Bouchier said joyously. Jacques immediately replied, "Cognac," quickly followed by Zoe asking for the same and then, "I will have a small shandy," coming from Pascal. Pierre then turned to the waiter standing close by and spoke the order, "one large bottle of your best cognac with three glasses and a small shandy, oh and two pipes."

The Inn was relatively empty apart from a few men at the bar and the fruit and vegetable wholesaler sitting in the corner who works his stall every day in the town's market, and has done so for years.

With the drinks poured and pipes lit, one for Zoe and one for Jacques, Pierre raised his glass to give a quiet toast, "to the success of this new mission!" They all, except Pascal, drank back in one gulp and then looked for refills, Pascal took just a little sip as he didn't like drinking especially the way it made people lose control of their brains.

With the cognac now being drunk freely and at random Pierre went over the plan again. He asked Pascal if he was confident, and he replied, "If the house you have put us in lines up with the geography I have described and calculated then most certainly things will align correctly." Pierre Bouchier disliked Pascal and his young arrogance. But Pascal was not chosen by him but by his master Philip de Albret, Count of Morlaix, for reasons of his mathematical type genius and family ties. Pierre also disliked the way he looked at Zoe as Zoe was his and his alone and they had a private agreement together.

Zoe also didn't like Pascal as he kept looking at her breasts and smiling and licking his lips when she bent forward. She wanted to hit him about the head and for him to show respect but she is streetwise and plays the game, especially this game of cat and mouse. Sexually she would eat him alive and so each time he leered at her she would flutter her eyelids as if butter wouldn't melt in her mouth.

Jacques who was older and wiser of them all thought Pascal was simply impertinent and not up to the job. But Jacques was tired of this type of work and knew this would be his last task as he needed to get a life.

After a few more cognacs Pierre then said, "listen you three, your ship sails very early tomorrow morning for the Cornish coast of Sennon and it's getting late, are there any last questions you would have of me before I leave you." All three remained silent knowing the long difficult task that lay ahead which may take one or two years to complete and was classed as very dangerous. Each of them looked into their glasses and said nothing.

"Good then let's raise our glasses once again to success." "By the way," Pierre continued, "you have not heard the good news of last week's encounter in which our Navy destroyed the English assassins."

Jacques ears pricked up on what Pierre had just said and was the first to reply saying, "the word we got was that the English Galleon got away." "Indeed, it did Jacques but not before we blew up the little boat in which they were

19

escaping. It was destroyed with a direct hit after only two rounds of ranging fire at half a mile which is excellent and a credit to our gallant sailors."

"How can you be sure everyone died in the little boat," Jacques replied. Pierre, Zoe and Pascal looked at Jacques with quizzical eyes wondering why he was asking these negative questions. "Because Jacques after the cowardly little English Galleon ran away our Navy moved in to look for survivors and found none alive." Jacques realised his questions of doubt had spooked some kind of distrust and loyalty so quickly changed his attitude and responded, "My apologies Pierre for questioning you but sometimes I hear these things and the truth is sometimes very different. I just wanted proof of our success that is all." This seemed to do the trick and took away the puzzled looks from the others.

Jacques went on, "so let's raise our glasses to our gallant and heroic French Navy." They all obliged in unison except for Jacques himself who copied them all with the raising of his glass but didn't drink the cognac.

His heart had literally been cut in two as if that cannon shot had actually killed him.

Chapter 1

Joshua was standing by the window in his warm inherited cottage at Gunwalloe looking out at the cold wet windy weather. It was early in the morning and he was contemplating whether he should go to the beach or not. If he does he will sit for hours on the rocks and watch the world go by and let the spiritual vibration of life enter his mind and body. It doesn't matter to Joshua if the weather is terrible or glorious as it all depends on how you look at things. He always sits in the same place towards the right of the beach near the old church where the rocks are most rugged. He sits for hours until his body clock says enough, you have been rejuvenated through the power of the sea and the freshness of the air.

He also likes to think and visualise things such as the spray of the surf or a leaf blowing in the air or a squirrel running about. He watches and wonders on how are things made and thinks how life is just unbelievable.

Joshua moved away from the window and sat down by the fire to think about what he will do. Even though it was cold and rainy his mind was pretty much made up. Taking the boiling pot off the fire he started to make his tea and once done he fetched his tobacco and pipe. Taking a sip of his tea and a long puff on the pipe Joshua sat back and with an inner smile decided that yes he would go. Then weirdly as he said this an icy cold chill came at the back of his neck which then ran down the full length of his spine. Joshua shivered the cold chill away and put it down to the thought of going out in the icy weather. "Hmmm," he mumbled to himself.

His little cottage is situated about a mile from the cove set up high with lovely gardens of floral and beautiful views of the sea. From the front Joshua can see way out over the ocean and its beautiful aura of strength. The cottage has one bedroom and one work/utility room. There was also a kitchen come restroom with an open fireplace and good chimney. The back garden was full of trees and shrubbery and the front was laid to grass that sloped downwards away from the house. In the summer it's beautiful and in the winter it's beautiful.

After Joshua drank the welcome morning tea and with the smoking of the pipe finished he was ready. He got up and went over by the door to put on his coat and warm woolly hat. Then after making sure the fire was down and safe put on his boots and went out making sure the door was securely closed door behind him. When he feels at peace and the weather is much warmer he would take along Queenie and Cecil or being more precise they, his two Jack Russells, would take him. But as it was cold and wet they did not move from the fireplace and so he left them by the warmth of the hearth to await his return.

Once outside the front door Joshua says in his mind that he is ready for the day. So standing still with a straight back he starts to take some long deep breaths of fresh air mixed with some unwelcome rain. As he fills his lungs and exhales he then bends down and touches his toes. Stretching back to the upright position he swishes his arms back and forth and sticks his chest out. With the little exercise done he walks down the path to the little cottage gate which he opens and closes with a certain pride. At thirty-five years of age he feels pretty good and rather healthy he thinks to himself.

The beautiful thing about this walk is that the beach and the rocks are never out of his sight which gives him much pleasure. Joshua could also walk faster but now walks at a slower pace as he has slipped over many times before and landed on his bum which immediately humbles one.

The first thing he noticed when getting to the beach was it being empty of the human species which he was glad of as he needed this day to fully cleanse his brain and think. The old church set to the right on the rocks was being quiet and calm as usual but Joshua knew you only need to enter it and the spirit of the Lord will talk with you.

Joshua saw the tide was coming in with an off shore wind so the spray of the crashing waves was being held up in the air in slow motion. Lovely he thought just how Joshua likes it. After sitting down on a smooth rock that fitted Joshua's bottom posture just right the feeling of being comfortable started taking effect. He then started to stretch his eyes wide so he can get the full freshness of the chilled wind mixed with the cold wet of the rain deep into the eye sockets. This exercise always felt to Joshua like an injection of nature's medicine. When finished Joshua reached into his pocket and brought out his new technology miniature telescope which he bought from Bristol and now keeps on him most if not all of the time. Why he purchased such a thing he never really understood as just seemed a natural thing to do.

Joshua then relaxes for an hour or so just being himself with nature sometimes looking through the glass and sometimes just closing his eyes and doing nothing. This easy method allowed him to digest his problems in life of which gladly most were now put into a better perspective.

The cold isolation and freshness of the sea are giving him back a better feeling of patience, calmness and peace. As he smiles he notices a couple of tall ships out on the horizon. "What a beautiful life I have," he says to himself.

Drawing his legs up and resting his elbows on his knees he moved his telescope to his eye and steadied himself. He needed to be very still to focus on the ships and get a better view but they were too far off to get any real detail. So accepting this fact and keeping the scope to his eye he slowly started traversing the scope across the other side of the beach. Then gently gliding the scope to the big caves with mouths as dark as the night was when he saw a single person looking directly back at him.

Joshua immediately dropped the scope from his eye and rubbed it and then raised the scope again on the human target at around three hundred yards away. Even after sharpening the focus he still couldn't see the face as it was shrouded in a veil or something and then he saw he or she, Joshua wasn't quite sure, turn away and walk straight into the furthest and darkest cave.

"How can that be, what the, am I seeing things," he said to himself. Joshua works on logic but it felt to him as the person almost acknowledged Joshua seeing him. He rewound his visual brain to run over the sight again but this time in a slower motion. It was as if the person knew when Joshua had seen him or her as then the person's twizzled their right hand fingers like a magician who rolls a penny through the fingers. Was it some form of code? Joshua noticed the person was not smartly dressed but casual and appeared capable and confident but with no arrogance.

Joshua didn't move but started to rub his chin in deep thought and squinting in almost disbelief. What was that all about? He wanted to make a pipe and sit back to work this out but was still in awe of what he had seen and so kept his eye over the beach at the cave's entrance. All right I get it thinks Joshua, let's wait this out, I will sit here and you whoever you are you sit in the cave. "That's good Joshua a very reasonable solution," he said to himself.

Trying to act casual, Joshua decides to make a pipe and after fluffing the tinder up on top the tobacco flints it alight and takes a long slow puff. Joshua has also come prepared, just in case, with a hip flask of Cherry Brandy. These little naughty luxuries allow Joshua to fully relax and so in between his puffing, he takes a lovely nip. After a couple of these little naughty habits are completed Joshua picks up his scope and focuses again on the tall ships out at sea. However, even while his right eye is squeezed into the scope he cannot but open his left eye to peer over to the cave area.

After one hour had passed Joshua's curiosity is now on a high as the person who went into the cave should be out by now but, they had not. He was also getting very cold and so was thinking of heading back to the warm cottage. However, his mind kept being drawn to the cave but then an instinct of inner defence kicked in, it could be a trap? Overreacting doesn't do it for Joshua, calm and logic are his way.

However, he cannot hold his curiosity back anymore as his brain says it is not logical for someone to go into a cave and not come out especially, after all this time. He decides this is silly and so after getting his gear together he gets up and walks confidently over to the lion's den. Once across the sand and getting near the entrance of the cave he shouts, "Hello there!" There was no reply so he moved closer and stopped and repeated, "Hello there!" Again there was nothing. Joshua was now totally confused, if someone went into this cave and did not come out then they must be in there.

Joshua took a deep breath and inched forward to the cave's mouth. He looked in and around but saw no person but he did see a shiny object located on a small rock about ten feet into the cave. He carefully moved forward towards it and then saw it was just a bloody tin box. He started to chuckle to himself and thought how innocuous a simple tin box is. But then thought, if something means nothing, it must mean something and that's what was drawing him ever closer to it. Still very aware that the unknown person had simply vanished, which just cannot be, Joshua got himself to the tin box and as he bent down to take a closer look he saw the words in bold lettering, 'Hello Joshua.'

Joshua stared in utter amazement at his name and then quickly looked about the cave for the other human who came in before him over an hour ago. Joshua was now alarmed and knew he had to get away. Quickly picking up the tin box he ran out onto the open sand. Once outside and a safe distance away from the cave he stopped and took a deep breath to calm his mind down and take stock.

'Alright,' he says to himself, 'I'm in the open and I have escape routes' but for some reason, he still felt that someone was looking at him. However, the feeling was that whoever was watching him was not menacing, more observational.

Joshua then decided that enough was enough and return to his cottage so turned about and started making his way back up the beach. While Joshua walked he kept thinking and shaking his head in bewilderment at what he had just seen and then at the same time trying to make sense of it all. After ten minutes of gentle walk and still in quiet thought Joshua arrived at his front gate and as he started to open it, he heard, "Hello Joshua."

Looking up he saw a woman standing by his front door with her arms by her side and moving her fingers like a crab. Bemused he blurted out "Good day" as natural as one would to an attractive lady. He always feels very comfortable around the opposite sex, fully believing they are better creatures than the male. Maybe that's to do with his beautiful mother and her loving simplicity versus his experience of brutal pub brawls and the knowledge that some males have bad attitudes and big egos. Nevertheless, he must be on his guard. You never know.

Joshua closed the gate and walked toward this unknown lady but she showed no sign of anxiety. She appeared calm and friendly with a posture of openness. She was about five foot four inches tall with good body shape, strawberry fair hair, and a full featured face with lovely green eyes and full lips. She looked around thirty three years of age and all in all, very attractive. The rolling fingers type motion was the one he saw the person on the beach do whilst looking through his telescope. What is this Joshua thought, what is going on here? If she is the person on the beach, and he can see that she is, as she is holding the large hat and veil he saw through his telescope, how did she get to his cottage before him?

"I apologise for surprising you at your cottage but have you the time for a chat, it's very important," she asked in a nice tone of Cornish but with a hint of something else. "Yes of course, please come in and I will make us some tea. I hope you like dogs as I have a couple of Jack Russells." "Thank you, yes I like dogs, my name is Rebecca Pendarve," she said with a certain sigh of relief. "I am Joshua Pendragon," he said with a certain formal pride but it still came out warm and friendly. "Yes," she said, "I know."

Once both inside Joshua noted that although the fire was warm it needed building. Rebecca sat on the window ledge which is about two feet thick and as with most of the cottage, whitewashed. Joshua was going to mention the ledge being cold but she didn't seem to mind and was looking thoughtfully out of the window. Queenie and Cecil liked her immediately and were at her feet sniffing away, quite extraordinary thought Joshua.

Rebecca then calmly turned her head towards Joshua and said "I believe our families are connected in some way dating way back to Henry IV." "So we are distance cousins then, completely removed over four hundred years," Joshua replied with humour. "Cousins, no, not cousins," she says with a soft chuckle, "more, how can I put it, more related through a tight code of quiet cooperation and protection"

Joshua just shrugged his shoulders and said, "I'm sorry you have lost me." He then handed over the cup to her with a saucer and then thought, funny that, with a man, it would have been an old chipped mug but for some unknown reason he automatically made the tea with cup and saucer. Since leaving Bristol Joshua didn't have much in the way of excess and pretty much lived day by day. He often thought about his dear lovely wife who went to the Lord whilst giving birth many years ago.

He had so many questions to ask he didn't know where to start so he sat himself down by the old wooden table and started to fix up a pipe. "Ooops sorry Rebecca," he said like some school boy asking if he could go to the toilet, "do you mind if I smoke?" "No of course not, I like the smell, it reminds me of my Father before he passed to the Lord when I was very much younger." "And you're Mother?" Joshua asked. "Unfortunately, my Mother passed away two years ago somewhere in Holland, they said it was typhoid or something, but as I was away in Plymouth I didn't get to know the full the circumstances."

"I'm sorry Rebecca I didn't know, it's not easy sometimes, my Father also passed away two years ago." "Thank you Joshua it isn't easy and I still miss her every day."

"Rebecca may I ask why you are here, sorry, before I ask that, was it you on the beach by the cave earlier that I saw with my telescope?" "Yes, it was me." "Well at least I now know I wasn't seeing things which is a relief but how did you get to my cottage before me as you never left the cave, or I didn't see you leave it. In fact, how is it you know where I live?"

"Do you mind if I sit at the table with you," she said. "No of course not", he replied. She gently got up and walked over with the dogs following at her feet. Putting her tea down she looked around and then silently looked and studied Joshua and he silently studied her.

"Before I answer any of your questions Joshua may I ask, do you own this cottage?" "Yes, I do." "And may I ask how that came about?" He described his Father's last will and testament and the clauses therein. "Hmmm," she said, "it's curious don't you think that my Mother and your Father also passed away at the same time two years ago." "Not really Rebecca, it could be just a coincidence." "Ok, if I then said that my small holding in Marazion was bequeathed to me from my Mother with the same clauses in it as yours, at about the same time as yours, would that be a curious thing?" "No, not really, most parents do this."

"Please Rebecca, if you could just explain things clearly and in truth, perhaps we can discuss things a lot better." Again she started studying him as if waiting for something. Then she leaned back, looked out of the window then turned her head back again, breathed deeply, and said, "Alright I will., "Last week while I was sitting on the rocks on Marazion beach in the complete open air with many people about, a man came directly up to me. For some reason, I wasn't afraid as his demeanour was very simple, sincere and polite. He was well-dressed and politely presented himself as George Kernow. He then went on to explain why he was here, something about my Mothers work and how lovely she was. He further explained that the project she was working on was not finished and would like me to help a colleague, being you, and to carry on this project to completion."

"Did you say, Colleague?" "Yes I did Joshua, that's what I mean, it was mentioned in my Mothers will, that should someone say this to me, do not be afraid and trust them." "That's exactly what was said to me in my Father's Will."

Rebecca nodded and continued, "I was to go to Gunwalloe beach this very day at around ten thirty in the morning and wait outside the furthest cave on the left. He said he will meet me there and introduce me to the colleague in question. He also said he knows this all sounds a bit secretive but assured me that in fact, it is and I believed him."

"I got the ferry to Porthleven and then rode over here this morning and did as the gentleman suggested. When I was about twenty feet away I noted that he was already standing inside the cave just out of sight. When he saw me, he spoke brightly and cheerfully saying, 'good morning Ms Pendarve, please stay where you are.' He then said, 'if you would kindly look over to the other side of the beach you will spot a man looking through a telescope.' He then started motioning his fingers on his right hand like a crab and said, 'once the gentleman looks over, please copy what I have just done with my fingers as it is a sign of safe identification,' again I did, as asked."

"He then invited me into the cave and said, 'well done Rebecca.' For some reason, I just wasn't nervous about this man. We then went to the back of the cave to the top where a sealed hatch was opened and I followed him upwards through a neat symmetrically square tunnel, all the way up here. He talked in the reassurance that your name was Joshua Pendragon and your Father worked with my Mother. I was to wait at your front door for you to arrive. I was then to introduce myself, explain what had happened and what was said and, if you agree, we are to meet this same gentleman later today in the same cave at teatime this afternoon, meaning three thirty prompt."

Joshua's jaw dropped many times in utter disbelief as Rebecca was talking to him but once she had finished he simply said, "would you like another cup of tea?" With a heavy sigh of relief she smiled and said "yes please Joshua, thank you, I need one."

Whilst making the tea an atmosphere of tense quiet came about the cottage which felt uncomfortable but Joshua's brain was still busy trying to work out all of what she had said and put it in some logical form. He also felt this lady Rebecca didn't like the quiet atmosphere either but gave her the time and space she needed.

With refreshed cups of tea in hand Joshua said, "Rebecca, you believe this man?" "With what he knew of my mother and the openness in which he talked then Yes I do believe him. May I add that since meeting you only half an hour or so ago, I feel that you also are a good man but what you make of my tale is yours to decide."

Studying her through his silent thoughts, Joshua twists and turns his brain to try and give a logical answer but just says, "Thank you Rebecca and you too seem a good woman too and may I say a brave one at that, what would you like me to do?" "What do you suggest Joshua," She responded.

"I say we try and eat something and then gather our thoughts and be outside the cave for three thirty. We will then both find out exactly what these people want with us." He then added, "however, this time when we meet these people, I will have my pistol with me primed and ready."

Chapter 2

So there they both were Rebecca and Joshua outside the cave at the allotted time. When the tide is in, this particular cave's entrance is unapproachable, however, the tide had receded just enough. Being brave and a gentleman Joshua went in front of Rebecca and then stopped about fifteen feet away from its mouth.

Suddenly and unexpectedly out of the other cave next door came a voice. "Good afternoon Rebecca, Good afternoon Joshua, please both come over if you will."

Joshua looked at Rebecca in puzzlement but together went over and entered. Just as they got inside the man came forward and kissed Rebecca on the cheek then turned to Joshua and, standing a little more firmly, extended his hand and said, "Joshua, I am George Kernow, good afternoon, thank you both for coming." Joshua felt immediately relaxed with this man and could see how Rebecca wasn't afraid as this fellow oozed confidence but with not a shadow of any arrogance. When Joshua looked straight into his eyes he felt warmth.

George then said, "I do apologise for the little deception about not being in the right cave for this meeting but one cannot be too careful. By the way, that person over there," he pointed to someone in the shadows at the back of the cave, "that is a good friend of mine as are a couple of other persons located on the cliffs outside."

Joshua and Rebecca were both surprised that others were involved and felt a dread of fear so Joshua immediately went for his pistol as a means of protection and comfort.

George saw Joshua's reaction and quickly said, "Please do not worry Joshua they are only here to advise and protect." "Do any of them have telescopes?" Joshua asked. "Yes of course they do," George replied. "Ok, now let's get down to business shall we," said George. "Please both take a seat on the rock over there and I will sit here opposite you both."

Once all seated, George looked over to the person at the back of the cave and with a nod of approval turned to Rebecca and Joshua and with an openness of clarity said, "We require your help, both of you, and hope that you will accept." He continued, "we have reason to believe that enemy sleepers are in the towns of Newlyn and Mousehole and are executing a plan of hurt towards our good people of the Cornish in the hope of softening our defences before a full scale attack. Their success would increase the probability of them winning future attacks and also reduce their casualty rate. We do not know exactly who these people are but believe them to be French or Spanish, with help from some English hands who are sympathetic and who wish harm against us and our beautiful Queen Anne."

Joshua kept his mouth quiet and listened intently as George went on. "You may wonder why I have been so open in such a very short space of time. The answer is, we trust you both as we trusted your good Mother and Father, God rest their souls." "You worked with my Mother?" Rebecca asked in confusion. "Yes, we did." "How can that be," she responded. Joshua was all ears and listening with keen interest.

"Rather than go into the details now I promise that all will be made known to you Rebecca in due time and with full courtesy and respect as your Mother always gave me." Joshua was going to ask the same question about his Father but expected the same answer so said nothing and carried on listening.

George continued, "The information we have is that these so called sleepers have been in place for some considerable time and appear to be dug in deep. Therefore, we wish for you two, using your intelligence, logic, and life experiences to find them and flush them out. Time is not on our side and our department's only objective is keeping this realm safe for our hard working and loyal people, guided by our good Queen Anne, God Bless her." Joshua interrupted with a calmness saying, "And your department is?" "Hmmm," George mumbled back and without saying anything else turned his head to his shadowy friend at the back of the cave for a sense of support but got nothing. So he turned back and said to Joshua, "The Diplomatic Department in Whitehall, London." Joshua didn't reply.

George then carried on, "with the wars in France, Spain, and America, our defences are stretched to the maximum. That is why we, in keeping things close and tight, have personally come to see you as well as sort some other things out here in Cornwall. Penzance, Falmouth, and St Austell are very strategic places of importance to us and the enemy as they give excellent bridging status, close to their shores."

Joshua and Rebecca didn't say anything as they didn't know really what to say so silence prevailed until George again took the lead. "I don't mean to rush anyone on such an important matter but we do need to get going quite shortly and ask you both that on the brief information I have given, will you help us? Money, authority, and good people will be on hand to help where necessary. You only need to say yes at this stage and a date and time for the initial briefing will be suggested and coordinated for you both sometime early next week, at Mevagissey. You will of course have time to ask questions, which I would assume you have many." "One question to you Mr Kernow before I give my answer; did my Father trust you?" "Yes, he did and I him Joshua," George said with conviction and truth. "I also have one question Mr Kernow; did my mother work with Joshua's Father?" "Yes she did," he replied.

Again silence but Joshua felt an endearing feeling about his lost Father and the thoughts of him working with this man, Mr George Kernow. After rubbing his chin in thought and weighing up the logic of the loss versus gain and the yes versus no scenario, Joshua decided to go first by saying "Yes, I will help you, subject to verifications on further questions and answers." Not long behind came Rebecca with a yes as well.

George got up and said "Thank you both. Now let us say our goodbyes and let you two enjoy the rest of the day together. We will see you both again in Mevagissey next week, God willing. If you would both like to exit the way you came in, I and my friend will wait a little while in here."

When Rebecca and Joshua were out of sight, the supposed George Kernow turned to the shadowy figure at the far end of the cave and said, "Well Mr Kernow how was that?" "Very good Henry, I truly believed you were me, now let us be off from here and move to our next rendezvous." Once Henry had gathered his things he asked Mr Kernow, "When would you like me to deliver the information about the meeting at Mevagissey?" "You mean St Just, Henry?" "I thought you said Mevagissey?" "I did Henry but we must keep one step ahead at all times, just in case." George then said "Oh and by the way Henry the meeting is not next week it is tomorrow."

Both men then went to the back of the cave to a side access point leading through to the adjoining cave but then the real Mr Kernow stopped and turned to Henry and asked, "What are your initial thoughts of those two Henry?" "I believe them to be good people and once I advise them on their parents, I think they will be trustworthy and capable of doing a good job. Joshua is strong and logical and Rebecca is wise and thoughtful." "Just like their parents then," said George. "I think Rebecca's Mother was a little more head strong, but other than that yes you are right."

"Good," George replied, "please get a message to them both within the hour that we will see them again tomorrow at the Star Pub, St Just, at ten o'clock, a room will be made available under your name. I will see you Henry this evening in Helston at the Red Lion at eight o clock. Now let us get through this damn opening and back out through the tunnel away from here."

Once through the opening and into the main cave, both men stood at the back opposite an access door to the tunnel leading back up through to the cliff tops, the one Henry showed Rebecca to go through only a few hours ago. Henry couldn't help but think how very simple the Cornish tunnel worker's code of direction was. If the main access point to any tunnel had a carved single digit, it was a straight tunnel. If it had a carved V-type impression, it was a tunnel with a single fork. If it had a carved trident, it had two forks, right and left, not left and right and you knew where the forks were by a large square indentation on the tunnel's left wall, always in intervals of one hundred paces. So no torches were needed, simple but effective. This tunnel had a V shape and so groping the left wall and reaching the first hundred steps, George felt the indentation and barged to his right which opened the access fork and on they went.

Once George and Henry were both safely out of the tunnel they turned and waved to the two protection lookouts, who after acknowledging the signal to join them, withdrew to their tethered horses.

On getting back to the cottage Joshua opened the front door to allow Rebecca to enter first. On entering, Queenie and Cecil came rushing up as happy as can be. Joshua said, "please make yourself comfortable, I will take these two out for a quick walk and maybe on my return we could talk further." "Alright," Rebecca replied, "that sounds good I will boil some water and make us a nice cup of tea."

Rebecca looked around the cottage and noted how manly and bare it was with no creature comforts, more workable and simple. However, the cottage did have a warm feeling she thought and situated by the hearth were two snug chairs right in the line of the fire.

After a brisk ten minute walk Joshua came back with the dogs safe and refreshed. Joshua noticed that Queenie and Cecil went straight and laid down by where Rebecca was sitting and not in their usual spot. It would seem they prefer Rebecca to him, Joshua thought. But he accepted this rebuff with a smile and then took a deep breath and said, "so what do you make of it all Rebecca?" "I'm not too sure Joshua, my brain is trying to make sense of it all, only early this morning I was in Marazion thinking how lovely and simple my life is, and now I am all over the place. One thing I do know is, George Kernow knows an awful lot more about us than we do him."

"Hmmm," Joshua mumbled aloud, "and what about the person in the shadows in the cave, do you know anything of him?" "Nothing, I didn't see his face so I have no idea why or what he was doing there." Once again "Hmmm" came out of Joshua's mouth. Joshua needed to make sense of the situation. "Shall I run through the facts as we know them and we can start from there?" "Alright, that would be good Joshua", Rebecca said, "but I can see this is not going to be a short conversation and I have left my small gig and Lilly, my horse, back on the beach behind the church as I walked to the cave from there this morning."

Joshua realised then that he had forgotten his manners, apologised and suggested they both walk back down to the beach and fetch her horse and gig and bring it back here in safe surroundings. He then said, "we can then relax and talk openly and when you feel you are ready you could ride home or if it gets too late, I could either escort you home or you could make my bedroom yours for the night and I will rest by the fire." "That's very kind of you Joshua, I have no one reliant on me in my cottage for a night or so but my chickens would need attention soon. So let's see how we get on and if it's not too late I will take you up on your escorting me home." Rebecca didn't mention the other option of staying the night.

Once they got to the gig Rebecca allowed Joshua to sit next to her and when he was comfortable she instructed her horse Lilly to 'push on,' heading them back to Joshua's cottage. Joshua hadn't been alone in a riding gig with a woman for many years and found it strangely tamed and calm.

Once back inside and with tea and pipe, Joshua started, "now let's look at the facts. We are both about the same age, both live alone in cottages given to us by our parent's last will who both passed away two years ago. Since then we have been pretty much living by ourselves, is that right Rebecca?" "Keep going Joshua." "So, this very afternoon we meet an unknown person called George Kernow." "You didn't say stranger then Joshua," Rebecca said. "That's right Rebecca I didn't, how strange, hmmm." Joshua continued, "Anyway, with George was another man who we couldn't see, and also two observers on the cliff top with telescopes. George said he had worked with our parents and knows of a plot to hurt our good people and we are to flush them out."

Joshua paused for a while and Rebecca carried on. "We also know, which we didn't yesterday, of these secretive tunnels, and an odd way of moving one's fingers for whatever rhyme or reason. Also, this George person not only worked with our parents but trusted them and, what is more to the point, we both believed him!" Rebecca and

Joshua both fell silent and together as twins do mumbled in harmony, "Hmmm."

Whilst looking at the fire in silence and trying to make sense of what was happening to them, both Queenie & Cecil suddenly leaped up and ran over and jumped on the window seat. With both looking outside they started growling and waging their tails at the same time.

Quickly glancing at each other, Rebecca and Joshua got up in unison to see what the fuss was about.

Coming through the gate was George Kernow who tipped his hat and carried on walking to the front door. Like an aged wedded couple, Rebecca instantly and comfortably said, "I will boil some water." Joshua went to the front door to meet George. Queenie and Cecil went with Rebecca as if not a care in the world.

Standing at the door step, Joshua opened the front door and greeted George who responded by saying, "Hello again Joshua, may I come in and talk, I trust Rebecca is still here?" On confirming both, George entered the cottage and as he did so took his hat off in respect.

Rebecca had already moved a chair from the table to the fire area while Queenie and Cecil busily started sniffing George's feet but then got bored and went back to Rebecca. All was pretty quiet whilst Rebecca wrapped the towelling around the handle of the kettle pot which was on the metal grill over the fire. She then poured the contents through the strainer with the tea leaves into a cup and casually asked "milk and sugar?" To which George replied, "both please and thank you Rebecca." Joshua sat back quietly and pleasantly looked on.

When the tea was poured and all had their cups in hand, George started. "I presume you both been wondering what is going on. So I have come here to truthfully explain to you both as best I can with the information I am allowed to advertise, should you both wish?" Joshua took the lead and said, "we are all ears, as they say."

"I am not George Kernow, my name is Henry Hosking. George Kernow is the person who was sitting in the shadows at the back of the cave when we last met. I have worked for George these past many years and can safely vouch and say he is a good man but with heavy responsibilities. He takes his position very seriously and yes he does work and report to a government or royal office department; very nice tea, may I say Rebecca." "Thank you Henry if that is your name?" Henry then fidgeted a little and realised they were only listening out of courtesy and, now not believing as before. He knew before he went any further he would have to reassure them both to believe what he is saying is true and take stock of what is happening.

"Alright," Henry said, "let me go back and explain why all of us are here, drinking tea in an old cottage overlooking Gunwalloe Cove with the pretty Church, how's that?" "That would be a good start Henry," Joshua said and Rebecca followed by saying, "Yes please do Henry if you would." It was time for Henry to be clear and precise.

It was then that Henry's mind raced back in vivid thought to the very time he had last seen Rebecca's and Joshua's parents. He remembered it all like a recurring nightmare.

43

The twin mast Galleon which was to take them away from French soil was lying out in the foreign inlet and he could see the anchors were straining to hold her steady. It was two o'clock in the morning and the sky was dark and the sea deep. Henry, Jeanne, and John were in the little rowing boat struggling to get through the rough sea from the shore but eventually after a long while attached itself to the ship's side. Henry went up the awaiting ladder first to hold it steady for Jeanne and then John to follow last. He heard the boson shout, "Quickly, get a move on, hurry up."

Then Whoosh! A canon opened up from an unidentified ship coming round the rock point. Missed; Whoosh! The small rowing boat which Henry had just gotten out of went up in the air. Henry looked down mortified. The Captain immediately shouted the order to hack away the anchor ropes. Within an instant, the Galleon drew the wind and turned on its axis flowing freely out to sea and away from the wrath of the incoming cannon fire. Henry leaned over the side of the ship but couldn't see John. He saw Jeanne bobbing up and down as the ship passed her by. He heard her shouting something over and over but with all the noise and commotion he didn't quite hear it properly. Then she went down, he thought it sounded something like Ante...

Joshua and Rebecca remained still and quiet waiting for Henry to carry on and explain things but, were bemused as Henry whose eyes were now closed seemed to be in some sort of trance. Rebecca looked at Joshua and shrugged her shoulders, so Joshua spoke up, "Henry, are you alright?" Henry quickly opened his eyes and rubbed his head saying, "Sorry Joshua, sorry Rebecca, I was just thinking that was all." Henry then took a sip of his tea and went on to explain.

"Jeanne, your Mother Rebecca was a beautiful woman with strawberry blonde hair and fiery spirit." Staying with Rebecca he continued, "Richard, your Father, was sometime in the Royal Navy and you all lived in Saltash." Rebecca stayed silent as Henry turned to Joshua. "Joshua, your Father John, was a good man and Captain, also sometime in the Royal Navy when he married your good Mother Charity and, you all lived in Plymouth." Joshua stayed silent and then Henry looked at them both.

"Rebecca and Joshua, both your Grandparents lived in these cottages after serving the crown in the Royal Navy. Also, you're Grandparents, and Cornish bloodline forbears, have a written alliance of accord with King Charles 1st and to his heirs and successors for their loyalty and support in times of need. In simple terms, both your family's quiet loyalty dates back to Edward the fourth."

Still looking at them both he carried on, "For the reason of better communications, both your Grandparents, including the wives, were ordered to London and unfortunately, all died tragically of the virulent plague in 1665. At this time both your Fathers were young and away from these shores serving in the Royal Navy and when home from duty were both working out of Plymouth. Due to your grand parents' deaths, The Cornish cottages you now live in became vacant and were passed and demised to your Fathers. Shall I go on?" "Please do," they both said. Joshua and Rebecca were listening intently and taking it all in.

"Your Fathers became good friends and on return from duty, both were secretly briefed of their family's obligations and duty to the safety of the realm, outside of their Royal Navy services. Both were delisted out of the Navy service, given a good pension, and brought into the services in which the real George Kernow and I work. Richard, your Father Rebecca, married Jeanne, and John, your Father Joshua, married Charity. The rest you probably know but I feel I need to carry on to reaffirm our close ties and bond of communication. You Rebecca and you Joshua are both single children having no brothers and sisters and both Richard, your Father Rebecca, and Charity, your Mother Joshua, passed to the good Lord through ill health in 1689.

Rebecca, you were around nineteen years of age living and working in Plymouth and unmarried. Joshua, you were around twenty-three living and working in Bristol and married. It was when your Father Joshua informed us that his best friend and confidante in this service had passed to the Lord. He was then subsequently advised by us whether Jeanne, his wife, could step in and help in the continuation of their work.

With John's positive report back and blessing, Jeanne was duly enlisted and all ownership of everything that your good Father Richard had, was transferred directly into her name. "Henry, feeling exhausted with recalling all this information then said, "Have I now successfully convinced you both that I am genuine because I really do need another cup of tea. I am also conscious of time as we all have a rendezvous tonight at ten o clock in St Just with George Kernow?"

Joshua and Rebecca looked in disbelief and Rebecca said, "You said this afternoon it was to be at Mevagissey sometime next week?" "I know I did Rebecca and I apologise. It is what George Kernow asked me to say and then when you both left the cave, he changed the time and venue for tonight in St Just. He is very security minded and always likes to be ahead, just in case. Although it is intrusive and irritable, he plays these quick moves all the time and assures everyone that it saves lives and, I am positive it does."

With a pause in proceedings, they all then heard a muffled voice from outside and Henry quickly got up and looked out through the window. "Just a moment," he said, "I think this is for me" and with that walked quickly to the door, and out he went. This gave Rebecca and Joshua a quick moment to discuss what had been said and quickly ascertain what they wanted to do.

Rebecca was first to say, "I am intrigued and want to know more, my life has been very quiet these last years since returning from Plymouth, and have pretty much kept myself to myself living off my Mothers inherited monthly allowance. What say you Joshua?" "I also am interested, like you I have done pretty much the same since coming back from Bristol and wish to know more of what they expect of us."

The front door opened and Henry walked back in and looking at them both said with a huff, "the venue is not St Just at ten o clock anymore, it's now The Blue Anchor in Helston at seven thirty. If you are happy with what I have said so far we best quickly finish off and get moving as time is pressing on." Both Joshua and Rebecca were happy with what he had said so started to get their things together for the ride into Helston.

Just before they were about to leave, Henry turned around and said, "are there any last questions on your mind you wish to ask before we set off and meet George Kernow?" "Just quickly," Joshua said, "you know an awful lot about our parents and grandparents, what do you know of Rebecca and me?"

"Quite a lot actually, and in brief what I can and am allowed to say is that you Rebecca, while in Plymouth worked for Samuels Ship Builders as secretary to Mr Samuel Junior. You wrote frequently to your Mother and returned here in fullness nearly two years ago. You Joshua, after ten years in the Royal Marines, resigned your commission and moved to Bristol where you worked in a Munitions Company. Apart from your initial wayward and public fighting hiccups, we shall say no more on that subject you met your good wife and settled down. You returned here living quietly for the last two and three quarter years. Now can we please get going?" Rebecca and Joshua were astounded and realised these people are for real.

While Henry went outside, Rebecca contemplated asking Joshua a question or rather not, as it may be a little too delicate, but she quickly weighed it up and decided to ask it anyway as it would bother her continually if she didn't. "Joshua, are you married, where is your wife?" "Sadly Rebecca, when living in Bristol my lovely wife died giving birth to our lovely still born daughter. I must say Rebecca I loved her deeply and still feel the loss to this day although it helps to know she and our daughter are with the Lord." Standing alone together inside the front door Rebecca laid her hand on his and said with true tender compassion, "I'm so sorry Joshua I didn't know."

It was then that she looked at him differently and more deeply, being six-foot-tall with black short length hair, strong shoulders and a lovely determined face. His nose was straight and was clean shaven and, for all his show of manly bravado, she could sense something of a child inside him. 'Quite nice she thought, beware my girl.' As she thought these thoughts two beautiful butterflies coming out of nowhere flew between Joshua and Rebecca's faces and straight out through the open door. Rebecca smiled and thought back to the old Cornish rhymes her Mother had taught her when she was a child.

Chapter 3

As Joshua knew where the Blue Anchor lay, Henry bid his farewell. Due to the change in timing and location to meet the real George Kernow, Rebecca decided to take up Joshua's offer to stay over as it would be extremely late when they got back. So with about an hour to spare before they set off Rebecca started to make herself at home in the bedroom with the minimum of sundries a lady could work with. Joshua took this time to take Queenie and Cecil for a brisk walk and when he returned he got on with making something for them to eat. He also made a pipe for a smoke.

"I think once we get this meeting out of the way tonight we can then fully evaluate what is what and decide what to do, what do you think Rebecca?" "I agree with you Joshua, but I will need to sleep on things before any final decisions are made, I think that's my Mother talking.
They decided to leave Rebecca's smaller horse and gig at the cottage and take Joshua's stallion, named Harry, and his larger gig. Once all was in order and Rebecca was sitting comfortably they set off at a nice slow pace. Rebecca was pretty quiet enjoying the view and ride but Joshua couldn't help but ask question after question. This was Joshua all over, get the facts and analyse which will give better actions.

"Rebecca, something has been bothering me since we met this morning. You said you went through a tunnel to get to my cottage which I understand, but could you explain what is was like and where it exited?" "I was thinking when you were going to ask Joshua as I would have asked you hours ago" Rebecca then took a breath of the fresh air and said, " At the back of the cave there is an entrance to a tunnel that leads straight to your cottage in the back garden with the exit shrouded with shrubbery and brush." Rebecca carried on, "I have heard so many tales of these so called tunnels of smuggling that I just accepted it as natural, how odd is that?" "That's very interesting, so my cottage is the proud owner of a smuggling tunnel but like you Rebecca, I don't feel the least bit surprised especially here at the bottom of Cornwall and the cottage being so close to an isolated cove."

As they arrived outside the Blue Anchor in Helston a young boy employed by the Inn went to them and asked if they wanted him to guard the horse and gig. These young boys work for the landlord and are known to be reliable and trustworthy. "Yes, thank you" Joshua replied, "how much?" "Penny an hour Sir paid on the exit at the bar," he said confidently. Outrageous he thought but then again what else could they do. "That will be fine, thank you", Joshua replied.

 As Joshua and Rebecca went through the front door of the Blue Anchor the first thing they noticed was the place was buzzing with drinkers. Going a little further in and looking around they then caught sight of Henry to the right at a table with two other men. Henry saw them and got up and waved them over. As they got close Henry pulled out the end bench and invited them to sit and as soon as they did one man immediately got up and walked to the bar. Then the man sitting next to Henry turned his head and looking straight at Rebecca and Joshua said, "Good evening to you both and thank you for coming on time, my name is George Kernow." Rebecca said good evening back and Joshua followed. He carried on, "I will not take much of your time, would either of you like a drink before we begin?" They both asked for a small cider. Kernow waved his hand to another man standing close by who immediately went to the bar to order and collect. No one said anything until the drinks were laid on the table in front of them. Then the man who was the real George Kernow spoke again, "Now I am going to say and ask some things of you both tonight, please could you answer individually with Rebecca being first, is that acceptable to you both?" Quite naturally Rebecca said, "that is fine" and Joshua followed saying the same. "Good, then let's get started as we have only eighteen minutes before things happen." Rebecca and Joshua did not get the eighteen minute thing but didn't pry and let it go.

George continued, "On the information you have heard today do you believe what we say is true to your ears and extremely confidential to ourselves?" Rebecca and Joshua acknowledged as agreed. "Do you also recognise that what I am about to divulge is one hundred per cent secret and you promise to keep it that way?" Again, both agreed yes with their reply.

Taking in their positive responses George paused and after briefly looking at Henry said, "So be it, we would like you both to work together on behalf of the department to flush out these enemy sleepers and traitors in the area of Newlyn, possibly Mousehole or Sennon, not fully confirmed. Once you have found these heathens with categorical evidence on who they are and what their dastardly plot is, then and only then, report this to me, understood?" "Yes, but how do we report?" Rebecca said. They then all waited for the same response from Joshua but nothing came from his lips, so all fell silent. Joshua noticed that all three were looking at him. Realising his mistake, he apologised and copied the same answer as Rebecca had given. With that George Kernow nodded and carried on and picked up on Rebecca's last question. "That is up to you and Joshua my Dear to work out and implement your own strategy to achieve the desired result. Henry here will assist and be the go between but will not work in the field anymore as he once did with your good Parents. Now, we have done some homework for you both and surmised that these sleepers would not have been installed more than two years ago hence we have checked the subsidy and parish rolls and found that many unknown families have moved into the Newlyn area within this time frame. However, saying that, we also know that many unknown families have moved into the area without notifying the authorities also." Well, that cancels that information out thought Joshua.

George continued, "we are not saying any of these families are the people we require but it is somehow a start. I apologise for being sparse and vague but exact information is rare and extremely hard to get in our line of work. However, we do believe these sleepers to be three in number either all male or one female and two males. There is also evidence of a traitorous heathen about, who we believe to be a Cornishman of the old faith with deep sympathies to the French."

Rebecca and Joshua listened in total stunned silence as George carried on. "As for your money and tools required, Trevean and Trevean Solicitors, who you already know through your Cottage Title deeds and monthly pensions, will advance you fifty pounds each and raise your monthly income from twenty pounds per month to twenty-five pounds from immediate effect. How does that sound to you both?" They both nodded and Rebecca said calmly "Thank you Mr Kernow," to which, Joshua concurred. "Then we are all agreed, thats good, I believe that then does it for tonight." George then went on to say, "Please do not under estimate the enemy and be very careful and diligent. This assignment is categorised as dangerous so use all your skills and inner tact in achieving the results we need. We believe you have a one to two month time window. Good luck to you both."

George then advised Rebecca and Joshua to look to their left. They shall see three men and a woman at the bar drinking together. The largest man will turn to face you in a very short while and please do the same to him. Please do not take your eyes off each other for at least one minute. Just as they thought nothing was going to happen the man turned around and eyed balled both Rebecca and Joshua without a flinch. After what seemed an eternity and an embarrassing one minute, the man turned back to the bar. Joshua noticed the others around him didn't turn away from the bar and, understood what this man was doing. Surreal but professional, he thought. George then said "we are finished, if you both could just wait one minute before leaving that would be appreciated. Henry here will make contact shortly." With that, as if on cue, a commotion started over the left side of the bar and the lady with the three men started shouting abuse to some other men and all hell broke loose. George, with a glee in his voice then said, "the diversion is in progress if you would both like to slip out now the way you came in that would be good and once again thank you, and take care."

Chapter 4

The Chateau Morlaix, near Brest in Brittany, is owned by Count Philip De Albret, a model in charm and richness. The Chateau oozed money and extravagance. Only the very best attended here. The gardens were delightful and cut to perfection like a razor. The foliage colour, even in winter, was beautiful. All carriages that visited Chateau Morlaix passed through very expensive massive front iron gates. They then travelled along a mile of fine gravel which had been exquisitely laid through acres of lush green meadows giving the carriage occupants a feeling of self importance. It also showed that the owners of the Chateau had indeed truly made it in the highest of French society and, its nobility. The owners were distant cousins of the Duke of Brittany with friends and associates at the very heart of the French King and his protectors.

Time was moving on and Philip Albret had to get back to the card game. With Philip were two other men all sitting in silence in the sombre smaller inner room adjoining the library. Philip had left his card game and entered the room through the main library door whilst the other two had entered from a back door away from any prying eyes.

Philip broke the ice, "So, are we saying we are not ready?" "Not exactly," said Pierre Bouchier, who was a man of medium height, jutting chin and teeth. Bouchier also had a receding hairline but wore a full brown beard thinking it made him look virile to the ladies.

Bouchier is Count Albret's right hand man on the ground and has only one interest, being his self importance which was always only shown when he was away from his master. However, saying that he gets the tasks done whatever Albret asks and, he is ruthless. Bouchier continued, "We have after long investigations into the geography and lay of the lands, now identified the initial target and worked out how it will be done. But due to hitting an unsuspected heavy granite underground seam, our sleepers have had to move location which is dangerous but necessary to achieve success. We also understand our sleepers have successfully completed phase one in opening up the mines entrance and now wait in receipt to proceed further on your approval tonight."

Seemingly content with Bouchier's response Philip turned his attention to the other man, "And what say you, are you ready with your participation?" The alchemist was an older man of bald head and tubby features but known as an expert in chemicals and worked out of the Abbey of Landerneau, in which Philip Albret is the main sponsor. "We will be Sir," he replied with confidence. "Enlighten me where exactly you are then?" Philip asked. "As you know, we experimented with some scoundrels and paupers in Paris, at your request, and the germ worked well with no suspicions even after a thorough autopsy. However, the cloning agent required to be attached to the germ to achieve zero status in smell, colour and taste for the larger operations needs more work. So we anticipate full completion ready for delivery in the quantity you require to be a month or so."

Philip was listening with quiet confidence and then asked, "How much of this so called germ agent is required for this initial target in Mousehole and how are you going to transport it?" The alchemist didn't answer, instead turned his head to Pierre Bouchier, who then took up the discussion. "As you know Sir, there are many disgruntled people in Cornwall who are true believers and are prepared to fully cooperate with our ambitions to rid their country of the new faith and return them to the true way, irrelevant if it costs lives." "Yes I am aware of this," Philip responded.

Pierre continued, "We have recruited a reliable agent called Mr Ashley Ward, a pig farmer in a very satisfactory coastal position near Sennon. He will receive the goods from the sea and then transport them inland to the new location for the sleepers. Mr Ward has worked for us before and had proved very reliable. We also have another favourable agent in Penzance who is being considered as a backup. This so called germ agent will be delivered in false bottoms in our brandy kegs. For every four gallon keg of brandy, half will be the agent. We require two hundred gallons of this agent and therefore one hundred kegs. These one hundred kegs will be delivered in one single delivery, minimising risk exposure."

Philip Albret fell silent and contemplated the situation. He then spoke to the alchemist again. "How many people are aware of your work?" "You asked me a year ago that the work I was to undertake this work for the defence of France and by the King himself and that its success would bring the true faith back to us all if done in absolute confidence."

The alchemist continued, "Therefore, the answer is only one and that is me, apart from my two apprentices, who know nothing of the reason for the work, believing only they are experiments of the sciences." "Good," replied Philip, who then glanced at Bouchier who, looking directly back into Philip's eyes and without moving a muscle gave the very slightest of nods that only the keenest of eyes would have seen.

Philip Albret answered Bouchier's ever so slight movement of the head by saying, "Agreed." With that, a door in the wall behind where the old Alchemist was sitting opened and a large able man appeared. With pure confidence, he walked up behind the alchemist and without so much as a word, through a loop of wire over his head and garrotted him to death. Once completed, Philip smiled and said calmly, "Thank you my man, now take him away and dispose of the body."

Once the body was removed, both Pierre and Philip looked at each other with calm satisfaction of their professionalism and the known brutality of the game they were in.

"Now Pierre, having listened to all information and however much I do not like chemicals and germs, this is the future. I and my family will make history in its first ever use over the enemy. Once we have our first successful bridgehead in England I will be made the highest knight in the land. Therefore, I decide that you proceed."

With that, Pierre responded, "It will be done Sir, we will make contact with the sleepers and Mr Ward immediately. The germ will be completed on time with activation in a few weeks with the bigger target set, subject to this initial success, early summer, as projected."
"Good" said Philip, "that fits most nicely with our ships time tables and rear echelon supply schedules. Our dear beloved King will be most pleased. By the way, how is my

prisoner?" "She is safe Sir, as you requested." "Thank you Pierre, now I must get back to the cards I am on a winning streak." They both chuckled.

Chapter 5

While everyone's attention in the Blue Anchor was on the fight and chaos at the other end of the pub, Rebecca and Joshua slipped out unnoticed into the brisk cold night air. The young boy, who had attended to them on arrival, was there holding the gig and quietly talking to Harry, Joshua's lovely black stallion which he bought some two years ago.

"Thank you," Joshua said, as he helped Rebecca up into the seat. The young boy handed Joshua the reins and then slipped his hand into his pocket and reached out a sealed envelope. He then reached out his hand and said to Joshua, "I was to hand this to you directly Sir when you leave but only if you and the lady were together." "Thank you, may I ask your name and who you work for?" "My name is 'Little George,' I am in the service of Mr Henry Hosking." With that, Joshua pocketed the envelope and jumped up into the seat next to Rebecca. Then once they had both blanketed themselves warmly Joshua flipped the reins and in respect nodded to the young boy.

The ride home was quiet as they were both tired from the day's events and had much to think about. Harry seemed to be enjoying the exercise in trotting very graciously through the town and out towards the direction of the Lizard. After a couple of miles out of the town, they changed direction heading due south for Gunwalloe and Joshua's comforting little cottage.

Queenie and Cecil were pleased to see them and once they had taken their hats and coats off, Joshua stoked the fire and asked Rebecca would she like a little glass of brandy.

"Yes please Joshua that would be nice but a large one would be much better, thank you."

As they sat around the fire they began to relax. Rebecca suggested they both need a good night's sleep to take in what has occurred over this last day and to wake early and then discuss their thoughts. Joshua agreed and mentioned that he will get his things out of his bedroom in readiness to make it her's for the night.

On his return, Rebecca was quietly staring into the fire with both dogs by her feet and looking very thoughtful. Joshua then said, "I have done my best to make things a little more comfortable and have lit the candle, I trust it will be acceptable." Rebecca turned and smiled and said, "I am sure it will be fine, thank you. By the way where are you going to sleep?" "I shall pull out some rugs and lay by the fire, it will be most comfortable", he replied.

With that, Rebecca said her goodnight and got up with little Queenie following her. Cecil didn't know what to do and so reluctantly stayed with Joshua but his eyes were on Rebecca. Joshua inwardly felt that this little Jack Russell also wanted to be with her.

Once all the movement in the cottage had calmed the night became silent. Joshua looked into the fire and felt its spirit, especially with the flickering flames and spits of crackling sparking against the dark granite walls. He then drew in the ambience of peace thinking how comforting it was and how protective he felt knowing that a woman was within these walls and sleeping. He then remembered the envelope.

Knowing he couldn't wait till morning to find out what it said, he got up and went to his coat and retrieved it. He moved to the table and after sitting down and relighting the lamp opened the envelope.

R & J
Look in both your scrub areas to find a stone slab marked V which is yours to use as with your Mother and Father. A colleague

He flipped the page over looking for more writing but that was it, short and sweet. Joshua replaced the letter in his coat pocket and realised that whatever is in the slab V can wait till the morning. His mind was all over the place and knew he couldn't at this dark hour and being extremely tired, think straight, he needed sleep. So, lying back down by the hearth and covering himself over with rugs he released his thoughts. Through quiet breathing, he then stretched his body as though dispelling any tension, laid his head down and after only a few minutes was asleep.

Cecil woke Joshua up by loudly scratching at the front door at seven o clock. Joshua hadn't slept well with constant dreams of trying time after time to swim through a torrent of water and getting nowhere.

Throwing back the rug, he got up and let Cecil out to do his business. He then went over to stoke the fire and put on the pot water to boil some water for his morning tea and wash his face. He then thought that he better fill the pot up more as to leave enough for Rebecca. However, there was no sign of Queenie or Rebecca.

While the water was boiling he took the envelope out of his coat pocket and walked over to the bedroom door and knocked gently. On hearing Rebecca's sleepy voice acknowledging his knocking he asked if he could enter.

As he entered Joshua felt an immediate sense of gentleness as he saw Rebecca under the bed clothes with Queenie by her side all snuggled up. On rubbing her eyes and attempting to wake up, Joshua walked over and handed her the note explaining quietly that she should read it. He then said he would go back out and bring in some tea and a bowl of warm water and that once she was ready perhaps they could both discuss what it means. With sleepy eyes, Rebecca quickly read the note and with a quizzical looked up and said, "Thank you Joshua, you are very kind." On seeing Joshua turn and start to leave the bedroom, Queenie jumped down and followed him out wanting to join her mate Cecil outside. Joshua obliged and let Queenie out the cottage front door.

On delivering both the tea and the wash bowl to Rebecca, Joshua went out to the scrub area of the cottage to get himself cleaned up. Trying to discipline himself not to look until they were both together, he couldn't help but roam his eyes across the whole area trying to locate the V slab. Eventually, after pouring the water into the bowl and washing his face he started to dry himself before noticing in the left corner of the floor, tight up against the outer wall, a slab marked with a single deep scratch. The iron bath tub was covering the rest of the mark so pushing it aside he saw the full mark of the V. 'Unbelievable,' he said to himself.

He wanted to shout eureka but thought better of it, then heard the footsteps of Rebecca walking in. "Have you found it Joshua?" "I believe I have, shall we investigate?" "Where are the dogs, maybe I should bring them in first?" He agreed with her logic and Rebecca went and opened the front door to call them in.

They were both now standing side by side looking at the slab wondering what they should do. Rebecca suggested they clean all around it and then try and get it raised. Opening the back door, Joshua found an iron bar next to the privy and on his hands and knees started scratching and digging at the slab. Rebecca helped by brushing all the debris away. Once completed, he jemmied the slab up which left a two by two foot open gap with a large chamber below. Rebecca fetched a lighted candle for him as if knowing he was going to go down first, which in fact, he was thinking that anyway. So with a lighted candle in hand down he went.

The chamber was very well lined and dry, about ten feet long by six wide and six feet high so Joshua could just about stand up but what he saw was amazing. Everything you could imagine to be self contained in times of extreme trouble, including swords, muskets, flintlock pistols, maps, wine, water, all types of clothing including a most beautiful long range micro telescope. Once he understood what was down there he pressed himself back up through the gap and suggested Rebecca see for herself. So taking the candle, down she went sliding easily into the chamber.

On helping Rebecca up, they dusted themselves down and moved into the front room with the warm fire to sit down and decipher what they had and what they were going to do. It was now time to set and agree on the plan.

Once the dogs had been fed with the scraps of the leftover meals and then themselves with fresh porridge, they both sat down by the hearth and began to chatter about how they are going to do things moving forward.

They agreed on three critical points. Point 1, they should not work alone and be isolated but work together at all times. Point 2, they should alias themselves as husband and wife. Point 3, as the targets may probably be in the Newlyn area, time wasn't on their side so would need to be closer and therefore they would move today to Rebecca's cottage and make it their base. Queenie and Cecil will have a holiday with Mrs Stephen's family in Cury just over the way.

Being in the marines and working in munitions, Joshua knew about weaponry and self defence but he was worried about Rebecca. With that thought, he turned to her and said, "Rebecca, have you any experience in weapons or fighting?" In which she laughed and looked at him as if he was on a different planet, even Queenie and Cecil strangely looked at him. Rebecca replied, "Joshua, the closest I have ever got to hurting something is preparing a rabbit for a stew. As for guns and things, I have never fired one in my life. Now Joshua, if you ask me what I can do apart from not killing people, I will tell you. I can organise, read, understand mathematics, write, stitch, have sex and understand that life is about discussion and cooperation, not female subservience!"

Nearly choking on his pipe, he said, "I think I get it Rebecca and thank you." Joshua quickly thought that Rebecca comes across as a quiet lady until she feels undermined or threatened then, watch out. He will remember that in future.

However, as they were going into dangerous territory, he felt it necessary to convince Rebecca that she should at least learn how to load, prime and fire a pistol and to wear both a dagger and pistol on her person at all times, just in case. She looked at him square in the eyes but knew that his warning made sense, if not for her protection but his as well and therefore she nodded with agreement.

Not knowing what was needed or not needed, they decided to load the gig with pretty much most of the stuff from the V chamber. Rebecca had chosen a fine dagger and sheath for herself that fitted snug and was not too heavy. Joshua chose a small flintlock pistol for her with the latest all in one ball and powder cotton bag for ease of loading and reloading. Then taking five cotton bags they walked to the side of the cottage out of sight but still able to see the beautiful sea over the cliffs. Joshua set out an old bucket for Rebecca's first target practice about twenty feet away just below and against the outer garden wall.

Rebecca was a very receptive trainee and took immediately to the seriousness of why they were doing this and listened with the intent to get it right quickly.

Rebecca got it straight away and was not all conscious of the fact that ladies don't do this sort of thing. Steadying her grip for her first shot and aiming with both hands on the butt, she pulled the trigger and missed. With a bit of encouragement and two musket balls later, she was on or near the target and ably confident in the loading and firing procedure. "Well done Rebecca," Joshua said.

Rebecca then simply pulled up her long skirt and casually strapped the gun to a skeleton strap holder just above the knee. Joshua didn't know where to look. Rebecca then said, "Pity Anne Boleyn didn't have one of these." He just looked on in bewilderment.

With everything ready, Queenie and Cecil jumped up beside Rebecca in the gig. Joshua decided it would be wise to take his horse and so jumping up on Harry, they both left the cottage with Joshua leading. On arrival in Cury village, Mrs Stephens was very glad to see Joshua and more than pleased to take the dogs off his hands for a few weeks as if it was of no bother to her whatsoever.

Explaining to Mrs Stephens about Rebecca was another matter and Joshua sort of stumbled his way through as if they were engaged or betrothed or something. Mrs Stephens was lovely and just cuddled him and said, 'you two go off and have a lovely fun time together.' "Thank you Mrs Stephens," he replied.

Jumping in the gig next to Rebecca he asked if she was ready and she replied, "Yes, I am ready Joshua, let's do this and let's do it well." With Harry now tethered to the back, they waved to Mrs Stephens, turned the gig around and went off to Rebecca's cottage at Marazion.

They kept a good steady pace and the countryside passed by crisply with rugged beauty. Helston lay slightly to the east of their route to Marazion so it wouldn't have taken much to pop in to see Trevean Solicitors. They could then ask for their monies but Joshua thought it better to head directly to their destination as agreed.

On heading North West along the smaller country paths, they soon hit the main Penzance road. Passing through Breage and Rosudgeon they were now only a few miles from Marazion. A couple of quick miles later they met the turnpike where Rebecca announced they should bear left and then half a mile on advised taking the next track on the left. With a little pull here and tug there, Joshua guided the gig well.

A couple of minutes later Joshua could see the track ahead was coming to an end when Rebecca pointed to her Cottage on the right. When the gig came to a halt she jumped down and opened the gate for Joshua to bring the gig forward. With Rebecca walking ahead and taking the lead, things slowly came to a halt by the front porch. "Welcome to my home Joshua," she said. "Leave the gig there Joshua and come in while I get the fire lit and put some tea on." Joshua did as was told and jumped down but before he went in he quickly got some water for both their horses.

Joshua thought the Cottage was lovely, very much like his own with a granite build but bigger with two bedrooms. However, the main difference was the soft furnishings. Joshua's cottage was just the bare minimum whilst Rebecca's was home just like he had had in Bristol. A woman's touch just amazes him. He decided to help Rebecca with the lighting of the fire and ask if there was anything else he could do to help. But she seemed to have it all under control and suggested that he could unbridle her horse and put her and Harry in the barn then come back to rest and have some tea.

Joshua went out and completed what Rebecca had asked and then went back in. While Rebecca was still organising things Joshua decided to stand and look out of the window for a while. Although the cottage was tucked high above and away into some trees about half a mile west of the village, he could see the beautiful wide bay of Marazion with St Michaels Mount to its centre left, and Penzance and Newlyn off to the far right about three miles as the crow fly. "What a lovely view," he said. "Yes isn't it just lovely," Rebecca replied.

Once settled down with tea in their hands and the fire looking brighter and catching well, they started to relax somewhat. "Joshua, I know we are going to go about acting as husband and wife but I have two bedrooms here and one should be for you and one for me, I just wanted to get that out of the way now." Joshua started to laugh and said, "of course Rebecca, I understand completely, but when we are out and staying the night somewhere we would have to share one bedroom, do you not agree?" "Yes I understand that, but that is different, that's business."

"By the way Rebecca, talking about husband and wife, would you have a couple of spare rings for us both so we can display them to others?" "I do have a small jewellery box and am sure I could find us something suitable," she replied. "Thank you Rebecca," he said sincerely. Even though they were acting, Joshua didn't like to belittle the sanctity of marriage. Rebecca left the room and after a little while came back with two rings.

"How about these," she said. "They are not wedding rings, more for decoration but I think they will pass." With that, she passed one to Joshua and waited for his response as if knowing that they must put the rings on together at the same time so as not to demean the Lord. So as they both started to put the rings on they looked at each other really not knowing what to say, so they said nothing.

Looking around the room and contemplating his thoughts, Joshua found himself feeling very comfortable with what Rebecca had done in making the place feel very warm and cosy. Joshua remained in quiet thought but then noticed that Rebecca too was in quiet mode.

Time was moving on and Joshua felt he should go out to Harry and comfort him a while and start bringing in the belongings. It was then that Rebecca said, "If you want to bring the things in I will put some supper on and tidy your bedroom to make it comfortable for you, how does that sound?" "Sounds good to me," he responded.

With all the baggage in and supper eaten they sat down by the roaring fire quite exhausted. Although the atmosphere had been calm and pleasant, Joshua had always been thinking about how and when they are going to achieve their mission. Analysing this and visualising different scenarios his mind was working overtime and he believed it now to be the right time to ask Rebecca what she was thinking and, how she saw things.

Rebecca's response was thoughtful and calm. "I may look as though I am quite happy with this but I am worried. We are amateur's Joshua and have no plan, no strategy and what's more how do we get the information back to

Henry or George. I am also concerned for our future as if we succeed or fail, do they just leave us alone and we get on we our lives as normal?"Rebecca's response, Joshua thought, was a good one which left him quiet but then after a little time to think he decided to speak. "So then let us together start building a plan step by step. I think the first thing I shall do tomorrow is to ride into Helston and talk with the Solicitors about the monies we are owed and somehow find out how best we contact Henry."

"Agreed," she said, but one thing I have learnt in life is confidentiality. What I mean Joshua is not to say too much to anyone, people only need to know what we want them to know. If you go to the Solicitors and start asking questions about Henry too soon, the whole of Helston will know we are on his payroll. So may I suggest you hang about by the Blue Anchor, no drinking mind Joshua, find the boy in his service and say that we need to talk to his Paymaster and arrange a meet."

Joshua was a little taken back by Rebecca's suggestion that he might talk too much. However, even after ten years in the Royal Marines with all the fighting, bitching and biting, he knew she was right to remind him of the importance of working undercover.

"By the way," she said, "earlier on when we first arrived and while you were giving water to the horses, my curiosity got the better of me. I went to my scrub room and think I found a slab with a V scratch by the back door in the corner. The problem is the big iron tub is on top and I couldn't move it to find out more." "Shall I try?" "Yes please Joshua" With that they both got up and went to the scrub room and on pushing and shoving the heavy water butt aside they uncovered the full V. So just like at Joshua's place they jemmied the slab away and saw that it was full of equipment all usable for tasks of their pending adventure. "Quite unbelievable" she said. "Quite," Joshua replied.

They both agreed that what was found in the chamber should stay in the chamber until tomorrow as what was important now was for both of them to get a good night's sleep and be fully refreshed for a busy day tomorrow.

Rebecca showed Joshua the outside privy and the other wash area away from the main inner scrub room. She then wished him a pleasant good night's sleep, as Joshua did her.

Stripping off his clothes and getting into his new soft bed, he found everything to be much more comfortable, unlike his bare bedroom and much harder bed. Even the sheets and blankets felt softer and warmer. Laying still and letting his mind wander on what was happening he drifted off into a much needed sleep.

Chapter 6

Waking early, Joshua got up and used the outside privy but then came back inside to wash in the scrub room. It was once again very cold both outside and in. Rebecca was still asleep in her room so he lit the fire and got the water on for the morning tea. Whilst the water was on he checked on Harry.

Coming back into the cottage Joshua stood by the front window for a while and admired the view. He thought he had a great view at Gunwalloe but nothing quite like this. Gunwalloe was a cove, this was a massive bay with ships of both the line and merchant and on the far right side was the fishing fleet of all shapes and sizes.

Joshua made the tea and was starting to make a pipe up when Rebecca looked in and said "Good Morning Joshua." "Good morning" he replied, "the water has boiled, would you like a cup of tea?" "You and your tea! By the way Joshua, I don't mind if you want to smoke." "Thank you Rebecca, I've just made it ready to light."

Rebecca got herself ready quite quickly and they both sat down by the fire. Joshua spoke about the agenda for today, as agreed by them both yesterday and said that he should really start making tracks shortly. Rebecca suggested he have some warm porridge before setting off. "What will you be doing while I'm away in Helston?" he asked. "I want to give this place a good clean then go through all the things in the scrub chamber and better organise them so we can identify exactly what we have and store them accordingly."

"By the way Rebecca, I have been thinking, it would be a good cover story if we could start our move nearer to the target area as a new couple who wants to celebrate by the sea town of Penzance. We could find ourselves a room at an Inn and work the area from there for a while, how does that sound?" "I think you are right, it's a good simple cover story. Maybe when you get back from Helston we could go through and practise things so we are singing from the same hymn sheet, as they say. "Agreed Rebecca," he replied approvingly.

With the day's itinerary established, Joshua set out. With the gig ready and Harry bridled he flicked the reins and trekked off. Rebecca had already opened the gate for him to pass through and as he did they waved to each other.

The weather was cold and the ground very hard so Harry was moving steadily at a relaxed walking pace. Joshua anticipated that the journey to Helston would take at least two hours. The ride was lovely and relaxing and gave him time to think. Although he saw some people walking and riding it was in the main, a quiet journey.

Joshua saw the sun was now up and trying to make some sort of effort to heat the earth but the cold freshness of the air was having none of it and wasn't giving it a chance. However, it was a nice thought that the spring was coming. Reliable Harry kept his pace well, in a strong controlled manner.

He thought about Rebecca and her composure in the situation and did admire her courage and fortitude. It was then that he promised himself he would use all his skills and Royal Marine's experience to achieve what was needed and more importantly, protect her. He felt good about that.

The village of Breage was coming up ahead when Joshua noticed a steady rider heading towards him. It was the boy at the Blue Anchor. "Good morning Mr Pendragon," he said, as they both stopped side by side. "Good Morning Little George, how are you?" "I am well, thank you. I went to your cottage at Gunwalloe but you were not there so I thought I would push on to see Ms Pendarve in the hope that you were there. I have a message to give you from Mr Hosking."

"How did you know I would be with Ms Pendarve?" Joshua asked curiously. "Mr Hosking said if you were not at Gunwalloe then I was to push on to Marazion to Ms Pendarve's. Am glad we met halfway as Suzy my horse is getting a little puffed out." Suzy was a lovely looking well kept horse and Joshua's stallion, Harry, kept trying to get a better view but Suzy kept her stance ignoring him.

"Well then, that is good we met," Joshua replied, "what is the message?" "Mr Hosking's said please could you meet him for lunch in the Coach Inn at Breage?" Joshua knew there wasn't time to get to the Solicitors in Helston and then get back to Breage. Weighing things up he decided to forsake Helston and head directly for the Coach Inn and wait there if he had to. Little George waited politely for his response. With his decision made Joshua replied; "yes of course he will go directly."

"Thank you Mr Pendragon," Little George said, "Would you mind if I accompany you as my master Mr Hosking is already there?" "That will be my pleasure Little George but I would not get Suzy too close to my Harry as he sometimes thinks he is our good King Henry the Eighth when around young fillies." Little George had a nice soft laugh and they escorted each other to the Coach Inn

The Coach Inn was a large fronted white washed Inn, set back from the road with a friendly warm appearance to accommodate any traveller. Little George volunteered to look after Joshua's gig while he went in and met Mr Henry Hosking. On entering, Joshua saw Henry by the fire with another man whom he recognised as the man at the bar who caused all the havoc at the nod of George Kernow's head when he and Rebecca were at the Blue Anchor in Helston.

Henry noticed Joshua coming in and waved him over. "Good morning Joshua, let me formally introduce you to my friend, Bull." With that, the man called Bull got up and held out his big hand which Joshua shook and said, "Good day Sir," and Bull responded likewise with a heavy Cornish accent.

"Right," said Henry to Bull, "I think our business is done for today, have you any questions?" "None Mr Hosking, I get the situation and understand my responsibilities and bid both of you good day." Still standing, Joshua again shook his hand and then nodded their approval to each other as if somehow knowing their paths will cross again.

Henry then turned his attention to Joshua. "Right Joshua, I am famished, shall we eat? Please take a seat and I will order us an early hearty lunch and then we can talk." This Joshua accepted gladly as he was also hungry. Henry waved to the maid who took their order whilst pouring Joshua a large cider. Henry also refilled his wine glass.

"Before I forget Joshua, these are for you and Rebecca." He handed over two heavy purses containing fifty pound coins each. Joshua took them both and laid them by his side and said, "They are heavy but you have just saved me a trip to Helston, thank you." Henry nodded and then continued, "I presume you got my message about the underground stores." "Yes we did, Rebecca at this very moment is organising things."

"Good, one thing you may find strange if you haven't already are the undershirts made of cotton with a mix of plated iron and tin plate sewn in strategic areas to protect the vital parts of the body. They are light enough to wear and I assure you they are very worthy garments and can stop a blade or a glancing musket ball." "I have not noticed these items yet as we have been a little rushed, but I'm sure Rebecca will come across them, thank you."

Joshua explained to Henry their plan to enter Penzance as husband and wife tomorrow and then to evaluate the situation and work from there. "Good," he said, "I will make arrangements for a room to be ready for a happy couple at the Turks Head in the town." Joshua looked at him quizzically as he felt it important that they work alone. "Don't worry Joshua; I know it's important to work quietly and alone but let's use the resources we have and not leave things to chance. I will send Little George over now to arrange things." Joshua could not but agree with his logic and therefore, Little George was tasked. "Now, there has been some further information come in from abroad, a person related in some form to this espionage plot has been killed or removed. I bring this to your attention for two reasons, whoever is behind this is deadly serious for its success, and so please do not under estimate their brutality and ruthlessness to achieve their aim." "I fully understand" Joshua said.

"Also Joshua, we are no further forward with information on their planned scheme except for what you know. So, while we eat you can ask any questions of me and I shall answer as best I can."

The stew was delicious and whilst eating Joshua capitalised on the openness to ask questions. "Who is this man Bull you introduced me to just now?" "Bull is of extreme reliable character and has an enviable reputation in a fight, especially in defence of our good Queen. He is what we call our backup in times of need'. If you are in trouble or need help, Bull and his compatriots will be there." 'That's fine," Joshua says, "but how do we communicate if we need to get word to you?""Yes of course, good question. I have a house at 10 Lemon Street in Truro, you can always leave a message there. If not, find Little George who is usually found at the Blue Anchor working both for the Landlord on my behalf." "By the way, who is Little George?" "Little George and his not much younger sister Christine entered into a pauper's house five years ago and three years before that their Father died at sea fighting the Spaniards. When their Mother passed away it was when I saw them begging in the streets. I could see they were decent and very polite children and immediately took a shine to them both. I took over parental rights to get them out of the pauper's house, made them comfortable in mine, and looked after them ever since. Christine works and has a room at the Turks

Head in Penzance, where you and Rebecca will be getting a room."

"Henry, may I ask what is the setup, I mean who are you all?" Henry smiled nicely and understood the question completely. "As you know we are now called Great Britain. This is a great Country but being great means we much rely and thrive on information to keep it that way. George Kernow is responsible for the complete South West internal security and reports to London direct. As you know, I was like your Father and Jeanne, Rebecca's Mother, doing the frontline stuff. After that George Kernow asked me a while ago if I would manage Cornwall and come away from frontal activity. I agreed and was asked to handle three cells, one of them being you and Rebecca. I also have some support operators, loyal to the Crown, who help in the field, as and when required, one of them being Bull whom you have just met."

"Thank you Henry, now it's all starting to fall into place. And what about the tunnels?" he asked. "The tunnels are a long standing asset to our means of success. There are many more around Cornwall and only known to us. As time goes on you will get to know more of them." "Has Rebecca a tunnel?" "No, Marazion bay is too busy, we like secluded coves like Gunwalloe. Any more questions Joshua?"

Joshua continued, "I have loads more Henry but one which keeps coming to the forefront is, what happens if we get caught or injure someone or even kill anyone in our work?" Hosking's nodded, he understood where Joshua was coming from. "The Cornwall justices are aware of our presence in only the vaguest of forms, in other words, they know we exist for the benefit of safety to the County and Country but have no idea how or who. Should you or Rebecca maim or kill anyone whilst working it's as if you were back in the Marines. The only difference this time is, it must be formally asked by the injured party or by proxy if death occurs, which rarely occurs."

Henry continued, "We well understand this may come to pass and if it does, we will support you both. We will discuss to find out what happened and get on with things. However, if you are caught doing things which are illegal but feel must be done to gain the information, be conscious the local Constables are not aware of you or your work. Should you be caught and cannot get out of it then you must do what you have to do."

"I understand," Joshua said then carried on, "One last question Henry I promise, what of this rolling fingers thing I saw you and Rebecca do?" Henry burst out laughing. "That was brought in three months ago on the advice of someone in London, something to do with secretly knowing each other. We tried it but made a decision yesterday to throw it out as it's just too Walsingham and doesn't work. Also in Cornwall, we either very much know each other or we don't. So if anyone does it, as from this moment on, I would run."

With that they chatted idly about the weather and things and then parted. Joshua needed to get back to Rebecca and explain what he had learned and deliver her money purse.

Chapter 7

Joshua arrived back at Rebecca's cottage late afternoon and once he had looked in on Harry, who he thought had done really well apart from his boyish behaviour with Suzy, went into the Cottage only to find that Rebecca wasn't at home.

The cottage looked really clean and walking on through he entered his bedroom and noticed that the gear from the scrub chamber had been laid out all across the bed, floor and even in the cupboard and all in an orderly fashion. He went into Rebecca's room and found her things also laid out in the same way. He decided to make a cup of tea and have a smoke. He would then sit and wait by the fire which was still alight and only needed a quick poke and a couple of logs to flare it up.

It was thirty minutes or so when he heard the door and Rebecca walk in offering a nice, "Hello Joshua, I wasn't expecting you back for quite a while, did everything go well?" "I didn't get to Helston as we planned, shall I make you a cup of tea and explain all?" "Thank you, that would be nice," she replied. Making another cup of tea Joshua explained everything in full detail about what had happened and handed over her purse of fifty pound coins.

"I'm glad," she said, "it reassures me that Henry and George Kernow are who they say they are and that we are operating within a team albeit a very small quiet team across Cornwall. It makes me feel part of something as over the last couple of years I have been quite lost as to what to do with my life. How about you Joshua, how do you feel?" "I feel the same, I also have been at a loss of what to do with mine."

With that Rebecca explained where she had been as though he needed to know which to be truthful he was curious about where she had been. In truth, she had gone to the small village a couple of miles away to fetch milk and bread for supper and breakfast for them both.

Rebecca continued, "By the way, I found some more interesting things in the scrub chamber like a smaller lighter pistol with a holder that will fit into the small of my back rather than my thigh." "That's a pity," Joshua said cheekily with a grin, at which Rebecca laughed.

"Also, I found some strange intertwined under vests with yards of material, maps, a compass and curiously an outfit for a man that would fit me. I instantly tried them on and with my hair up and hat pulled down thought I could quite easily pass as a man which we may find useful Joshua, what say you?" Joshua said, "yes," anything that can give us an edge is good.""Rebecca, you are quite something" he said proudly. "Thank you Joshua, I feel my Mother's streak of adventure is coming through me."

With that they decided to pack the things they needed into the luggage cases ready for loading onto the gig for the morning off. Rebecca suggested Joshua sort Harry and Lilly, her mare, to be also ready for the morning trip to Penzance. They thought it best to bring Lilly along with them as an extra means of transport if required.
Once everything was completed and they were happy they had all the things relevant, they sat down to discuss and agree on their cover story. They decided that they had

met in Exeter three years ago at a dinner party whilst Rebecca was working in Plymouth and Joshua working in Bristol.

It was through a Charity that they both supported for ex-Navy personnel that guided them together. Also finding out that being both Cornish was another sign. They kept in touch and met as frequent as they could and decided to marry only a few weeks ago in Exeter where they first met.

As their parents lived in Cornwall they decided to carry on the tradition, hence their first vacation of being man and wife would be by the sea. Rebecca reminded him that knowing the Cornish they will delve and pry further as to where our parents lived and, if we stutter or stumble in reply they will know something is not adding up. So they agreed that they will mix truth with lies and that their parents did indeed live here in this cottage and Joshua's at Gunwalloe and they came down often to stay with them. However, as they have passed to the Lord they now manage the cottages between them as best they can until they know exactly what they want.

As they had both pretty much kept themselves to themselves, people in their respective areas may know them by sight but would not know the full details of their lives. Therefore, the scenario they have now created would probably pass any basic scrutiny.

However, they changed the traditional bit of this being their first real time away together by the sea, to having a break from managing both the cottages. It didn't seem so cavalier, more boringly mundane which sounded good to them as if they were bored then it will bore the inquisitor even more. They went on to discuss their likes and dislikes and the reason they are not in full work at the moment which they agreed was due to the monies left to them in their parent's will.

One thing they left out of the cases was the weapons they needed. Joshua knew how his pistol worked and thought it wise to question Rebecca about her new pistol and had she tested it yet. "I have only put it around me for fitting purposes but no I have not fired it yet." Joshua, like at Gunwalloe, felt that the risk of her not practicing was too much of an unknown certainty and said "we need to be sure Rebecca." As it wasn't too late they got the pistol and cotton and ball charges and went out back as far away as they could to quickly practice. Rebecca did very well and both pistol and loading went smoothly as with the tree she hit on her second attempt.

Going back into the warmth of the cottage the only thing that needed to be done was to try on those protective under shirts. Joshua took off his tunic and under vest which left him standing with a bare chest. Rebecca was looking at him as if it was natural for a man to be stripping off in her cottage. She passed him the protective vest and he awkwardly tried to put it over his head. Rebecca jumped up laughing and came to his rescue. "Maybe if you undid the shoulder straps it would be easier Joshua?"

Once the vest was on and the straps tied down it fitted him quite snugly without much weight at all.The protective plates were over the heart, each side of the kidneys and in the back behind the heart. "Now it's your turn." Rebecca got up and went into her bedroom and said, "I will be two minutes."

She came out with the vest over another cotton vest. "I put an under vest on as the metal plates rub a little under the heart but what do you think?" She then did a little twirl and Joshua could see the plates were all in the right places and settled except the front one which, was protruding due to her bosoms being, he believed, on the more firm side. He tried to say something about this but started to go a little red when Rebecca said, "I know Joshua, we need to bend the metal slightly in the front to blend in with my body but other than that it feels like a garment I could wear without too much fuss."

So with her protective vest eventually mended accordingly, they both sat down each with a large glass of brandy and Joshua lit his pipe. Time was moving on but there was no rush so they enjoyed a quiet evening relaxing.

The morning was fresh and they arrived at the Turks Head in Penzance around midday being met by Little George and his younger sister Christine. Little George introduced his sister who they found to be delightful and liked her instantly. Being at the end of the street the Turks Head had good stabling facilities to the side of its buildings. Christine showed Rebecca to their room while Little George and Joshua did the stabling and the transfer of their belongings. They agreed to meet the girls in the bar area when they had finished.

The room was on the first floor to the side and away back from the front of the Inn and its main drinking area. On entering they found a cosy main room, warm with fire already lit, a little wash basin area and one bedroom. The main room had one window overlooking the stable yard with a small waste land in between.

At the bottom of the stairs heading away from the bar and towards the main stores, was a locked back door.

Little George had selected their room well knowing they would need access and exits without being seen at any time through the day or night. Joshua said, "Well done Little George, you have chosen well." "Thank you Mr Pendragon and here is a duplicate key for the back door." Joshua thought for a young lad he is very bright and a good asset to have.

They then both went to meet Rebecca and Christine but only found Rebecca sitting at a table close to the large open fire. The bar was quite busy with a few men getting jolly. "I'm glad you've arrived as I was being eyed up by a couple of men over there," she said. "That's because you're very pretty Rebecca." "That may or may not be the case Joshua or it could be that I am the only woman in here, which is more likely."

Joshua asked where Christine was and advised that she had better get back to work which somehow he thought was a prudent move from this young girl. Little George did not sit down and Joshua could see he was slightly anxious when he said, "Would you please excuse me, I also have work to attend to?"

"Before you leave Little George, how long are you staying at the Turks?" "Until tomorrow, my sister and I are to head for Truro to be with Mr Hosking for a couple of days. We are to return here after that to assist my sister for a short while in helping you and Ms Pendarve. I am to share lodgings with her here in the Inn and if necessary work alongside her which will benefit the landlord, Mr Rosevear." On hearing this, Joshua asked if they both could come to their room early this evening.

Joshua and Rebecca then had their drinks served and a lovely mutton stew. They noticed as time went on that the men at the bar were drinking further and getting rowdier with song. Joshua suggested they should get their coats and start the process of their mission in getting to know the layout of Penzance and also practice their visual skills in seeing anything which seems untoward. "Are we to go as husband and wife or would you like me to dress as a man," Rebecca said with a smile. Joshua couldn't tell if that was a real question or a subtle way of saying to him to calm down but he replied, "I think Husband and wife."

So they both drank up and went out to fetch their warm clothing from their room and then set off. Joshua thought it funny that when he was in the Marines how much easier it was to see the enemy. Also, you can prove your courage in an open fight or show how good you are at shooting. But seeking out an enemy of sleepers completely embedded into a civilian population is a completely different ball game. He had never done this type of work before and neither had Rebecca so he was taking things seriously.

Walking arm in arm through the streets of Penzance as two newlyweds felt very interesting to Joshua and he thought anyone who was watching would be unaware that they were not. Appearances can be very fooling he thought.

Rebecca played the part like an experienced actress on the stage. He chatted to Rebecca about what he was thinking and how easy it was to see the enemy when at war when he was in the services. She replied, "yes I can understand that, I am also at a loss on what we are looking for and how we find whatever we are searching for. Maybe we need to sit down and start working things out and maybe put ourselves in the enemy's position and work from there." "Alright," Joshua said, "that sounds a really good idea, let's walk around a little more and get the layout of the town and then go back to the Inn for some tea."

The town itself was bustling as was the quay area and only started being more peaceful the further out you went. The main industry was fishing and a busy port for anything else you care to name. Unlike Truro, which seems prosperous and fine, Penzance was a working town and the sea was a major player in the town's life. Again, unlike Truro, which now had the new trendy tea shops, Penzance was a rough and tumble town serving ale and brandy in busy Inns and the place was full of them.

However, there were still some lovely spots where they could sit and watch the world go by. Joshua thought the place itself had around two to three thousand people with about three to four hundred houses and cottages in all sorts of shapes and sizes. Most of which were located on small side streets in tightly packed rows. 'Hmmm' he thought, 'there is no rhyme or reason to any of this, just a busy town trying to grow. But one thing he did notice was that it definitely had a roguish element to it.

As they got back to the Turks Head they were greeted on the way in by a well-dressed but slippery looking man. "Good afternoon Mr & Mrs Pendragon, I hope your room is satisfactory?" Rebecca immediately replied, "The room is very nice thank you, are you the Landlord?" "Yes, Mr Rosevear at your service Madam," he said proudly, "I am just on my way out but my wife is serving if you require anything."

Joshua then replied, "We are off to our room now but may come down later this evening for refreshment." "Good, hopefully I will be back by then so may see you both later, have a good afternoon."

"I do not trust this Mr Rosevear at all" Rebecca said, as they closed the door to their room. "I tend to agree, there is something not quite right about his manner, but maybe we are a being a little too sensitive at the moment." "Joshua, we need to be sensitive and use all our skills including spiritual and inner feelings if necessary, do you not agree?" "Yes, I agree Rebecca, we can question him this evening and then discuss our thoughts once we have returned to our room."

They also agreed they would like to ask Little George and Christine a few questions so Joshua went out to find them. He found them together cleaning the yard. Little George suggested they should be with them within the hour when they had finished their chores.

Joshua went back to the room, stoked the fire and put some water on the boil to make some tea for them all. Rebecca finished the unpacking and started organising the bedroom as she felt it was needed. Joshua sat by the fire and let his brain wonder then cross wonder which made him come out with a mix of things no better off than he started. He needed to get a grip on this and start focusing.

It wasn't long before Rebecca joined him. Joshua asked if she had any ideas about finding these sleepers and the traitor. "Not really Joshua, and to be honest I am looking and trusting you to lead us. Don't get me wrong Joshua, if I feel that your decisions are questionable then I will question." Somehow Joshua felt relieved as his feelings of tenderness and protection towards Rebecca were maybe blurring his decision making and they badly needed some firm direction. However, to meet Rebecca half way and to ease his conscience he said, "Rebecca, your right to question is important, especially in these circumstances we find ourselves but I feel we must tread carefully."

With that, they went over what they knew, which wasn't a lot. They agreed there were only three people they could trust, being Henry Hosking, Little George and his younger sister Christine. Also, the vague information gained from George Kernow suggested that the unknown families to find and uncover are most likely in Newlyn or Mousehole, not Penzance where they were. They also both did not trust this Mr Rosevear, their Landlord.

After an hour or so of chatting, they heard the knock on the door. Joshua got up to answer and seeing it was Little George and Christine they were welcomed in. Once all were sitting down with tea in hand, Rebecca went first with questions to Christine on how she knew Mr Henry Hosking. Her reply mirrored that of Hosking's evaluation. Rebecca went on and further asked why she was working in the Turks Head in Penzance and not some place closer to Helston.

Little George interrupted and replied on Christine's behalf. "My sister and I work and are boarded in this Inn as well as the Blue Anchor in Helston. Our guardian Mr Hosking explained to us that in his work, information is very important to him and asked us both if we were willing to be his eyes and ears in two places where drink loosens the tongue. Christine and I discussed it and knew it might be a little dangerous but due to Mr Hosking's kindness, after our Mother passed to the Lord, we agreed."

"How old are you both?" Joshua asked. Little George said, "fourteen" and Christine followed by saying, "I am twelve and a half nearly thirteen." "Do you enjoy what you do?" They looked at Joshua strangely, then Christine replied, "Mr Pendragon, we are not silly children and if it wasn't for Mr Hosking's offer of us being useful, with lodgings and food included, would still be on the streets begging. So whether we enjoy it or not we had no other choice. But to answer truthfully, I would prefer to be at school or an apprentice in sewing and I know my Brother Little George would like to be an apprentice in the stables or Blacksmiths, anything to do with horses."

Joshua was silently pleased that this little girl was like her brother, Little George. They both had that grit when needed. Rebecca asked them about Mr Rosevear, the Landlord, and what they thought of him. Little George said, "We do not like him or trust him but Mr Hosking says he is valuable and we must stay close as we can but not put ourselves in any undue danger."

Joshua continued, "In that case, what do you think of us?" Christine immediately responded and said, "We find you both very favourable." Little George echoed saying, "Hear Hear." "And what do you know of our visiting Penzance?" Christine said, "We do not ask, only that Mr Hosking has said that you are both to be trusted, are loyal friends and we are to help in any way we can but we must keep him informed of what you are doing."

"In that case," Joshua said, "I must tell you that we feel we have made a mistake coming here to the Turks Head and must head further into the Newlyn, Mousehole area. We have decided that we will be leaving as soon as we can, probably in a couple of days. We may require some help while we are there, would one of you be able to do this and maybe act as a son or daughter or something?" Little George looked at Christine and said, "Yes of course, but we will have to explain to Mr Hosking tomorrow of this."

Joshua noticed that Rebecca didn't say anything when he mentioned their moving to Newlyn so he took that as a good decision made. With that, Joshua got up and made them another brew of tea and lit his pipe.

When Little George and Christine left the room, Rebecca said she was tired and wanted to lie down for an hour. Joshua wasn't sleepy so decided to go and check on Harry and Lilly. When he had finished with the horses he then went for a walk around the town again. After the town was done he went to the quayside to see and feel what was happening there.

He sat on an old stone of granite which he presumed was meant to be some kind of artistic design, in the so called new world of art.

He noticed that the only ships on the quay were various fishing ones and all were laying quiet. It seems the only activity here was in the pubs behind him with the sailors and fishermen enjoying themselves. He sat back quietly and with more focus gently scanned the bay around. He was not looking for anything in particular but once again found nothing, all was quiet. With that he got up and strolled back to the Inn and Rebecca, thinking about their meeting this evening with Mr Rosevear.

Rebecca was already awake and moving stuff about as only women can do. "How was the town?" she asked. "All pretty quiet and empty, except for the public houses," he said. "You look cold; I will boil us some water for a nice hot cup of tea." "Thank you Rebecca, that would be very welcome."

Once rested it was now nearing the time to go downstairs to eat and drink and also meet the landlord and his wife. Rebecca was already dressed and looked fine. However, Joshua needed to change his shirt and asked if it was alright for him to go into the bedroom. Rebecca replied "Yes the bedroom is ready and all your belongings are laid out on the far side of the room." As he went into the bedroom he saw straightaway how very well prepared everything was and thought, she is so organised.

He found the fresh shirt easily and put it on over his protective vest which he was now getting used to. He then noticed that Rebecca had put a big wooden divider in the middle of the bed which made him chuckle aloud, 'she thinks of everything this one'. Coming back out of the bedroom he asked, "Rebecca, you are wearing your protective under vest?" "Yes Joshua, we agreed that we would always wear it, thank you for asking." She was expecting him to say something about the bed divider but didn't say a thing.

Before they left to go downstairs they looked at each other and Rebecca said, "Remember Joshua, we don't trust this man or the people here so let's be on our guard." Joshua nodded and said "We are also husband and wife."

Mr Rosevear couldn't have been more inviting, reserving a lovely cosy table by the fire away from the other drinkers. Christine then came across with pewter of cider and bade them a good evening. She then mentioned that Little George was putting Harry and Lilly down for the night.

On chatting about nothing a lady then came across carrying two plates of lamb and roasted potatoes. She introduced herself as Mrs Rosevear and said, "Should you need anything more just holler." Joshua's initial gut feeling was she was a likeable good woman blinded to working hard for her husband. He also felt she was unaware or had no interest in the outside world including her own husband's interests. They also got to know the Rosevears had a young daughter about Christine's age who was working hard cleaning the tables and serving the meals.

Viewing the customers around them they noticed several small parties all chatting or whispering then laughing aloud and ordering more drinks. This very much reminded Joshua of when he was in the services going abroad with his mates to fight the French or the Spanish or indeed any other country we argued with. But that was then and this is now.

They ordered another jug of cider and even started to enjoy the atmosphere. Someone brought out a harmonica and a fiddle and started playing tunes and people started joining in the songs. Joshua looked at Rebecca expecting some sort of unhappy face or waiting to be told that they should go home to their room. Instead, she just smiled and started tapping her feet and started humming along with them. 'Is it me', he thought.

It wasn't long after Mr Rosevear came over sat down with them and immediately started asking questions. He was subtle but direct asking things like, how was the meal, how is the room, how long have you been married, what was Rebecca's maiden name, where do you live etc. Both answered alternatively and calmly as practised and it sounded good and real.

However, one question which he asked and they hadn't practised was, "So how do know Christine and Little George?" Rebecca, to her credit and calmness, responded straight away with, "Oh we were friends of their Mother's family, such a pity, lovely children." "How do you know them Mr Rosevear," she rebuffed. "Hmmm," he said, "I know their guardian and help them out as best I can." "That's a really lovely thing to do Mr Rosevear, you are a good man," she replied with sweetness. Not knowing where they were going with this, Joshua decided to ask how long he has been the Landlord here. "Nearly nine years, we moved in January 1699."

"Why do you ask," Rosevear replied quite stoutly?" "No particular reason just thought I would ask as you seem to have a healthy amount of clients." "Hmmm yes we do, they seem to like my beer and my wife's cooking." "Joshua," Rebecca butted in, "Stop asking silly questions and let's have another drink, I'm enjoying the singing, we are on holiday you know." She then leant across and kissed him on the cheek and then turned her head towards Rosevear and rolled her eyes. He laughed and hollered to his wife who brought another jug across. "I'll leave you two love birds alone, enjoy the evening." He then got up and went behind the bar with his wife.

With more songs, drinks and merriment, Rebecca turned to Joshua and said, "Joshua I don't feel very well, would you please escort me to our room." Joshua was just getting into it taking Rebecca's lead in smiling and singing. "What's wrong," he asked. "I think I am drunk and I need to be sick." On that they retreated to their room worse for wear but, they had achieved their aim of not saying anything untoward other than two newlyweds having some fun.

Joshua let Rebecca be sick in the bed pot and then rolled her into bed fully clothed apart from taking off her laced boots. She was out like a candle light. He then went down to the privy and emptied the pot and washed it out. On coming back in from the backyard he bumped into Little George. "Hi Little George," he said. "Good evening Mr Pendragon, is everything alright?" "Yes, thank you Little George, Ms Pendarve, I mean Mrs Pendragon has had a little too much cider for her own good and has been ill." Little George, although young, identified Joshua's error but chose to say nothing and simply said, "I am sorry to hear that Mr Pendragon; I hope Mrs Pendragon gets well soon." 'What a quick intelligent young man' Joshua thought.

Joshua went back to their room and decided to quietly get undressed and ready for bed. On checking Rebecca was alright he was just about to jump in but due to the big wooden bed divider, he had to walk back around his side to climb in. With candles out and the room very dark, he could hear Rebecca's quiet breathing which sounded reassuring and somehow nice. Joshua hadn't slept with anyone for many years and definitely not a drunken woman. That made him smile. He leaned back and put his arms behind his head and started thinking. Rebecca got him out of a little hole tonight and he must remember to say thank you for her quick wit.

Chapter 8

"Ashley we are not going to get into trouble, are we?" "Of course not woman, how can we when we are doing the Lord's work." "I was just thinking that was all, you know how I fret and worry." "My dear all will be well, we have assurances that no harm will be done to us and that assisting our Cornish friends back to the right way is a good thing to do, what you say woman?" "Yes of course Ashley if you say so," she said and then went back into the kitchen. He shouted as she walked away, "They will be here soon woman, make ready the refreshments and the ales and make sure the brandy is to ready serve." Nothing came back but he assured himself that she had heard him. He hadn't told her about the five hundred pounds and a small settlement he was going to get as a reward for his gallant work in allowing his farm at Sennon to be the pivot of their operation.

Pierre Bouchier was getting nervous as he disliked having to go into the frontline, but he had no other choice. Philip Albret, his master, would not take kindly to the word failure and so he needed to get his message across and find out exactly what the hold up is. The three gun sloop had sailed round the coast off Lands' End and was now laid off at Sennon. The ship's Captain was very able and like Pierre, won't take chances when he doesn't have to. Therefore, he laid back the ship a little further out from the shore for Pierre's liking but would not budge on getting any closer. Therefore, the small landing rowing boat crew had to earn their living and row a little more.

Pierre was in the rowing boat with a devout priest of the right way and had briefed him on exactly what he wanted to happen. Two sailors from the ship were rowing hard and two marines with muskets were also in the boat, just in case. When Pierre did something, he did it right and took precautions. He had learnt the hard way.

Whilst Pierre was coming from the sea, his team of sleepers were coming on land from the east. He was looking forward to seeing them again and to praise their courage, especially Zoe. She was a fine woman he thought and one day she would be his. As for the other two, Jacques and Pascal, well they need a kick up the arse. The meeting had been arranged for midnight at the Sennon Farm.

"Why is this meeting necessary?" asked Pascal, in English. "Because that was what the message said," replied Zoe, also in English. They were disciplined in their speech as when in England they spoke English and when in France they spoke French.

Zoe and Pascal lived in a cottage in Mousehole which they had only recently moved into. Their appearance was as Brother and Sister and were both now awaiting their colleague Jacques to come so they could all ride together to Sennon. Jacques on the other hand had taken residence in Penzance and lived alone as this gave him more freedom to move about without notice to anyone. When Jacques finally appeared they then all rode at pace to the rendezvous at the Sennon Farm of Ashley Ward.

Ashley Ward looked at the clock and then went outside to give the signal. Both parties were in their respective places waiting for the signal to move. Zoe, Pascal and Jacques were in the woods to the east. Pierre Bouchier, the Priest and marines were on the dunes below, by the sea. Then on seeing the signal for the all clear both parties made their way forward and entered the farm from their opposite sides. Ashley Ward greeted them as they came into the Farm House and escorted them to the large room with a roaring fire and cool refreshments. The two marines stayed outside on guard.

On seeing the Priest, Ashley Ward immediately knelt and kissed his hand and said, "thank you for coming Father, thank you." Mrs Ward was not to be seen.

This was the first time all had been together in enemy territory and everyone was looking at everyone else but really not knowing what to say. Pierre took the lead. "Thank you all for coming, we will first all take Mass and then I will talk to you all individually as instructed by my superiors. Mr Ward would your wife like to join us for the Mass," Pierre asked. "Thank you Mr Bouchier I am sure she would be delighted, we have waited so long for this."

With that, Ashley Ward led them all to a private chamber underground. When the service was over Pierre took Mrs Ward to one side and thanked her for her hospitality and friendship in the right way and for the strength she gives the Cornish people. "Thank you" she replied. "Now Mrs Ward," he continued, "We have some business to attend, so may I ask you to tend to my friends while I discuss things in the large room with that lovely fire?" "Yes of course" she replied.

On settling down in the arm chair, Zoe was the first to enter. Pierre immediately got up and kissed her on both cheeks but in truth, he wanted to do more. "Sit down Zoe, how are you?" "Well, that depends on how you look at things Pierre. If you mean how the project is going, I would say slowly and if you asked, have we embedded ourselves in the community, I would say excellent." "Good Zoe, Good" he said. "And what of the project, why is it going slowly?" "Pierre you know I am not responsible for the project's success or what it completely entails, only to act as cover and use my wit and knowledge in helping both Pascal and Jacques achieve theirs." "I understand Zoe, is there anything you need?" "Money as always and tell that bloody Pascal we are brother and sister, not husband and bloody wife." Pierre didn't like Pascal and this type of behaviour increased that dislike.

"Zoe, when this is finished you will be rewarded as you know, with your very own holdings of your choice and I will make sure that you are looked after in every way." "Thank you Pierre, but when will it be finished as I can't hold on much longer here with these savages who only eat things called pasties and drink bloody cider all day, bloody savages they are." Pierre could not help but chuckle and said, "I would say not too long now my dear, just get us to early spring then all will be done and you can return to our lovely France and we can dance forever." Before she could reply Pierre lowered his tone and said, "you do have the poison Zoe?" "Yes, I do and will use it on him as ordered when the time comes, as we agreed." "Well done Zoe, now take this purse of one twenty pounds." As they got up Pierre went forward and he kissed her on the lips. The meeting finished.

He then saw Pascal and Jacques together and listened intently as they explained the situation to date. When they had finished he questioned them thoroughly and both were professional in their responses. Pascal is an excellent geologist in mining and Jacques was the team leader. What concerned Pierre was the timing and their audacious move to another cottage which could have raised eyebrows in the community and jeopardised their cover.

In Pascal's opinion, the move was absolutely crucial to achieve the necessary results he had been tasked with. The mining direction had become impossible due to an unforeseen large seam of granite. The tunnel direction also needed to be changed and recalculated to exactly match the underground river in accepting the chemical germ correctly. Pierre then asked Pascal in a more definitive tone, "So are you saying we are now on course?" "Yes, most definitely," "Good, I needed to hear that directly from your own lips Pascal."

Pierre then turned his attention to Jacques. Jacques, please could you tell me the reason why you have moved to Penzance?" "When Zoe and Pascal left the last cottage in the middle of Mousehole and went further north of the town, Penzance was now closer and with its bigger size and population offers me more cover to move more freely. Also, it lays more direct and quicker to get to Sennon using the main road." Pierre thought this was a very reasonable thing to do and so responded with a simple, "Understood."

"Is there anything you both need?" "Money," they said in unison. With that Pierre handed each a purse of twenty hundred pounds. Pierre then went on to discuss how they were to receive the shipment of the chemical. The germ will be mixed and dispatched in one hundred Brandy Kegs and when you are ready to receive them you must send a message through the same channel as before. You must also give at least two weeks' notice in preparation for delivery. "By the way Jacques, is this farm under Ashley Ward still the best place to receive this chemical consignment?" "Good question Pierre, I have been looking at alternative places for this drop and think I may have found one at the Turks Head but am still working on it."

Jacques continued, "The owner has smuggled before and is still doing it but whether he can take a hundred barrels cleanly and move them on quickly without risk from the authorities, I would say I am not sure. If he can, then the Turks Head would be ideal and if I feel he cannot, then the Farm here would be best. Either way, I will get word to you once I have my conclusions." "Thank you Jacques."

Pierre got up and whilst shaking their hands said, "you are very brave men and doing your Country of France proud. Your rewards will be waiting when the project is completed and successful, may God be with you." The meeting was finished.

Pierre went to find Ashley, who all this time had been with the priest. Once he found him he made sure he went over the top in thanking him for his duty to the Lord. "We will be in touch soon with the required shipment to spread the word of the right way, so thank you again Mr Ward, is there anything you need?" "I would like to buy some pigs for the farm," he said with a wink. Pierre dipped into his pocket and handed over a purse of a twenty pounds saying, "I trust this may go some way to help?"

Pierre, the Priest and the guarding marines then set off to the small rowing boat waiting at the sea edge for their voyage back to Brest.

Chapter 9

The night passed quietly and Joshua slept well, maybe the drink helped. As he leaned over the big bed divider he noticed that Rebecca was already up and her side of the bed was all tidy.

Joshua got up and went into the main living room. He saw Rebecca sitting in the arm chair with the fire alight and looking much refreshed. "Good morning," he said. "Good morning Joshua, the fire's aglow and the water is boiled," she replied. "Lovely, thank you Rebecca, what a beautiful way to start the day, how are you feeling?" "Well, I have felt better that's for sure but the sleep was good and I have had some tea and am feeling much better, thank you."

Once Joshua was settled down in his chair and watching the morning fire, he said, "I think I owe you a big thank you for getting that Rosevear man off my back last night." "I had to do something Joshua and although it made me ill in the night I was rather enjoying myself. Seriously though, Rosevear was probing for information and I could sense something was not right."

They discussed things in a little more detail and apart from a few ominous characters in the bar and Rosevear's questioning, nothing really was out of place. However, they now both agreed that moving away to get closer to Newlyn or Mousehole as quickly as possible was the right thing to do.

They decided to stay until Little George and Christine returned and until then keep themselves to themselves except for eating in the bar area. As the hours passed, they started to take some time to dry practice the use of their flintlocks in aiming, loading and unloading. Joshua also wanted to make sure that Rebecca was comfortable wearing the new flintlock in the small of her back. He helped her adjust the positioning and tension so she could take it out and replace it easily without any hindrance. The daggers were also practised. As Rebecca is left handed it was agreed that this particular weapon is moved to Rebecca's lower left leg and her long dress or skirt would cover all.

Once lunch was taken in the bar, they went out and walked the town in a leisurely style. As both were wrapped up well they quite enjoyed the walk and fresh air. However, unlike before, when a walk was just a walk, they now had to start to take everything in and learn what they had seen. In other words, they had to remember all that was fine and all that was slightly not. Joshua found this to be light hearted fun but it was good training and Rebecca bought into it as well.

The day passed rather quickly and after dinner, which they shared with a small diluted cider, they went back to their room with a bottle of brandy. Mr Rosevear was not there and so they were served by his wife and daughter. They asked Mrs Rosevear about the whereabouts of her husband and she said, "Talking and drinking with his so called friends at the Fisherman's Inn as he always does on this evening, he will be back in a while."

Joshua felt an inner shudder and didn't like it. He had learnt that anything that doesn't fit or feel quite right, alarm bells start ringing inside him. Once back in their room, he shared his gut feeling with Rebecca who, bless her, said, "Joshua I agree it didn't and doesn't feel right, I feel that something is going to happen to us, what do you suggest?"

"Discretion is the best part of valour, I say we pack up and get out of here quickly and quietly and leave through the back door which I have a key, thanks to Little George." "Where do you suggest we go." "I do not know Penzance well enough, so I say we head for the forest and sleep outdoors tonight." "But it's bloody freezing Joshua!" "Yes, I know but we can take the warm blankets we have here and with our other stuff we should be alright. I think it better we live under the stars for one night rather than wait here any longer unknowing our fate. We can assess the situation in the morning, what say you Rebecca?" "I say let's get on with it."

They packed quickly and quietly and having the room at the farthest end of the Inn gave them an exit to the stable yard without distracting anyone. While Rebecca was finishing off, Joshua went to get their carriage and their horses ready and sorted. While he was at it, he took as much horse feed as he could carry.

After a short while, Rebecca then came down to meet him wearing full double clothing, looking like a puffin that has eaten too much. "Don't laugh Joshua because I am not going to get cold for anyone, especially the likes of Mr bloody Rosevear." Joshua did as he was told and hurried back to the room to get the remaining bits and pieces. Once satisfied they had everything, he glanced around the room just in case. He decided to lock the door and take the key.

With Rebecca and their belongings safely in the gig, he gave a gentle tap of the reins and a quiet sounding shhhhh which Harry seemed to know meant tread softly. So without a further word spoken they slowly and quietly left the Inn. On studying the map beforehand, Joshua decided it was best to head west by northwest towards a main cross junction. Once there the cross bearing would be Sennon due west and Helston due east. If you went south you would cut down to Newlyn and due north is the safety of the forests where they would camp.

Mr Rosevear was indeed at the Fisherman's Inn with a belly full of beer and mouthing off about his beloved Turks Head and only the best in society stay there, unlike this place, which is the pits. The Landlord and fellow drinkers were all loudly agreeing with tongues in cheek and laughing, especially two of them. Quietly through all the loud banter, Rosevear gestured the Landlord to come closer and then whispered in his ear. He quietly mentioned the arrival of a newly married couple who had just booked into his place. They had money and informed him of the room number. The landlord nodded his approval and during the agreed hand shake, Rosevear slid the back door key into his hand and then drunk up and left.

The Landlord took the key and after a quiet chat handed it over to one of the two men at the bar. As he was just about to take it the Landlord slightly held his hand back and said quietly, "fifty, fifty?" The man nodded, took the key and put it in his pocket. The Landlord then gave them more free drinks in anticipation of his cut.

Jacques, a tall able looking man sitting quietly in the corner, was watching and listening to all that was going on but said nothing. He always drinks cognac and lives alone as this gave him freedom, which he likes. He doesn't mix, just gets on with things and comes in when he wants and leaves when he wants, with no time table. He causes no trouble but people feel he is capable so simply leave him alone apart from a nod here and there.

After an hour or so the two men at the bar left the Inn to get their burglary tools including an iron bar and daggers. Once they were happy with their equipment they headed quietly in the dark to the back stable yard of the Turks Head. "Bloody fool that Rosevear, thinks he owns the place," said one to the other. "He didn't say much about his smuggling mates though, did he," the other responded.

The key went smoothly into the back door of the Turks Head and turned without a hitch. The men looked at each and smiled. After a little wait of silence, they went straight upstairs to the room pin pointed by Rosevear. Again they waited in silence just in case. Ever so gently and quietly they started to pick the lock knowing at this time of night the lady and gentlemen would be in the back bedroom and wouldn't hear them until it was too late. The lock then clicked open and they entered noting that the main room was empty as they expected. They then moved quietly over to the bedroom door but this was already ajar and as they peered in found it also empty, nobody was inside. "Empty, bloody empty", they gruffed aloud, that bloody Rosevear."

Rebecca and Joshua got to the main road. It was now past midnight and very cold. They saw the forest over the other side but couldn't find an entry point wide enough for the gig. So they had no choice but to carry on towards Sennon and just before the road branches off to Newlyn saw a good but tight entrance to the woods.

Joshua urged Harry onwards and although it was dark the clear night allowed visibility albeit not fully. Harry pushed forward through the woods keeping to the centre of the track as best he could and Lilly followed obediently.

After a few more minutes in the gig, Joshua pulled the reins and said, "This should do Rebecca." Rebecca looked at Joshua with a thin smile but didn't say anything. However, Joshua felt she knew and understood there was nothing else they could have done and although cold, they were alive and far away from the danger they both felt at the Turks Head.

"If you would like to unpack the warm gear, I will get a fire lit and see to Harry and Lilly," he said. Rebecca replied, "Alright Joshua, I will also try and make some sort of cushioning for our sleeping." Joshua didn't feel any threat was to come to them like they were being hunted as it was more just getting out of a danger zone. Therefore, going fully covert tonight without warmth was just not worthwhile. They both got on with their jobs and after a few swearing words heard from each of them, eventually got things sorted. Once all then had quietened a while Joshua said, "As we are newlyweds we have a great excuse should we be found, in that we are exploring the wilderness of love." Rebecca replied, "As long as I am warm Joshua, I don't care what excuse we use but the tale does sound good."

The fire was small but done its job and then Rebecca declared the bed was ready. As they both sat quietly around the fire listening to the dense woods an earthy feeling of contentment came about. In other circumstances, Joshua would think it would be quite romantic. Rebecca then broke the silence and said, "Joshua do you have that brandy bottle?" "Yes, I do." With that, each had a good couple of nips and once warmed inside decided it best to retire to the so called bed of warmth.

When Rebecca woke, they were huddled together like bear cubs. Without a word she quickly unfurled herself and got up. It was early and very cold but thankfully dry. Joshua then also started to wake and got on his elbows to look around when he saw Rebecca walking away through the trees. With a smile on his face, he got up and checked the horses and gig.

On her return, Joshua announced, "Morning Rebecca, sleep well?" "Good morning Joshua, well let's put it this way, I have slept better and a lot warmer but I must say I feel a lot less anxious than I did last night." "I fully agree, shall we both freshen up and get dressed as best we can. I will then relight the fire and we can then chat and consider our next move?" "That sounds good Joshua."

Although they had nothing to eat or drink they sat by the fire warming themselves and with minds now coming alert Joshua began. "I feel this thing we are on Rebecca is just starting and getting in closer to find our enemies is a must but risky. But I am still not sure whether it's Newlyn,

Sennon or somewhere else." "George Kernow mentioned Newlyn and Sennon and also Mousehole so let's concentrate on these for now. Like you, I thought we could move to and fro from the Turks Head but even if we could I now realise we wouldn't gain the information we require, so I agree we do need to get closer." Rebecca continued, "I have also been thinking that if we are to find these so called sleepers, we must work smart rather than brawn. What I am trying to say is that if these people have embedded themselves into the Cornish community then we must play that game as well. The only thing we don't have on our side is time." "I'm impressed Rebecca, any suggestions?"

"Well Joshua, every time I think of something that I imagine may work an obstacle comes up and blocks that idea out So no, I haven't any suggestions at the moment other than to try and play their game better." "So, what we need is a way to mingle with the local people, ask questions without raising suspicion, and when we have the required information we then engage and do what we have to do." "I agree with the first two bits" she replied, "but as to how we engage, I think we should wait until we achieve phases one and two." "Rebecca are you sure you were not in the Army or Navy?" This is different Joshua, these people are using mind games and tactics to mislead and manipulate good Cornish people of which I am one." "Good Point Rebecca." They then both looked at the fire in silence.

After a few minutes of silent thought had passed, Rebecca broke the ice. "Maybe we should go to Newlyn and get ourselves a room with a view of renting or buying a property. This will allow us to get in and probe and start asking questions about the town and its people. Normal people would do that if they were thinking of moving into the area. We could also enquire into setting up a little business there as again that wouldn't raise any real suspicion. In fact, we could say that as newlyweds we are selling our cottages to fund the move as a new opportunity for us both."

"That sounds good to me Rebecca. What sort of business were you thinking?" "Well Newlyn and Penzance are up and coming and the fishing industry is booming in both towns so money is becoming more readily available. Don't get me wrong, I know this is not London or Truro but I was thinking of something like what Christine said, sewing or embroidery. I also understand that coffee and tea shops are becoming popular in Truro so why not here. It's not as if we intend to do it long term, just as cover for the very short term."

Joshua suggested that Christine and Little George would be very useful to increase and further their validation of cover. They could even have them employed as apprentices in the business sense. "Yes, we could, that would fit well but we would need to seek Henry's approval first as he may have other things he wants them to do."

Both in agreement Joshua poked the fire and said, "Shall we make haste and find some suitable accommodation then?" "I am ready when you are Joshua but why don't we enjoy the warmth of the fire for a little while longer as it's still very early." "Agreed, but first I will make ready the horses and gig and pack away our things including our lovely bed and come back when done." Whilst Joshua was busy packing it gave Rebecca a chance to think things over. Although she was confident in front of Joshua she was really quite unsure about all of this and where exactly is it leading. Joshua she now knew was a good man albeit a little alien and insecure around women but was sure he could very much hold his own against other men and at that she felt safe.

She also thought that their communication together was equal and nice without fear and then a warming little smile came over her. She looked around at the beautiful silent cold forest and suddenly felt a sturdy resolution come over her to protect Joshua and get the job done.

Joshua returned and said, "All packed and ready" then sat down to warm himself and relax a little. "Are you alright Rebecca, you look deep in thought?" "Yes I'm fine, just thinking about things and how they are going to pan out. I am also starting to enjoy the silence and solitude of these woods."

She continued, "I have also been wondering about Little George and Christine and how are we going to get a message to them?" "Yes, I have also thought about that and think that sending a message to Christine at the Turks is a little risky so maybe once we are settled, I will gallop over to Penzance in the night and give word with her myself." "That would be good Joshua as I have an endearing feeling for those two."

Joshua also mentioned that early tomorrow they ride out to the Sennon coast. Yes, Newlyn or Mousehole is thought to be where the main problem is but in the back of his mind Sennon kept nagging at him. There was something about its coastline and its closeness to Mousehole. He didn't know what but felt the need to go there sooner rather than later.

Having got everything ready, Joshua helped Rebecca up on the gig. Once she was comfortable, he walked forward and took the reins and led Harry and the gig out of the woods on foot with Lilly bringing up the rear.

Nearing the clearing but still just in the woods, he caught sight of a rider off to his front left galloping fast along the main road about hundred yards from his position. He halted, turned his head towards Rebecca and put his finger to his lips. The rider carried on without noticing, forcing the horse faster. Joshua watched to see which track he would take at the cross junction assuming it would be either Newlyn or Sennon. The rider took Newlyn.

Joshua scratched his head and thought two things. One, it is very early to be riding fast and two, the rider looked familiar not his looks but the manner or his posture or something like that.

After waiting a little longer, just in case, Joshua pushed forward into the clearing and then got up beside Rebecca. "What was all that about she said?" "Don't know, I just feel we need to be careful and something in me decided it was wise not to be seen. The funny thing though is I thought I recognised the rider in some way." With that, he gave Harry a quick tap of the reins and they were off. "Don't forget Joshua, the first thing is accommodation and warmth." He liked her when she was in this jovial authoritative mood.

It was good to be on the move and once at the split, guided Harry left on to Newlyn. After about fifteen minutes later Newlyn appeared and so Joshua slowed the gig to a walking pace. Newlyn itself was definitely a fishing port in its own right. The town itself was very tightly knit and compacted with granite cottages and houses close together in no specific order. The town is also on a slope heading downwards towards the sea. Newlyn was on the up and Joshua noticed that to accommodate this upsurge, new roads and houses were being built. Newlyn and Penzance have never really got on with each other even though both were prospering. Penzance always acted like the bigger brother.

They were looking for an Inn to take them in, including the horses and Little George and Christine, if needed. On seeing a couple of Inns on the way, they both shook their heads knowing they didn't seem to fit what they were looking for. They felt these Inns were too far out and isolated and maybe it should be something in the centre where it was all happening. So getting closer to the quay area they came across the Sailormans Inn which was a large substantial building seeming to offer all that they needed.

Although they stopped and looked for a little while, they decided it was too close and too busy without any good exits in emergencies so they pushed on. Just as they were coming out of the town heading towards Mousehole they spotted the 'The Anchor Inn.' This seemed the perfect place within a few minutes walking distance into town and good exits away from the town and with stables. Not too far out and not too far in.

The Landlady also seemed very nice and efficient and, she had rooms available. While holding hands, Joshua and Rebecca explained their situation and their need to be alone away from the main hub of things. Being a romantic, the Landlady understood without any questions. As Joshua went into the bar area for refreshment the Landlady showed Rebecca the room.

On her return, Rebecca asked for a small cider and both warmed themselves by the fire. Breakfast had already been served but some bacon and fresh bread rolls were brought out, especially for them, which were heartily eaten.

Rebecca had chosen wisely the furthest rooms away on the first floor with the rear exit of the Inn just by the stairs leading up, very similar to the Turks. She had rented two rooms next to each other with an adjoining door that could be locked. Asking for a fortnightly term, Rebecca paid the Landlady in advance and explained that her sister maybe joining them. "Sister," Joshua said. "Joshua, we must be cautious and not mention Little George and Christine as we don't know where they are and how they are going to help. The important thing is that we have a room for them and I am sure the Landlady wouldn't mind if it were my sister, brother or nieces." Joshua understood her caution and suggested another cider and then he will organise the horses and start bringing their things in.

Little George and Christine arrived safely at Mr Hosking's house in Truro and were enjoying the couple of days rest with their master Henry who lived alone except for the housekeeper and maid. His job to the crown didn't much allow a loving relationship but that was his decision and he accepted it. He had only loved one person and that person was gone but he thought about her often which gave him peace. He knew he could never love another as he had loved her but she never knew of his intentions of heart, as he never dared to tell her.

His thoughts passed to the last time he had seen her and the three of them together, John Pendragon, Jeanne and himself. It was when they were trying to get aboard the ship in the early hours of that dark morning with a savage wind in the little rowing boat, rowing for their lives.
They had completed their operation in Morlaix and had ridden quickly north to reach the waiting ship which had been arranged by George Kernow and where they would all sail home safely to Cornwall.

The covert operation had gone well and the mole they went into France to find and if necessary kill, had been achieved. When they had eventually found this so called patriot they also uncovered information that he was being funded by one, Philip de Albret. John had eventually shot him dead whilst he had held Jeanne in front of them both with a knife to her throat. He was threatening to kill her in his bid to escape from us. Although he had his musket aimed at the traitor's head he couldn't fire the shot due to his emotional loving intent for Jeanne and his aim was shaking terribly. John Pendragon had no hesitation.

It was only when they entered the open sea on their escape and saw the French Galleon coming around the west coast that they knew they were in trouble. The French knew their jobs well and literally didn't make haste to catch their escape ship. Rather they slowed to balance their ship's buoyancy for more accuracy of fire. Henry remembers John Pendragon shouting, "They are targeting us for range, hurry up." Attaching the little boat to the ship Henry rushed forward to get up the ladder first to steady it for Jeanne and remembered thinking, at least now they were safe. Then whoosh! Why didn't he let Jeanne go first, was it his cowardice. If he had let her go first she would be alive now and this guilt he lived with every day would be no more.

He thought they should never have gone to France in the first place. Their job was to protect the Cornish people on Cornish soil, not go abroad in foreign territory. But George Kernow insisted they finish the job whether it be here or there across the waters.

John Pendragon was Henry's friend and close work colleague and knew he had strong affections for Jeanne. However, as they were not lovers on the sexual side of things John accepted it as flirtation and said, "If it doesn't affect their effectiveness to work together he had no problem with it." Henry also thought that George Kernow may also have known but again he had never said anything.

The problem is when Henry reminiscences it becomes deep and thoughtful and when he comes out of it, he honestly can't remember how much time has elapsed. Not only does he miss Jeanne, but he also thinks he has some form of shellshock or trauma which was becoming a little known issue with men coming from these battles of warfare.

Henry shook himself out of his thoughts and went down to see if Little George and Christine were up for breakfast. Both were sitting at the table and as entered they said their good mornings. Henry sat down and advised them both, as his wards, that he had indeed thought things through and it was indeed time for them to head back to Penzance and help Rebecca and Joshua.

Little George and Christine had briefed Henry straight away on their arrival a couple of days ago. Henry had been silent and listened intently to what they had to say and said he would think on it. Little George and Christine, although young in age accepted this type of working method as a way of life and knew that utter confidentiality and any intelligence gained must be accurate and delivered without passion. They had learned well.

Henry continued his orders, "Now don't forget you are to be very careful with this Rosevear man, do not put yourself in any danger. We understand that he is double crossing for his own gain. Act as brother and sister and nothing more. I want you both now to concentrate on what Rebecca and Joshua are doing. Although they are a little naive they are purposeful and loyal. For your protection my lovely children I have put a friend on alert that we may require his services in the near future.
I also will move into the Blue Anchor in Helston tomorrow so you can reach me more speedily. I have a letter for you to give the Landlord there before you push on to Penzance."

Little George and Christine listened intently to what Henry was saying and took everything in. Henry was extremely proud of them and how they respond with affection and loyalty towards him. However, he was concerned about their tender age but the alternative to not helping him in his line of work was the workhouse, which made him feel better.

After breakfast, Little George and Christine got ready with the help of the maid, whom Christine adored. Little George packed his things himself as he was nearly a man. With the morning moving to lunch time they were ready. The housekeeper had packed them both food and drink.

Although Henry knew that Mr Rosevear would not dare jeopardise the safety of his wards, for if he did he would be hanged, pure and simple. But he is a slippery fellow and could with the help of others organise something away from the Inn to harm them, should they hear, see or do something they shouldn't.

Little George was on his horse Suzy, waiting and raring to go and saddle bags packed. Henry helped Christine up to sit behind Little George and ride pillion. He then handed Little George a note to give to Joshua and just like he had been trained, tucked it into a slit in the reins. He shook Little George's hand and kissed Christine on the back of her clutched fingers and said, "I am very proud of you both, take care and be wise, you know where I am and will see you in a few days."

Pushing Suzy on, Little George felt very proud of himself and his little sister. Christine looked back and saw the maid waving her arms and hands like a happy butterfly which she thought was lovely and made her feel warm and wanted.

Once out of Truro they made good to Helston where they stopped outside the Blue Anchor. Christine got Suzy some water while Little George went into the Inn giving the Landlord the letter from his master Henry, as agreed. He thanked Little George and requested that Christine come in too and both have some refreshments.

On leaving the Inn, the Landlord said, "Make good speed, keep your eyes sharp and do not stop for anyone that you do not know." This they understood as the Penzance road was becoming quite horrid with people getting robbed by highwaymen.

Although Christine was the youngest, she was bright in mind. Holding her arms tightly around Little George's waist with Suzy gentling trotting out of the town, she said, "If I was going to rob someone on this Penzance road I would do it in that horrible dip going through the woods at Porthleven by the brook. I never liked that place and it gives me the creeps." Little George, being the bigger brother squeezed her wrist and said, "Don't worry sis, I agree and don't like that place either."

A couple of miles out they reached the area where Christine had mentioned. Now surrounded by a forest on both sides Little George reined in Suzy and stopped. Christine waited for what Little George will do. Suzy also waited but was twitching with impatience and her ears were up and alert.

The feeling inside Little George wouldn't go away, something was not right. He could either hear something or feel something but whatever it was made him nervous. He thought about what his master Henry always said, never put yourself at a disadvantage and always listen to your inner feelings.

122

With that, Little George turned his head to Christine and said, "hold on." He turned Suzy sharply right to the north and galloped quickly across the heavy shrub area as fast as he could. He was taking a chance and all their safety depended on Suzy dodging scattered granite boulders and pits as best she could. They carried on for over two miles until they came across a narrow clearing heading west towards Penzance, which they took.

A further ten to fifteen minutes of steady galloping brought them eventually into the known village of Breage. Little George was disappointed as he thought they would be further on than that but at least they were safe and far passed the brook which caused so much doubt. Without stopping Little George got back onto the familiar main road. He would remember that detour route, just in case.

They arrived at the Turks Inn later than anticipated, just after tea and the night was drawing in already. They met Mrs Rosevear who greeted them with kindness and told them to put away their things and for Christine to help out in the bar area. Little George was asked to help in the stable yard as quickly as he could.

This they did and it was always the same feeling of sadness that they were away from the big open house at Truro and now back in a dark room which was small and just fitted the two beds. But it was clean and they were working for Henry which pleased them. Christine went off to the bar but Little George decided to check on Mr & Mrs Pendragon.

When he got to their room the door was open and the place was empty, cleaned and ready for new arrivals.

Little George hurried to the yard but again found no sign of Harry or the gig. They had gone but where and why. They said they would be here waiting for us. Little George was confused. He didn't like being confused but couldn't get to understand any reason.

Christine came running into the yard and saw Little George sitting down upset. "They have gone haven't they Little George?" "Yes they have and I don't understand it." "Well, Mrs Rosevear said they just got up and left yesterday evening and no one has seen or heard from them since. Mrs Rosevear was quite jolly as they had paid her a week in advance and the room was still clean. She wished all guests could be the same."
They sat down together and cuddled each other and knew they just had to get on with it but what to do for the best was something they didn't know. So they decided they would be brave and carry on, as usual, say nothing and give word to their master Henry in a few days, as he advised.

Rebecca and Joshua were concerned about not being at the Turks when Little George and Christine returned and knew they had to get word to them. But things weren't that simple and had to prioritise the importance of their next step. They decided that staying low and resting was the most important. Therefore, with a day or so holed up in the Anchor they decided to walk around Newlyn and get a feel of the place, arm in arm of course. Joshua would go to the Turks tonight and find them.

Like Penzance, the village town of Newlyn was busy but not as dense. Again, it overlooked the bay of Marazion which is nice if you could see through the mass of sails in the harbour.

They agreed to go to the Sailorman's Inn for refreshment and start their investigation but soon noticed that the place was crowded with loud conversations. As they entered a couple of men pushed others aside to make way for the lady and Joshua to sit by the fire.

They ordered wine and listened to the chat. Rebecca leaned across and said in a quieter voice, "Joshua, we need to get some soothing cream for my back as this pistol is chaffing my skin horribly." Joshua smiled and said "of course my dear."They then chatted about nothing with more intent on listening and looking.

Joshua suggested he go to the privy and whilst there check out the stables as he wanted to look at the horses. He felt it important if he could start seeing identification marks which could be of use later in some way or other. "Don't be long," she replied, "I feel I am the only woman in here who is spending money, rather than making money."

"So he's left you then as he," said a man who just walked up to her as bold as brass and smelling of liquor. Rebecca ignored him and kept looking at the fire knowing that conversation would only encourage him, which she didn't want. He leaned further into her space and said, "Excuse me madam if he can't afford you I can, what sort of money are we talking and what do I get for it?" Again she stayed focused on the fire. Then tapping her front shoulder he said in a louder voice, "Have you no tongue woman?" She wanted to punch him on the nose because not only was he rude, he was ugly.

"Leave her be," one of the other men said aloud who had earlier moved up to make room for her and Joshua. "Her hubby has gone to the privy and will be back shortly." The man immediately turned about and snarled, "Who's talking to you, bird brains?" Both men squared up to each other in silence. After an eerie long minute, both males looked away from each other to their respective corners of support. In no eagerness to confront each other yet at this early time of day, they all laughed and more drinks were ordered.

Joshua then came strolling back in and after smiling at Rebecca, offered her another drink if she wished. Rebecca couldn't wait to get out and so got up and taking Joshua's arm led him about turn, straight out of the front door. Once outdoors a big cheer erupted inside. "Bloody heathens," she said.

Joshua looked at Rebecca and said, "What's happened?". Rebecca explained what went on inside while he was away and how she felt like punching the loud mouth on the nose. Joshua didn't say anything and just smiled protectively.

While walking together arm in arm along the street an old woman was passing them by when Rebecca excused herself to her and asked, "if she knew of a place that sells soothing ointments." "Yes my dear, keep going straight and you will find Mr Pendricks shop, the last on the left, he sells all that sort of stuff." With thanks, they moved on.

"You are new to the town I guess?" Mr Pendricks asked very politely. "Yes we are," Rebecca replied, "but we are thinking of maybe selling our cottages and moving closer by the sea. We are presently on vacation, I suppose you don't get many new faces here?"

"No, not really, everyone wants Penzance as it's the in place to be. They got yet another approval for 'Market Town Status' and I also hear they got the royal seal of approval for building some sort of coinage mint. We get the fish, they get the gold.""Apologies" he said, "there's me carrying on, who do I have the pleasure?" "Mrs Pendragon," Rebecca replied, "And this is my husband Joshua. So do you have the soothing ointment?" "Yes I do but may I ask what exactly is it for." Rebecca explained about her lower back and how she had been carrying some iron goods home and it rubbed greatly leaving it red raw. "Arrr yes, I know exactly what you need." He then went into the glass cabinet and handed over a small pot of cream to be rubbed in twice a day.

They paid for the lotion and as they turned to leave Mr Pendricks said, "where about are you staying?" "The Sailormans," she lied, "it's a little rowdy but it will do." "Well, if you are looking for something a little homelier, I am renting out my little cottage?" "Thank you, but why are you renting it?" "Well business here is doing well and I have rooms upstairs for my bed and things. I get a little lonely in the cottage as my good wife passed to the Lord over ten years now." Joshua said, "We are sorry to hear that and thank you we may well take up your offer." They went on to discuss agreeable terms and said they would go away and think on it and come back with their decision on the morrow.

They decided to check out the cottage anyway and found Mr Pendricks single story little cottage a mile or so on the western side of Newlyn. It was just off the main road to Mousehole which was a very appropriate location.

The front looked very nice and pretty but lacked in love and care. The back had a stable yard exiting onto a lane heading north out of town and south edging back down to the quay. They could enter through either back or front but. The back access was especially important and was therefore glad to see the access was large enough for the gig and horses.

Returning to their rooms at the Anchor they discussed that although things hadn't gone very far, they were achieving their initial goals of moving into an unknown area without raising any suspicions. It seemed that their language and stories are being believed as just a new loving couple moving in.

This was good but they now needed to keep their ears and eyes open and play the quiet patient game and probe where they can. Rebecca showed Joshua the small of her back and asked could he rub in the lotion. Joshua smiled a cheeky grin and got the jar. She laughed and said, "just the back Joshua." He also adjusted the pistol holder and strap to make it more comfortable for her. They both agreed taking on the cottage was a good idea and would move in the following week. There they could have a base to operate more freely without prying eyes everywhere.

The afternoon soon ran into early evening when Rebecca said, "What time will you be off to see the children?" "I was thinking mid to late evening as I want to catch Little George on his own so we can talk." "Be careful Joshua, I have a funny feeling about the Turks Head and will be well pleased if they agree to come to us." He decided to double check his pistol and knife making sure all was correct, just in case. Rebecca now accepted these checks as wise and sensible. Once finished they went to have an early supper, he also needed to get Harry ready.

The Turks Head came into view and was about a couple of hundred yards away when Joshua decided to dismount. It was important not to be identified as he wanted to get in and out quickly with no fuss.

Walking the long way round and coming to the back of the stable yard seemed to take ages. Joshua waited quietly in the shadows just outside the yard for an hour but still no sign of Little George or anyone. Harry was also very quiet and liked the calm stroking. 'Patience Joshua, be patient and silent, he who waits will win,' he said to himself.

That's fine he thought but he couldn't wait all night and so decided he would give it another thirty more minutes and if nothing, had no option but to go into the Inn and find them.
Time passed and nothing so Joshua tentatively entered the yard and loosely tethered Harry. Also as he may need a quick exit he left the backyard gate open. As he entered the rear of the Inn he could hear the singing in the bar but went on walking slowly to where Christine had her room. It was then that he heard someone around the corner coming his way.

What to do? No time to run or second guess so had no choice but to front it out. He carried on walking but his tension was up and so slid his hand to his back and as he approached the corner was ready to draw his weapon. It was dark but not that dark and when he turned the corner he saw he was facing the daughter of Mrs Rosevear. Funny thing he thought, here he was all tensed up and extremely nervous and she didn't seem to have a care in the world. Get a grip of yourself Joshua.

"Good evening sir," she said politely intent on just walking straight past. "Good evening," he replied, "have you seen that boy Little George, he was meant to be looking after my horse." "He is in the bar area helping Mama with the drinks and food." Joshua then convinced her to fetch Little George as he wished to talk with him very briefly and will make sure he is back within the minute.

Joshua then went back out to the stable yard and waited by the door. Soon enough Little George appeared and when seeing Joshua, rushed up to him and hugged him tightly. Joshua bent down and hugged him back. He then explained to Little George the situation as best he could and asked if he and Christine would come to stay with them. "Yes we will gladly," he replied and then pulled out the letter saying, "This is for you, from Mr Hosking."

Joshua told him not to go back in but get his horse Suzy ready to ride and he will get Christine. "Christine isn't here, Mr Rosevear has taken her to the Fisherman's Arms." "Alright, get Suzy ready, I just need to read quickly this with some light."Joshua went back in where the light was better from a wall candle just inside the hallway. It read;

R & J
Get out and take the children.
Respectfully yours
A Colleague

So they were right, that bastard. Think Joshua, think. He put the letter back in his pocket and went outside to find Little George.

Little George was up and ready to go and once Joshua got onto Harry they were off. Joshua noted straightaway how his horse acts with a more confident strut every time Suzy was near. They were heading for the Fisherman's Inn.

Reaching the Inn, Joshua told Little George to stay here outside on Suzy ready for a quick off. He will go in and fetch Christine. Even while they were outside they could hear the laughing and merriment coming from inside. Joshua knew, as he had been in this situation many times before, that there was only one way to achieve what he wanted and that was the swiftness of action. However, he also knew he needed to locate a route of exit before he acted. Rebecca's words of caution were gone out of the window, for now.

Little George was still on Suzy but feeling worried as he seemed to know what had to be done. Joshua jumped down from his horse and passed the reins to Little George saying, "Hold Harry and keep ready as when I and Christine come out, we are off. If, I am not out in ten minutes then ride straight without delay to Rebecca who is at the Anchor Inn west of Newlyn as fast as you can."

Joshua entered the bar area through the front door and sized the situation immediately. His life depended on getting this right with no messing as he knew from past experience.

Rosevear and his cronies were at the other end of the bar, which was good. He caught sight of another man sitting quietly in the other corner closer to the entrance. This man looked very capable and noticed his jet black hair and icy blue eyes but, for some reason, Joshua did not feel any threat from him.

The exit route Joshua confirmed was the entrance, the way he had come in. He saw Christine serving ale looking tired and worn. Joshua was ready and so shouted, "Christine." She and everyone else in the bar looked around.

Nobody moved as the place went eerily silent. Christine immediately went to go to Joshua but Rosevear said loud and strongly, "Stay where you are girl." Stalemate, just what Joshua didn't want but the exit is still clear, good. Then Rosevear started, so all the pub heard, "What are you doing here Pendragon, why don't you go to that new little wife of yours and get her to warm you some milk for bed, with the big divider."

A loud gaggle of laughter came from everyone at the bar but it soon died away. Joshua didn't say a word but moved slowly forward with the exit remaining firmly in his head. Shall he pull the gun, shall he not, shall he pull the knife, no not the knife. If he pulls the gun people will be aware for future problems. He needed to act smartly as the seconds of silence ticked by.

Smash! Someone had thrown something heavy through the outside window where Rosevear was closest. All looked around in amazement which gave time for Christine to run to Joshua, who quickly picked her up and ran out with her under his arm. He saw Little George getting back up on Suzy and knew it was him who had diverted Rosevear.

Joshua put Christine on Harry as he jumped up behind her. Joshua was in two minds. On one side he was tense and alert to the violence that this Rosevear brings and was ready to do it. On the other side, he had achieved getting Christine out, albeit with Little George's help, but now had to run away like a coward. It hurt his pride but knew he had to run with the children.
One day he will get Rosevear, one day he will get him without anyone around, one day.

The man known as Jack was still sitting quietly in the corner drinking his French brandy and saw everything but didn't move. He too didn't take kindly to this Rosevear or his thugs for friends. But, he had been useful in the past with some stuff he wanted shifting and may be useful later so he will now keep him at arm's length with nods and smiles. However, this man Pendragon, whom he had never seen before, quietly impressed him with his courage and calm. He took another sip of the French cognac and contemplated things.

Joshua with Christine and Little George on Suzy galloped off at pace just as the Rosevear clan were coming out and jeering loudly. Harry led the way and Suzy followed. They were soon on the main road to Newlyn and keeping up a good pace of gallop meant it wouldn't be long before they could ease up and relax a little.

They got to the cross junction where the road split and as they went left to Newlyn they slowed the pace. Christine was shivering so Joshua took off his doublet and hugged it around her. Little George seemed good and was keeping up well.

After a further thirty minutes of strong gallop, they got to the AnchorInn at Newlyn and entered the backyard. Then after leaving the horses tied up all went in to find Rebecca. The horses were breathing heavy and needed a rub down. Joshua would see to them once the children were safe with Rebecca.

Rebecca had locked the door but once opened and saw them all, she made a big smile and both children ran to her where she cuddled them like a mother hen. Christine said, "She had no clothes or anything." Rebecca said lovingly, "Don't you worry my little sweet, tomorrow we will go out and buy you a new wardrobe, and you also Little George. Now tell me what has been happening and why do you both look so worn out."

Joshua started to cough in a gesture that he was also there. Rebecca responded by saying, "Joshua, you can tell me all about it when I have the children sorted and put to bed." "Have you the brandy bottle?" he asked. "Yes, it's on the table." "Then I will just tend the horses and come back and get tipsy if that's alright?" "Joshua, that is fine, I can see things haven't gone to plan so I will also make you a pipe."

Sometimes Joshua thought he wished he was born a woman as they always seem to say the right things at the right time making you feel lovely. Even though he had to go back outside again without a word of thanks for getting the children back safe and sound, he giggled to himself and thought women, unbelievable.

Chapter 10

Jacques, as he was known to his compatriots in his beloved France, or Jack as they say in English was getting tired of this cat and mouse game. For twenty years he had fought for his country behind the scenes. He knew he wouldn't get recognition as the Generals do with their sabre rattling prances but he was good at what he does and he knew it. But this new undercover germ of mass type killing was not his style, especially when it was not against frontline troops, more the underbelly of its supply chain. However, he was trained to do a job and the job he will do.

It didn't seem that long ago when you could gain good information and supply it to interested parties at the best price. He was told that times are changing and we must all change with them and this type of warfare was the way forward. He tried to convince himself that this was right but knew he was fooling himself and that he was ready to quit or retire, as he liked to keep telling himself, after this Cornish thing.

Bloody Cornish, bloody savages and all in bred. All they do is fish, bloody fishing, and dance around some bloody pole with soot on their faces and men in dresses prancing around like prats. With those thoughts held in his head, he took another large nip and chuckled inside.

He started to weigh up Rosevear of the Turks head and the advantages and disadvantages of choosing him to take the germ. However, after the Pendragon thing and his attitude with his louts, he decided he was too much of a security risk and therefore wouldn't use him. He was also a loud mouth double crossing cur who went about the town thinking he owned the place.

No, he wouldn't use him for his barrel running, decision made. That means he would not switch his tactics as he suggested he may. Yes, he would keep with the trusted sympathisers of the Wards at Sennon, so now needed to get this information to Bouchier as quickly as possible. However, getting that message away secretly was easier said than done. Taking the last swig of the brandy and feeling a nice glow of warmth run down in his belly, he thought about his boss Pierre Bouchier.

Jack had been drafted in to lead this project in Cornwall and really didn't know too much about him, only that his reputation preceded him as a ruthless man who had contacts up and down the chain ladder. Overall they had got on alright together but Jack didn't like being twisted and lied to. He preferred facts which Bouchier did give or, believe he gave.

But then Jack's experience entered his mind and knew that he doubted Bouchier's loyalty to people like him. Then thinking on the other side of the coin he didn't doubt at all the man's will to get a job done, no matter what. In other words, Jack could be wiped as easy as anything if Bouchier thought necessary. Jack got up and put his hand up to the barman in a salute that he had finished for the night and left the Fisherman's Inn in deep thought.

Jack's place wasn't too far away located in the middle of the town. He liked its position as with the hustle and bustle of everyone and everything going on about, he could be invisible.

He rented a room in a mediocre house where he could come and go as he pleased and tonight he wanted more brandy and a night of good sleep. He was on mining duty at the cottage the day after tomorrow which didn't inspire him at all and knew this had to change as well. Everything was taking just too long.

His room was small and sparse and as soon as he entered he immediately went straight for the bed and laid his body down. Being still fully clothed he grabbed the brandy bottle. After swigging a few large gulps he made every effort to hold the drink in his mouth and then slowly let it slide down his throat to the pit of his stomach. Soon afterwards he started feeling the effects of drunkenness which is what he wanted. Too long he has been here and too long being too much.

Jack drifted to thinking about his home and the women he had had. He wished he had a woman now waiting for him like every good love story he had been told about but, he hadn't. His job didn't do it for them, or him.

He made his mind up that when this one is finished he would go home to his little small holding in Southern France which he owned outright. He would also somehow find a woman to settle down with and take care of him.

His heart and soul just couldn't and wouldn't let him think about his real love. He was just starting to doze off when he awkwardly remembered to take out his pistol from the inside of his doublet. Laying it on the floor, within hand reach, he again lay back then full sleep took him.

On his waking, Jack felt drained with a heavy head. He made the decision last night about not using that big mouth Rosevear and nodded inwardly that it was correct. When he worked in his own home land whether that was in Austria, Netherlands or Germany, it was all so much easier to give and get information. But here in this bloody England, there was a massive channel of sea in between them and it seems that eyes and ears are everywhere. He knew then that he had to get to Mousehole and meet his contact. He needed to get to Pierre Bouchier quickly and with the minimum of fuss.

He got up and washed then went out to the market place in the town and bought a couple of pies. He then went to the local blacksmiths to pick up his horse, stabled at a fair cost and was looked after well. His horse was a big chestnut with a white patch on his rump and called Arc. When people here asked why he had named him Arc, they were given the beautiful soft answer, 'due to the rainbows in the sky.' But in truth, it was in remembrance of his heroine Joan of Arc.

Once on Arc, he felt the brisk air run through him which was what he needed. Then when he reached the main drag to Lands' End he opened Arc up to a full gallop and enjoyed the thrill. After a mile, the speed of the gallop had done its job and so steadied Arc down to a canter. The cobwebs were shaken off both man and beast. Getting to the cross tracks he turned left and headed on through Newlyn then pushed over through to Mousehole.

Mousehole was a funny little place. It didn't know if it was a town, village or port. It was a bit of everything. He knew where his contact would be if the ship was in. Reaching the wharf, the ship was indeed in the dock being cleaned and waiting to be loaded with sardines ready for the mainland European markets.

It really didn't matter which country he landed in as once he was abroad in his own territory, it was then just a matter of distance for him and Arc to ride. They could take which course or direction they wanted subject to circumstances permitted.Jack knew that having to expose his appearance in a small village like Mousehole and trying to hitch a ride to France, or as near as he could, was dangerous but it was the only way. The problem is the enemy know these sorts of things.

Cautiously he went into the Smugglers and ordered a drink. He then took a seat trying to mingle as best he could in being just another ordinary person.

He noticed his contact was already there and although they saw each other, they did not acknowledge one another. Then after about ten minutes had lapsed Jacques got up and went to the privy. Once there his contact came in next to him.

"I need to get to the mainland," Jack said quietly. "When?" "I need to get there as soon as possible both for me and my horse." "We set sail for Calais the day after tomorrow at high tide around five o clock." "Calais!" "Take it or leave it," the man said. Jack thought quickly, realising that Calais was hundreds of miles from where he wanted to go, but it was at least the mainland. "Alright, I will be here." "That's twenty pounds paid now." Knowing the exorbitant rates this man charges Jack paid and left without going back into the bar.

Jack needed to be careful now. He would need to go back to his room in Penzance and lay low. He was up very early tomorrow as he always was on these particular days of the week. Also, especially now after meeting a contact, it was always wise to withdraw and wait quietly. Experience Jack thought, which made him proud of what he did for a living.

Jack rode swiftly and got back to the stables in Penzance where the blacksmith's young apprentice took over Arc and his needs for water, food and rub down. Jack told the boy that once Arc was done to take him to the usual place next to his residence and tie him up for the night. The apprentice was used to this and was paid accordingly on top of the stabling costs. Jack went off to his lodgings and lay on the bed. Like clockwork, he got the brandy out and drunk himself to oblivion. He knew he had a problem but always justified it, once the first drops had started down his neck.

Zoe and Pascal were in the cottage as always, never leaving only in necessity and this day was a necessity. There was hardly any food and the water buckets needed filling. This was Zoe's job.

Pascal was underground tunnelling as usual with his weak arms but an intelligent brain. He wasn't built for digging, he was built for thinking and being romantic and thought all other men were cavemen in comparison and all had worm brains. How could women refuse his intelligence?

Zoe left the cottage to go down into the local market and get the groceries, nodding to people as she went. She

141

spoke perfect English without an accent and people accepted her as a recluse type person. She always paid her way with good cash and no one pried. She also knew that with her being of sultry nature with blue eyes and jet black flowing hair she caught the eye of many young men. This she could do nothing about but she did inwardly enjoy the way she rejected them all.

Once the groceries were bought she headed back up the town through the narrow streets. The cottage itself was to be found at the very top at the end of the terraces. It was located on the left with a little yard attached to the side and just enough room for a few horses to be tied.

The exact location had been chosen by Pascal through his so called intelligence of navigation to achieve the best results for the job at hand. The previous cottage was too far off from the target area and the veins underneath the deep earth were found to be of granite and also ran in the wrong direction. He boldly said that no scientist could have foreseen the underground problems that lay below, hence the need to move closer which did give some curiosity from the locals but no one said anything.

The next step for Zoe was the water so after dropping off the food supplies, she went back out to the nearest well. This was now much closer and also in line with Pascal's new judgement of the cottage location. Filling the buckets was easy, it was the bringing back that caused her aching back. In fact, on numerous occasions, people would say to her, 'why don't you get your Brother to do the water run Sue,' as she was locally called? She would then always reply with a roll of the eyes, 'Oh you know what men are like?' Then she would just carry on heading home without further discussion. However, in her mind she was thinking, 'bloody fools.'

She knew she had to be especially careful, as she was the only one of the three who had to mix with the locals when supplies were needed. However, she did not like or relish the close contact with them. This Cornish contract sounded good in France but never has she felt so on edge.

The thing that kept her here in Mousehole was the loathing of the English enemy and what they had done to her people in the wars gone by. She was doing her bit. But like Jacques, her colleague in this task felt it was a lot easier in France where she could mingle more freely.

Maybe it was a confidence thing. She didn't know but what she did know is that this was dangerous and Pierre better reward her as he said he would, otherwise she would kill him. As for his advances and kisses, she played him like an instrument for her own gain but she loves another.

Once back in the cottage she felt more secure. They had weapons loaded and the gunpowder placed ready to set alight in strategic positions by the windows and doors. The bolts on all entry points were also extra strong, just in case. The horses were again always ready to go at a moment's notice. Zoe however was tired. She recognised that this new method of warfare was taking a long time. She much prefers movement over long distances where she can run and hide when needed. She did not like being stuck in one place working covert in an overt way, and especially not working with smelly bigheads like Pascal.

She also likes to work alone specialising in single entities as her best forte. However, the reward for this Cornish job will out way the cost, she thought hopefully.

The day was moving on and Zoe was now working hard to clear and move the rubble and crap into workable heaps coming up from the ground from Pascal's so called digging. It was becoming apparent that they would have to start using the front room and kitchen area if they don't get to the target soon. Pascal then decided he had had enough for the day and will let Jacques carry on early tomorrow morning when he arrives for his shift.

Zoe had made some stew and she and Pascal ate together. One thing Zoe was good at and that is stringing people along and letting them believe she liked them until such time when they are of no more use. Pascal talked about how wonderful he is and how his own precise bearings and measurements are proving very beneficial to success. He wondered how on earth any other team could have done this without him. Zoe agreed like a doting pet, preening his ego all the way.

It wasn't that late but Zoe was too tired and wanted to sleep. Jacques would be here early and he liked a cup of tea before he started work. 'Sounds like an Englishman' she thought. Pascal too was tired and so they both went upstairs together but entered separate rooms.

In Penzance, Jacques waited and watched. The morning was very early around two thirty and the place was quiet and dark. He was just inside his lodgings with the front door slightly ajar. On seeing and hearing nothing after five minutes of wait he went for Arc. Then as gently as he could and without a murmur, they rode off to Penzance. If people had asked why he was up so early he answered that he was a fish cutter in the fish station at Newlyn and the hours were crap. They always laughed at the end bit and never queried further.

Although cold and dark the cottage in Mousehole soon enough appeared so he stopped and dismounted. Pulling Arc and himself into the shadows he again waited quietly and watched. All was good. It was just past three thirty in the early morning when Zoe heard the code, rat a tat tat, pause, tat, pause, rat a tat tat, on the back door. The code was correct and the timing right so she pulled back the heavy bolts and Jacques quietly slipped in.

When the door was safely bolted back into place Zoe turned around and hugged him and he responded. The water had just boiled so Jacques took the tea and sat down. "Pascal is still asleep upstairs," she said. "Good and long may he stay there." Jacques didn't do Pascal and knew the feeling was mutual. Zoe on the other hand he liked but was cautious. He knew that a woman to do this type of work was very resourceful in many ways. He considered telling her that he was off to France tomorrow to speak with Pierre about the delivery and the time this mission was taking. He also wanted to tell her that the role he was being asked to do was crap. Also the cursor was swinging above the acceptable risk of being killed, versus getting the job done and surviving. While they chatted he thought more on the subject and decided he would not tell her.

With tea and chat over Jacques got changed into his digging clothes. He then went to the hole located in the back room and climbed inside. The tunnel was small and went away from the row of terrace cottages into an exact direction he knew not, somewhere he thought between north and west. It didn't take him long before he stopped and saw the end of the tunnel. 'That bloody Pascal' he thought.

'That idle bastard.' If he thinks I am digging to make up for his bloody bone idleness he's got another thing coming. Bouchier is going to be informed of this. Things have got to change. He decided to dig but he was totally fed up. After filling a few buckets which lay in a line he dragged them back to the entrance. He then went back up into the cottage and decided to rest. Zoe realised something was up and asked, "You seem fed up Jacques, what are you thinking?" "I'm thinking that idle bastard Pascal." He was going to say more but kept silent, something was telling him that Zoe was probing for something or, was he being paranoid. Either way, he needed to talk with Bouchier first, that was the important thing.

"I agree with you Jacques, all he ever keeps saying is that he was built for intelligence of the romantic and field of science." "Well he can go to a bloody field for all I care and use his intelligence with the cows, this job is taking too long and the tunnel is not as far as it should." "What do you mean it's taking too long?"

Jacques realised he had said too much, Zoe had friends and knew Pierre had a thing for her. "Nothing" he said, "it's just that I'm not feeling so well this morning, I think I'm coming down with something. I will work through this day and tomorrow as best I can."

Zoe quickly sensed that Jacques was up to something as he seemed cagey and edgy. She was used to this type of character from men and also knew when it was out of place. "Jacques, do you still believe in this mission?" "Yes I do, I am just not feeling well that's all." She left it at that but her inner defence mechanism shivered a little. 'Be careful 'she said to herself.

After a good and peaceful night's rest, Pascal came slowly down the stairs mid to late morning. On seeing Jacques, he said, "Good morning Jacques, how are you this morning?" "Terrible actually," he replied. "He is not well Pascal, he thinks he is coming down with something," Zoe added. "Anything I can do to help Jacques?" he said. Jacques was just about to say, 'Yeah dig faster and work bloody harder you idle bugger' but instead said, "No that's fine, thank you Pascal."

Pascal then went on to speak about his hard work rate over his brain power and how he was not built for being a miner. They both nodded in agreement and acceptance of his dilemma, or so he thought. Jacques then said, "Pascal, how long will it take until we reach the target area?" "At the rate of which we are tunnelling and using the formula of time equals distance over speed, I anticipate the first point of contact would be three weeks." "What do mean the first point?" Jacques replied. "I mean once we hit the centre of the first point of ninety feet, we then turn eighty-seven degrees for forty-three feet at a fall ratio of one inch in three feet and that will take a further three weeks. Altogether, I would say eight to ten weeks maximum and within the time scales of Mr Bouchier's directive."

Listening to this entire baffle, Zoe butted in and said, "Then what?" "Then we inject the germ into the current

and allow that to feed itself into the mix and then, 'Voila'"
"And how long will that take before we reach 'Voila', as
you say?" "It will take three days from the point of
pouring the germ into the ground, giving enough time for
us to make our escape and let nature take its course."

Another two months more of this back breaking work and
keeping these guys safe while also watching for the enemy
outside was just not good, thought Jacques. He also saw
Zoe's face frown on learning about the length of time it
will take and seemed to take a reality check on her safety
that this was pushing things. How long before someone
got curious or a mistake was made? It seemed, the only
one not to feel threatened or at risk was Pascal and that
was because he hasn't and doesn't have to mix with the
local people. Or he is too stupid to realise the position he is
in. They may be Cornish, Jacques kept thinking, but one
slip could be the rope for us all. Bouchier has to be told of
our fears of safety. He then thought he should now inform
Zoe of his pending departure but something inside, yet
again, stopped him.

The day went fast and the digging slow. Jacques finished
around six o'clock and said to himself that was it. Zoe had
made a good stew for all and Jacques gulped it down.
Pascal didn't drink but Zoe did and liked a brandy and
knew secretly of Jacque's love of the drink too. Pascal took
over the digging duties for an hour or so but Jacques and
Zoe hit the bottle. Come late evening Pascal came out of
the tunnel with a face like thunder and after swiftly saying
his goodnights took for his bed and his books. Much later
after finishing the bottle, Jacques and Zoe went up to bed
together.

After telling Jacques many times that she loves him and that he was the best she had ever known, she said, "Two more months is a long time here, we may not make it Jacques?" "I know" he said, "That's why I'm off to France tomorrow to speak with Bouchier." "Well done Jacques, you clever thing but how?" "Contact in Mousehole, bloody expensive and can only get me and Arc to Calais." "When tomorrow, or more to the point when today?" as time had pushed by the midnight hour. "We set sail at about six this evening with the tide and so have got to be there for five. It will still be daylight as such, which I don't, like but it's the only way."

Well, he had told her now, he thought. She always seems to know exactly when and when not to ask things and like a bloody fool, he fell straight into it. "So how long will you be gone?" "I would say a week to two, why will you miss me," he said curiously. "Yes of course I will miss you my little sugar pumpkin," and then thought what a bastard he was for not telling her before. "You be careful Jacques my dear," she added warmly.

The morning came all too soon and Jacques was mulling over the voyage to Calais. Although he wanted to take Arc with him he knew that moving in daylight hours just wasn't good, especially boarding an open ship with an expensive good looking horse like Arc. Weighing up the risk he knew he would have to buy a horse at the Calais market and leave Arc here at the cottage. He would also have to dress down.

Pascal, as usual, entered the tunnel periodically throughout the day doing a little digging and more talking. Jacques found a gunpowder keg and set a cord to

149

it then placed the whole thing on the floor inside the entrance. Although tight, there was still room for manoeuvre. He said to Zoe and Pascal that he would be away for a week or two and if anything should happen, light the fuse and get out. They understood. He also explained to Zoe that she would need to follow him to Mousehole Harbour and bring back Arc.

When the time arrived for Jacques to leave, Zoe once again unbolted the back door into the yard and then both waited silently for five minutes. With the all clear they ventured out and after mounting their horses rode quickly away from the town.

They took the indirect route going out around the town. Although this took more time and was further in miles it was safer than going through the town of Mousehole. Jacques always preferred this indirect route, just in case.

Getting to the small wharf the contact and boat were there as promised, ready for sail. Jacques, saying his goodbyes to Zoe and looking like a pauper, briskly walked to the wharf, exchanged greetings and got aboard. The contact briefed him that the wind was favourable and should reach their destination very early morning which suited Jacques well.

Zoe turned around and went on her way back to the cottage with Arc in tow. She went the long way round mirroring the same way they went. When the cottage came into sight, and as Jacques had taught her, she got off her horse and waited. Feeling comfortable she then walked the horses to the back yard and gave the customary double tap code with pause rat a tat tat on the door and waited for Pascal to let her in.

But Pascal wasn't there, no one answered. She waited a further five minutes and knocked again. Again nothing, so she gently pushed the door and it opened. Cautiously she called his name and then tiptoed in but nothing. She went upstairs ever so slowly fearing the worst and then entering his bedroom found Pascal fast asleep. He roused when she shouted at him and said, "sorry Zoe, I must have dropped off." "Dropped off, dropped off!" She just looked at him in utter amazement.

How could he lack the basics of their covert working within the team? This guy just doesn't give a damn about anyone and is a serious health problem to her survival. He has only one concern on his mind and that is his bloody self.

Zoe slammed the bedroom door and stormed downstairs. She then thought about the consequences of Pascal's non interested attitude towards security. He should have bolted the door inside and waited downstairs for the code tapping for entry. Anyone could have come through the door and seen everything and then she would have been lynched. Without further thought, she raced back out the door, jumped on Arc, who was faster than her filly and went directly through the town heading for the wharf.

People noticed her speed of pace but she didn't care, 'that bloody stupid Pascal.' Getting to the wharf, she found she was in time as the ship hadn't sailed yet. Zoe then openly asked a sailor at the boarding plank where her friend was. He replied that her friend had gone for a drink before sail and pointed to the Inn on the wharf. Hurriedly she went over and on entering found Jacques sitting and drinking with another man. They looked at each other and he got up. "What's the matter, what are you doing here Zoe in broad daylight?"

She told him about Pascal and the breach of security which could have been a catastrophe. "Kill the idle bastard, I will square things with Pierre and get this sorted." She nodded, but just as they were about to part he whispered, "before you do this, get his book of coordinates first, do you understand Zoe?" "Yes, I understand." Jacques then gently took hold of her wrist and calmly said, "Zoe, I will get back as quick I can, don't worry."

With nothing more to be said she turned and left. Jacques will tell Pierre and he knew Pierre loved her. It may also bring some new ideas to quicken their goal.

Zoe got back to the cottage via the long way round but she was now feeling more relaxed after talking with Jacques. She also now knew what had to be done. On reaching the cottage she didn't bother doing the waiting thing anymore so just entered the backyard, tied Arc up, opened the non-bolted door and sat in the kitchen. She could hear Pascal was up digging in the tunnel but that cut no ice with Zoe.

Zoe decided to clear things up and relight the fire and get the cottage back into some sort of order. Her inner defence mechanisms were kicking in and she knew it. She felt alive with excitement and so made dinner for them both and put fresh water on for a brew. She made Pascal's favourite dish.

It was an hour or so before Pascal's head came out of the tunnel. Once again he apologised to Zoe for his lack of security in a way like a child talks to a parent. Zoe played the game well and said, "O that's fine Pascal, you have been working very hard and on top of that you have to somehow work out all the coordinates for success, it should be me being the one to apologise. Here, I have made your favourite skirt stew with dumplings. Go now and get freshened up and then come down and relax, let work go today, you have done more than enough for any man and I am very proud of you." Pascal just couldn't believe his luck. He knew one day she would come to understand his brain and, that day had now come. Feeling good with himself he swaggered upstairs as advised.

Having set dinner by the fire the two of them ate with a seemingly much better feeling of like and understanding of each other. Zoe chatted about her young days and Pascal responded with his days at college and how he had passed all exams and the girls he wooed. "I always thought you were clever Pascal but was too afraid to say it as I am not as learned as you and you may think me dim." Pascal accepted this, nodded and said, "I understand Zoe."

Zoe had changed her dress for dinner and was now showing a little bare leg above the ankles and her blouse was a little more open than usual, showing off her breasts. Pascal kept looking at both areas.

Zoe waited and listened patiently while Pascal drolled on about his life and science then, casually asked, "So how can a simple girl like me learn something like direction and coordinates of mining?" "You can't, you do not have the basic skills of mathematics," he replied. "Then teach me." "It's not that easy Zoe and it would take years." "Oh I see, never mind, it was a silly thing to ask of you, more tea?" "Yes please, thank you."

Once Zoe had tidied everything up, leaving Pascal to relax in the chair, she decided to head for bed and get an early night. She said her goodnights. "Goodnight Zoe and thank you for your new understanding of me and the extremely difficult job I have been singly tasked to do." With that, she up and went to her room.

Getting into bed she relaxed her thoughts and dwelt on Jacque's trip to France and her method for getting rid of Pascal. She could use the poison or, more simply the blade. Either way, she must first get his coordinate workings but every time he left his bedroom, he locked it. She then heard his footsteps outside her bedroom and stopped outside the door. She knew what he was thinking and so waited. After a minute or so she heard him move on to his own bedroom. Tomorrow it is then.

Chapter 11

Rebecca put the children to bed in their own room and stayed with them until they were asleep. On her return, Joshua was quite tipsy and feeling sleepy. "That bastard Rosevear," she said, "putting young Christine to work in not only at the Turks but in the Fisherman's too. She told me she had to scrub the privy every hour then clean and clean until her fingers bled, poor little mite. As for Little George, he worked him harder, taking over the duties of his daughter as well as the stables. If it wasn't by the grace of God that you went over tonight they would still be there. My God, it doesn't bear thinking about." She then finished by saying, "that bastard." "Rebecca, would you like a nip of brandy?" "Yes, a large one please."

Joshua discussed the letter he had received from Hosking and what had happened at the Fisherman's. He explained how Little George had bravely caused the distraction which allowed the stalemate to be broken and give time for Christine to get to him and escape. They both agreed that the children were resilient and very loyal to each other. Rebecca then asked, "Why would Rosevear do such a thing, knowing that Henry Hosking is their guardian?" "I have no idea," Joshua replied. "Probably ego and greed thinking he owns the place may have something to do with it. Also, he knew the children wouldn't say anything as to upset Henry, so they just get on with it."

Rebecca said, "Well it stops now, I won't have it anymore, these children are staying with us and I will speak with Henry myself. I will talk with the children tomorrow and ask if they wish this to be. If they do agree Joshua, are you in accord?" Without hesitation, Joshua just calmly and naturally said, "Yes Rebecca, I am in accord." "You are a very good man Joshua."

With that, Rebecca smiled and poured him another drink and reminded him that they have a busy day tomorrow so they had better turn in. Rebecca went into the children's room and got into their bed and cuddled them and then all snuggled up to each other like three peas in a pod. Joshua put the candles out and leaving the adjoining door ajar, went to bed. He thought about the whole situation and realised how a person's life can change course from a single moment and you then either go with the wind or not.

Joshua woke up early and was still in thought about what to do. It was coming apparent that he would have to take more control of the operation in which they have been tasked and more to the point, both of them had accepted. Christine he thought needed Rebecca whereas Little George needed a little more guidance as a man. His strategy started taking shape and he decided to put his thoughts to Rebecca for approval.

He got freshened up and sorted the horses out ready for the day. On his return, all three were up ready and dressed with smiles on all their faces. He was just about to say something when Rebecca said, "right Joshua, what you say we all head into Helston and have a day out shopping, we can also see Hosking and discuss things. The children have decided they wish to stay with us." "I couldn't agree more" he said with a broad grin.

Little George helped Joshua with rearranging the gig to be pulled by both Lilly and Suzy side by side. Joshua would ride on Harry up front. He felt that two people and two children in one gig were a little too much for one horse to pull. Once the gig was completed and the horses seemed happy with each other, Little George and Joshua went to meet the girls in the downstairs breakfast room and, once all were satisfied with their fill, they were off. The day was freshly cold and clear but the smiles on the children's faces were glowing with warmth and happiness.

Harry took the lead and it wasn't long before they were on the main route east to Helston. Helston is a Market type town and tries to compete with Truro. However, although there are some nice shops, Truro really was the place to go. On arrival in Helston they split up and it was left to Joshua to talk with Hosking alone. They would all meet up again a little later at the top of Meneage Street for a late lunch in the new tea shop. They left the gig and horses in the saddler's area.

Reaching the Blue Anchor Joshua asked for Henry. The landlord told him to wait. He then came back and escorted Joshua through the Inn, up the stairs to a back room. On knocking, Joshua was asked to enter. Henry was sitting at his desk with quill in hand and the man named Bull sitting opposite. 'That's the second time I have seen these two together, he thought.

Bull got up and shook Joshua's hand and stated he needed the privy, mentioning he would on his return bring back some refreshments. When Bull left the room, Henry and Joshua were alone which he thought how very discreet and polite of him.

Henry put the quill down and once Joshua was seated asked what was on his mind and how things are going. Joshua explained everything in detail about what had gone on. Henry asked how the mission was proceeding. Joshua went over their plans about moving into the rental cottage west of Newlyn on the outskirts of Mousehole to work from. Once in they would then have a base in which they can work more quickly and thoroughly. Joshua also explained their new strategy of a night and day observation type rota to get and understand the movement of people and then work from there with the information gained.

Timing was another question, as it always is with Henry. However, Joshua's answers seemed to satisfy this and that they were working cautiously too.

They also went over the facts of what Rosevear had done which begged Joshua to ask the question, "why Rosevear?" Henry apologised and explained the situation. It became apparent that this Rosevear fellow was a friend of a friend which allowed Henry to insert Christine into a place that was being suspicious in its activity.

Henry continued, "I know you may think me cruel to put a young girl at risk but I thought she was safe and believed she was in no danger plus the information she gleaned was extremely useful. Joshua, we now know for certain he is double dealing and we intend to raid his place very shortly, covered and disguised as we do, as a nasty bar brawl. That's why Bull is here to discuss tactics. My advice Joshua is to stay away from the Turks Head for the next two weeks until our job is done there."

"And what is to be done about the Fisherman's Henry?" Joshua asked. "Joshua you have been away for a long time being in the Marines and working in Bristol. The Cornish, as you know, are hardworking people and very much like to trade and smuggle, it just seems to be in their blood. Nearly every Inn across the county is doing things not quite right, including the Fisherman. But I will let the sheriff sort that out. As for that Rosevear, well he has pushed the boundaries over this limit of acceptability and if my information is found true, a traitor to boot."

They went on to discuss the children, and Henry, after listening to what had happened, reluctantly agreed with Rebecca's thoughts. One thing about Henry, he is practical. He knew the children needed more but his job just didn't allow this commitment type of love and attention. He also sincerely praised Rebecca as like her Mother, she would treat the children well and keep them safe.

Henry wanted to keep his title of guardianship as he felt a loving responsibility for them but confirmed they could live with Joshua and Rebecca for the foreseeable future. Little George and Christine would be a big loss to his gaining of gossip and information from around this town of Helston and the Penzance area so would need to recruit quickly.

The meeting over they shook hands and Henry said, "Well done to you both for getting into Newlyn and Mousehole and establishing a base without any noise or commotion and good luck with the strategy, it will work Joshua, I know it will. Remember Joshua, that whoever these people are, they are embedded deep so be patient and diligent and together we will get them." "Thank you Henry, and thank you for your kind encouraging words, much appreciated."On leaving the Blue Anchor, Joshua passed Bull with a tray in hand heading back to Henry. Joshua nodded his head with appreciation in now understanding that his job was as difficult as his own and, they were on the same side. Bull responded the same.

Joshua walked up the town but Rebecca wasn't to be found at the new trendy styled cake shop, so he sat at a table and ordered some tea. It seemed slightly strange to him not to order a beer in an Inn but like everything, times are changing and to be honest, Joshua felt strangely pleasant and dignified. However, it wasn't long before they entered and seeing Rebecca and Christine with new bonnets and Little George with a new hat made Joshua smile inside.

Joshua quietly discussed his visit to Henry with Rebecca. The children were not really listening, being too absorbed with the shop surroundings, until Joshua got to the point of the children living with them and in which Henry had agreed. They then became all ears and beaming smiles. Rebecca then put forward a suggestion. They should all this day push over to Truro and stay the night in a well to do Inn. Then they will all wake up early and shop all day and enjoy themselves together as a family. What could Joshua say but, "Agreed."

The evening and following day in Truro went too fast but all thoroughly enjoyed themselves. Rebecca was thinking ahead and taking ideas from both the tea shops and linen shops as to which area she may want to go into, in Newlyn or Mousehole. Christine too was very attentive. While starting the trip back early afternoon they decided on a quick detour to Rebecca's cottage in Marazion. Although it had been quite a while since Rebecca had been back, they found the chickens were still there babbling away. 'Hardy little fellows' Joshua thought. Having checked out the cottage and taking a few extra bits they decided to take the chickens with them and give them to the landlady of the Anchor, where they were staying, in thanks.

Rebecca and Joshua talked a lot about the children and although this was nice he felt that they were drifting and being a little too comfortable when they should be alert and diligent in trying to find these dangerous people. Rebecca accepted this observation and so agreed that this indeed seemed to be happening and they did need to sharpen themselves up accordingly. However, she suggested that let today be for the children's good spirit and once they were back at the Anchor they would revert to their low profile working until they were all safely in their new cottage.

So the next following days leading up to their move into their new cottage were intentionally quiet playing cards, talking and discussing things. Having then the final terms of the rental contract agreed with Mr Hendricks, they could now move pretty much when they wanted. Two mornings later that time had come and all having a hearty breakfast and with Little George and Joshua packing the last things up, they were off. The move went well albeit taking a few trips backwards and forwards due to the extra stuff they had collected along the way.

Although the cottage had only a ground floor, it was pretty spacious with one large room with come open fire and three other rooms. Two were bedrooms and a spare for all the clutter, tools and other things they had bought, and a scrub area.

Whilst settling in, Joshua's mind was on their next move, which was to come once they were settled, probably in a few nights' time. He needed to get an understanding of the sort of movement coming in and out of Newlyn and Mousehole. He also needed to get a better feel of the area and more importantly any unusual practices that became a pattern in which he could follow up.

Rebecca and Joshua were now getting used to wearing their protective underwear as Joshua made it standard practice between them. Although they were slightly uncomfortable they needed to get used to it, until their mission was completed, as with the pistols. Both weapons and protective clothing had to become natural parts of their day to day living. Little George and Christine, being so close, observed these things in their stride and knew it was part of their business. 'Bless them both', thought Joshua.

Early the next first morning, Rebecca made all a lovely warming stew with bread which went down a treat. Rebecca, with the help of Christine, also prepared dried food for Joshua's next move. They went over all the equipment they had gained to complete the tasks ahead and tonight he needed the warm weather and covert clothing gear. His musket and scope were also going to be needed. It was agreed that Joshua's task tonight would be done alone with Little George helping only in the insertion and extraction.

Little George got Joshua's horse Harry and Suzy ready for the task ahead. Harry would take Joshua and his gear and once in position, Little George would ride back to the cottage on Suzy with Harry leashed to the rear.

Once the horses were ready and the timing right Joshua said his farewells and he and Little George left the cottage quietly. They went out through the rear yard into the dark lane leading away from the town. The time was midnight and so if all goes well Joshua should be in place by no later than two o clock.

They slowly and quietly walked the horses for about half a mile away from the cottage before jumping on their backs and speeding on. After about twenty to thirty minutes later they got to the main cross section of the Helston to Lands' End road which forked north to the area of St Just and south to Newlyn and Mousehole. They got off their horses and waited and listened for around ten minutes. The night was fresh and the stars were out. The cold and stillness of the dark made the night awesomely crystal clear.

Joshua had beforehand practiced many times with Little George on what to do when entering a position of reconnaissance. He learned well and was doing everything correct and Joshua was extremely proud of him. Joshua also noted that Little George seemed to have a certain inner spirit of strength and knowing. At the cross junction, Joshua knew he needed to be on the other side of the road so he was facing the junction from the north east. He nodded to Little George and they moved on around until such time as they found the small break in the wood line then both silently slipped into the forest. 'So far so good', Joshua thought.

Once in the forest, they started to move through the woods closer towards the cross section, looking for a position about ten to fifteen feet inside the forest's exterior to suffice. When Joshua saw the cross roads section through the trees they stopped and got on their knees to rummage around to find the ideal observation spot for him to lay. They were looking for somewhere where not too much work was required and the natural habitat would camouflage.

Once found, they started scrapping and digging. When the scrape hole was completed they unloaded the gear required and put things in place. Joshua would be here for three nights so it needed to be as comfortable as possible as he would not, if all goes well, be standing up again for the next seventy-two hours.

While unloading Joshua started thinking of his marine day's way back on the Continent fighting the Spanish. However, that was then and this is now but he needed to be diligent, careful and use that experience well.

He laid down many times trying to get his position right. Once he felt comfortable and happy he fixed the small telescope and sighted it on the junction. He then checked both pistol and musket again and once happy put them in position. He then checked his food and water supply. The next thing to do was put on his warm weather gear which included a very warm woolly hat. Lastly was the over-blanket. Laying snug down and putting the thumbs up, Little George bent down and pulled over the groundsheet completely covering Joshua and his position with the earth line. He then put some stones to hold it down using only the natural habitat as camouflage. Little George's last job was to go all around Joshua's position and check all angles of the hide. Also, he was to cover any tracks or things that may have mistakenly been left. Joshua was in and so Little George took hold of Harry and Suzy and walked both back up out of the forest the way they had come in. Once out of the forest, he jumped on Suzy and with Harry tied to her saddle, rode off to Rebecca and the warmth of the cottage.

With Little George and the horses gone it only took a few minutes before the silence and eeriness came through the woods. Joshua was totally alone now and he knew through experience that from now on time took its own pace. Patience was needed.

The morning came quite quickly and soon enough the first light of day appeared. Joshua was happy and found that the extra clothing and cover were sufficient in keeping him relatively warm. Joshua wasn't hungry or thirsty, it seemed even his body clock was being toned down in tune with nature, in that things happen and grow when needed.

As noon arrived Joshua saw his lovely horse Harry pulling the gig with Rebecca and the children coming up from the Newlyn road to turn right to Helston. As the gig stopped at the cross section Joshua then focused his scope on Rebecca's face, as they had discussed earlier. Rebecca got out her handkerchief and rubbed her nose as a sign that all is well. That put a smile on Joshua's face. She waited a few more seconds then flicked the reins for Harry to lead on.

The night soon came again as with the chill but with his warm weather gear on Joshua was able to keep the cold at bay. Nibbling the food at regular intervals, which had been fully prepared at the cottage earlier, also kept the hunger back.

Throughout the day he saw both people and horses coming to and fro from all directions but nothing for Joshua to be anxious about. In fact, he started to think about what he was exactly looking for and question himself but then knew this was normal thoughts in fighting against the sanity of being in a hole, in the middle of nowhere. The funny thing was when he was in the Marines he always fought on land but always got paid by the Navy. 'Never understood that,' he thought, but there you go, it is what it is. Perhaps it was because they travelled with the Navy.Anyway, that's the way his thoughts were drifting and as time went on they drifted to Rebecca, Christine, Little George and others in a gentle but very explorative way.

Joshua kept assuring himself that time wasn't an enemy. If you have a problem to solve in your daily life it seems we have to have a solution as quickly as possible otherwise all will fail. Joshua knew that being in a hole, unable to move, and with time of no importance, lets you analyse at a pace with the birds singing or the squirrels looking for food.

Noon the next day Rebecca came again with the children. She once again blew her nose as the 'all is well sign' was given. Joshua felt relaxed and relieved for them but also for himself. There was only one more full night and one full morning to go then he would be home. He then thought had he achieved anything as at this moment he had not seen or heard anything out of the ordinary. 'He was doing well,' he said to himself, 'it's a process Joshua.'

Late that night a group of riders came bustling down from the St Just road and headed quickly left at the cross junction towards Helston. Joshua got a good view of the leader and swore it was Bull. They didn't seem like a bunch going to a tea party, more perhaps they were going to sort out Rosevear and his cronies in Penzance. 'Give him one for me' Joshua thought.

Joshua's mind drifted again towards all sorts of scenarios but sleep and tiredness were getting the better of him. As with this type of situation, he would cat nap throughout the day and try his best to leave his ears open for any unnatural sounds. That may work in the classroom but in the real world, when you sleep you sleep albeit maybe a little lighter. The night passed easily and untoward and soon enough the sun rose to start a new day as it does every day on this earth. How exceptional is that?

Rebecca passed a third time and signed in as 'all's well'. Joshua felt good that tonight was his last full night. At around two or three in the morning, Little George will come to help him exit his position, as practised.

He started thinking about the gear and the food which he had brought with him and felt what he had had was good enough. He was weighing things up for when next he would do this, knowing that he would, but using different locations. He also thought could he have bettered his performance over these last days which he analysed and then suggested to himself the answer to be no.

What he needed to do was now done, albeit no clear intelligence was gained to work with. But information was the cherry on the cake and the hide itself had worked and the mechanics to get in and set up had worked as well too. Therefore, he was satisfied.

Once again the night slowly came and darkness prevailed. Then midnight passed and it was now time to start his exit strategy. He gently started to wiggle and then squeeze himself gently up through the ground sheet like a slithering snake. What a feeling of relief his body felt when he started to move, stretch and stand up. All he wanted now was a lovely drink of brandy by the fire and a pipe to smoke; bliss he thought.

He calmly started to gather his equipment in readiness for Little George to come with Harry so they could be away from this place with no delays. He packed everything away and filled in the hole where he had laid and put the foliage back as to once it was, leaving no traces. Once he was happy, he moved away from the hide closer to the small path on which they came in and waited.

Joshua had hung one of his old scraggy hats on a branch which could be seen from the road. This was a visual message to Little George that all was well. If it wasn't there on his arrival at the said pickup point he was to gallop pass without looking back and go straight to Rebecca or Henry Hosking.

Joshua was lying at the forest edge waiting in silence when again he started to reflect on the last three days. Although he saw nothing untoward and gathered no useful information, he thought overall the hide went well and his mental state was good and still intact so with all said and done, it was a success and felt pleased. Then on cue, he heard horses and saw Little George sitting proudly on Suzy with Harry in tow heading towards him. Little George stopped, looked over in Joshua's direction and noting the old hat on the branch, remained still. Joshua with gear in hand got up and moved quickly forward towards them. Without saying a word Joshua quickly put his things over Harry and once he had jumped on both were off in seconds. It was only after they were well out of the way, in the middle of nowhere and about a mile from home that they slowed to a stop and talked.

Joshua asked Little George if all was well at home and he confirmed that it was and they were all awaiting his return. This was good news so Joshua said a 'well done' to Little George for being a good man and doing everything they had practised. Little George smiled with pride. As the cottage was getting closer they decided they should get down off the horses and carefully walk the last hundred yards whilst keeping their eyes and ears peeled.

Joshua told Little George that even after a busy schedule, no matter how tired he was, coming out and re-entering the home was to be classed as cautious. It was a time when many people let their guards down and more importantly, the enemy knew this. Little George listened intently to the advice as if he was learning a career.

Outside the back gate to the yard in the darkened lane they stopped again and waited a few minutes. Then creeping a little bit forward, they saw light coming from the back window and also saw the horseshoe on the window sill in the upright position. This was good as they had all made known that if there was a problem the horseshow would be turned upside down with the curve at the top. Feeling relieved Joshua patted Little George on the back and said again "well done, let's go on in."

Joshua didn't expect anyone to be up as it was very early around four o'clock but he was wrong. Rebecca was up and dressed with a lovely hot cup of tea waiting. Joshua's smile was bigger than his mouth could make as he was so very pleased to see her. Rebecca also was with a smile and although she was being more dignified and reserved than her outward emotions showed, he felt she was pleased to see him which made Joshua feel warm inside.

On taking the tea, Rebecca then gave him his brandy bottle which he gratefully took and poured a large amount into the tea. Taking a big gulp, he felt the brandy hit all the tubes in his body as it went deliciously down his throat. Then sitting down at the table he noticed his pipe had been already made up for lighting.

"Don't think this will happen every time Joshua, but in truth, I am glad you are safe. Now tell me all that has happened and then I will tell mine." Just then Little George came in with the bags and said, "the horses have been cared for and both are well, can I have a cup of tea now?" "Of course you can Little George," Rebecca replied, "you have been very brave, now come and sit down with us and warm yourself by the fire." Little George quickly sat down with a big grin and said. "As I have been brave like Joshua, can I have a brandy?" They both laughed lovingly aloud but then came a strict "No" from Rebecca.

When Little George had finished his tea he was told to get to his warm bed and rest, Rebecca will wake him up when ready. Back on their own they then sat for quite a while discussing things when Joshua suggested that he really needed some sleep. Rebecca also had been up most of the night and she too was tired. So with things still to talk about they let the fire down and retired. Although they slept in the same big bed Joshua saw she had once again put a divider between them and looked bigger than ever. However, he was just pleased to get into a soft clean bed and once he was undressed and in, he was out like a light.

Joshua woke up early afternoon and lying quietly thinking, decided to get up and have a good wash. Rebecca and the children were already up and by the fire talking. He said good afternoon to all when Rebecca suggested they all have a good scrub and she would warm some water for the bath tub. A lovely stew was on the way as well.

Scrubbing himself clean in the bath, he was thinking that Rebecca and he need to talk about their next moves and would broach the subject after dinner, without the children. Although it was important to inform them of what they do, he somehow felt they should be shielded as well. It was a continual dilemma for him to get the right balance. It was still early days for them all in this new type of work and he had learnt that somehow life has a way of letting these things develop in their own time.

As late evening approached the children went off to bed so with a pipe in hand Joshua and Rebecca, now alone, started picking up on where they left off. He explained to her that he felt the hide and three day static reconnaissance went well and that he should do the same again soon. Rebecca argued that the last few days had produced no new information and gained nothing to work on. Joshua had to agree with her observation and argued that all hides produce different things meaning sometimes they can gain you knowledge which can be worked and some not. It was a cat and mouse game, or hide and you shall seek.

They eventually agreed that the hides were really the only way to quietly gather information about movement but that the locations needed to be different. Rebecca suggested they put a minimum information value on future sites. In other words, if that minimum value could not be reached then that hide doesn't go ahead. Joshua was impressed and took his hat off to Rebecca as she sees things very analytical where as he sees things more as a challenge versus risk.

The loud knocking on the front door came early the next morning whilst all were in bed. Rebecca started rousing from sleep and on opening her eyes saw Joshua was already up and putting his protective vest and boots on. He put his index finger to his mouth, messaging a silent hush, then grabbing his pistol went through to the front door.

Standing to the side he asked, "Who's there?" A soft but determined voice replied, "My name is Connor and I have a message for a Mr Pendragon or a Lady Rebecca from Mr Henry Hosking's." With the pistol locked for action and aimed, Joshua tentatively unlocked the door and slowly pulled it back.
It was a young boy about the same age as Little George and Joshua felt straightaway he had an inward ability to think above his age, and had courage. Joshua also noticed the horse tied to their front fence. "I am Mr Pendragon,

what is the message?" Connor passed him the envelope and said, "I am to await a reply Mr Pendragon."

When the boy said he needed to wait, cautious thoughts went through Joshua. "I understand," Joshua replied, "Just wait there a little while and I will return." He closed and locked the door and then went straight into Little George and Christine's room. Little George was awake and already getting dressed. Joshua quickly explained the situation and asked him to sneak out the back and quickly go around the outside and look for any other riders. He will go back to the boy messenger and talk with him further.

Little George did as he was asked and Joshua went back to the front door. Connor was sitting down but stood straight back up when the door opened. Joshua asked the name of his horse and where he had travelled from. The horse was called Madam and he had travelled from Helston. All this was stacking up but he wanted to hear the 'all clear' from Little George first before he did anything. That even means not reading the message now which would take his inner thoughts away from the feeling of caution that a stranger gives, even a young one.

It wasn't long before he heard Little George coming up behind him. Joshua turned and looked at him when Little George said "all clear." Little George then moved to Joshua's side and together they looked at Connor. Straight away Connor said, "Little George, it's me Connor." And with that Little George quickly left Joshua's side to greet Connor as young adults do with slapping and laughs. "You two know each other I presume." "Yes we do," Little George said, "We were in the poor house together a long time ago." "I work for Mr Hosking's now," Connor said proudly.

With that Joshua let things calm down a little. Little George and Connor took Madam around the back yard to be fed. Rebecca was up and dressed. Joshua explained what had happened and showed her the envelope. She nodded and suggested he light the fire, whilst she makes the tea and they will read it together directly.

R & J
No 4 Bridge Street – Mousehole - One person –Alien
Be Careful
A Colleague

They went over it again trying to make sense of what, who and how. However, they are quickly realising that the information they gain is not always straight forward. In fact, it is becoming more apparent that things that come their way are more merely snippets of information from loose talk, sights or hunches, which they have to put together and make four.

Once all was discussed, they agreed on a plan that Joshua will go today and ride quickly by the house in question and check the area out. He would then report his findings to Rebecca and go from there. Joshua quickly got himself and Harry ready while Rebecca fed the children, including Christine, who was now talking non-stop to Connor and vice versa. It was agreed that Connor would stay in the house and await Joshua's return with a reply.

Harry was up for it and fresh as a daisy. Bridge Street wasn't far, just through the town on the South side of Lamorna Road. The day was fresh but chilly and not a lot of people were about which suited Joshua. Getting closer to the target area he eased Harry up, dismounted and started walking so he could take everything in. All was quiet, with Joshua noticing that the street in question was quite narrow, with normal type cottages and all terraced in units of ten.

Number four was nothing out of the ordinary. In fact these were simple lowly cottages with direct door openings onto the street. Probably fishermen's houses or something like that. The problem with this type of target is there is no room for manoeuvre or places to covertly observe as everything is too enclosed. With his passing done, Joshua remounted and spurred Harry on back home.

Connor was given his reply that the information will be acted upon by the end of the morrow. They then said their farewells and Connor was on his way.

Looking at all angles they realised that they could not devise a way to penetrate this No 4 without being noticed one way or the other. They also knew that it is one person. Therefore, the idea they kicked around which sounded very plausible was to act as Parish Council officials, without the Council's knowledge of course, checking subsidiary rolls throughout the street starting at No 1. Whatever they found at No 4 they could leave, overcome or take prisoner. Joshua liked the plan for its simplicity. Rebecca would dress as a man with the clothing they already had in addition to their protective vests and armed. Little George and Christine were to wait at the bottom of the road on the Lamorna Crossroads with Harry and Lilly just in case anything should go wrong and a quick exit is required.

They fully explained their plan to Little George and Christine and the rolls which they were to play. Rebecca insisted they must wear protective mailing vests such as theirs and she would make them today out of the spare material they had. These must be worn by all without fail before the plan is put into action. However, giving them pistols for their protection was out of the question for now due to their young age. When all were in agreement on what to do and what was to happen they prepared themselves. They decided that this operation would start late tomorrow and so all would get a good night's sleep tonight and move out fully prepared and fresh tomorrow afternoon around four o'clock.

The next day and upon nearing the allotted time to leave, Rebecca did a twirl looking quite naturally as a man. The children also showed they were wearing their newly made vests correctly. Joshua being the leader and now happy with the preparation, false identifications and job roles, suggested that it was time they were off.

As planned, reaching the crossroads at the bottom of the street, Rebecca and Joshua dismounted and then set off on foot to do their duty. Little George & Christine both stayed there sitting on Suzy while holding Harry and Lilly. If they were not back by the latest six o'clock they were to go straight to Henry Hosking's at the Blue Anchor in Helston. On nearing the target area, a couple of people passed them by but didn't really take any notice which Joshua found quietly encouraging.

Joshua nodded to Rebecca when they were at the door of No 1. "Are you ready?" "Yes Joshua let's do it," she said.

With that, he then knocked on the door. Within two minutes a lady came to the door and asked what they wanted. Joshua explained they were Inspectors of the Parish Council and wanted to know who lived here for the annual subsidy and census rolls.

Reluctantly, the lady agreed and gave some information which Joshua wrote down spending only a few minutes of her time. With the information obtained, the lady then firmly shut the door on them. However, based on this first call they were somewhat encouraged as their plan had shown plausibility and credibility. No 2 and No 3 went pretty much the same as number one.

Now it was No 4. On squaring up to the door as before Joshua knocked loudly and immediately felt he had knocked harder than he had with the previous. He was getting tense. Then he heard the faint but familiar click of a double pistol locking mechanism and a loud frightened voice shout from inside the door, "You Bastards!" And then, the loud back blast noise of a heavy double pistol fired off. Joshua immediately threw his full weight into Rebecca to get her out of the way and shouted "get down."

The person had fired through the door and Rebecca was hit. Joshua couldn't believe it. He was going to fire back but nothing was there. They were both on the floor and needed to get away quickly. What a bloody mess.

Joshua kept on the floor dragging Rebecca's unconscious body away from the door's entrance. Nobody came out of any of the nearby houses, nobody would, not yet. All became so very quiet. Once out of direct range of the house and into the cobbled street, Joshua got up and with all his strength picked Rebecca up and threw her over his shoulder. Little George was quick he would give him that as he was already coming up with Harry while Christine held back with Lilly. Joshua threw Rebecca's limp body over Harry like a rag doll and then got up into the saddle to hold her and galloped off at pace.

Little George and Christine followed closely behind as they all went quickly out of town and around the long way. Joshua couldn't afford, even then, to let people see which direction they were heading. When completely out of sight from everyone Joshua doubled backed around and headed into the backfields, eventually reaching their backyard to the cottage. What a bloody nightmare.

Chapter 12

Jacques was now once again back in his homeland of France and enjoying himself, he felt confident. He was at Calais and still a long way from Morlaix but all the same, it felt good. He didn't like England and the Cornish were even worse, bloody pasty eating savages he thought. As soon as he said those thoughts, his mind raced back to his grandparents and how they would be thinking of what he was doing. He quickly shook his head to get rid of this mindset but even then he ever quietly apologised to them. While a horse was being made ready at the stables he engaged himself to a few nice cognacs in the local Inn. Sitting by the window in the corner seat, he was quietly working out what he would say to Bouchier when they meet at the Chateau.

He thought of the job at hand and what is needed to finish it. Time was the main factor but nobody seemed to care. They just think a job is a job so get it done. Being in the front line is so different from being at a desk and organising missions with no bloody experience, although they think they have.

He thought about Zoe and Pascal and how she would finish him off. This was not his responsibility so why should he think like this? He knew it was the time dragging in completing the task. He also knew the English were not silly although they seemed to play it that way. His experience told him that their spies were good, which he reluctantly took his hat off too.

Weighing things up with more cognac, the more he realised he needed more men to finish the tunnel and then place the liquid germ and get out. Yes, this is what he would demand from Bouchier. More men and a quicker time scale to end the job. One other thing he must get to know is the exit strategy. Whilst still in deep thought the young stable lad came in and informed Jacques his horse was ready. On paying the boy, Jacques didn't move but started weighing things up about his life. He decided then he needed another good drink, he deserved it and one more day wouldn't make any difference. So he ordered a room and told the lad to take his kit up and he would pick the horse up in the morning at first light. With that, he ordered another bottle and relaxed through the next few hours with cognac and his thoughts.

Early morning came all too soon. He had slept like a log and the drinking session was a good one. He breakfasted and then went to the stables. He had paid over the odds for a good horse but wasn't disappointed. He was a big bay with good lines and strong in stature. The lad seemed proud of what he had achieved and so Jacques gave him a good tip.

Riding out of Calais gave Jacques a sense of pleasure. He had over a hundred miles to ride and would do it in five stages, possibly four, depending on the trail and how he felt. He wasn't going to bust a gut, especially for someone like Bouchier but something inside was niggling him that time itself should not be messed with or, taken for granted.

After a long first day in the saddle, he was nearing Caen and decided to stop for the night. He feasted and drank his beloved Cognac and again slept well. A few more pushes like today he thought and he would be there or thereabouts. One thing about Jacques that he was proud of, is when he wanted to do something, he had the determination to do it and not just say it. The next couple of days were the same but he was now getting tired and knew he needed all his wits about him when he meets his boss Bouchier. So with a good night's rest and not too much of his favourite poured down his neck, he would wake early and calmly go the last few miles.

The next day and on time Jacques entered the grounds of Chateau Morlaix which immediately brought home the fact that his employers were rich and powerful. On riding on through the grounds he was tasked by the guards at the main courtyard and ordered to wait while checks were made. Being cleared to enter an escort appeared who asked Jacques to dismount. His horse was then taken away to the stables and Jacques was then asked to follow the courtier around the back of the Chateau, on foot.

Jacques started thinking about his own mortality and how vulnerable he felt in this vast palace and its opulence. He was led into a quiet plain looking room and told to wait.

Behind the quiet plain room where Jacques was sitting was the library in which Bouchier and Philip Albret were having a meeting. "Against tough competition," Philip Albret said, "I convinced the Prince that my plan was the best to achieve their aim in softening the enemy. He accepted and kissed my cheek, so tell me Pierre, why has this fellow of yours come back to speak with you, before the objective is completed?"

Pierre gathered his thoughts and knew he was on dodgy ground as if he gave a fumbling type answer his boss

Albret would be ruthless. "One of our softer agents in the Cornish town of Penzance known as Rosevear has been taken away by the authorities but not before having a terrible beating by some local thugs." "So, what of it?" Albret interrupted. "We were going to use him for ferrying the germ and had already paid him some money. So now we are going to use Ward the farmer instead at Sennon." "Bouchier, I am not interested in the local goings on, what I am interested in is this plan working and on time as I pledged to the Prince. My name and reputation are of the utmost importance so let me ask you once again, what is this man doing here?"

Bouchier realised his boss Albret was not one to take to fiddling answers and so knew he had to just tell it as it is. "I believe he is here to ask for more men to reduce the time scale of the job." "That's better Pierre, and what are you going to tell him?" "That I agree and that we have men already earmarked and briefed to fulfil his needs." "So Pierre, what you are telling me, is that the plan is on course and the timescale is correct or shorter as the case may be, is that the case?" "Yes, Philip it is." "Good, then let us have our sherry and then you can leave through that side door."

Jacques got up when Bouchier entered through an opening in the side wall and not the main door. They shook hands and got the niceties out of the way. Jacques didn't like Bouchier and Bouchier didn't like Jacques but apart from that, this was business. Jacques got his views across and Bouchier listened.

They discussed the plan ahead in that four extra frontline men were sufficient to quicken the pace.

They too agreed that the four men were to deliver the germ to Mr Ward's farm, hopefully within seven to ten days. Once delivered, two men will remain and the other two will come back to France. Bouchier then mentioned that Jacques need not worry himself about selecting any of these new men as they had already been chosen.

The exit strategy was also discussed. The liquid germ would be poured into the ground and during the time it takes before the first victims are infected a boat will have arrived off shore at Sennon. They will then extract the five of them back to France. Bouchier had lied, he had no intentions at all of doing this but he would let Jacques keep thinking he was. Jacques was then going to mention to Pierre that it may be only four persons returning, not five, as Zoe was going to kill Pascal. But, as he would probably be already dead decided not to as the less Bouchier knew the better.

Once the discussions were coming to a close Jacques felt happier, knowing he had achieved his aim. He was advised to get lodgings in the town and await further instructions. As Bouchier said his last words a small butterfly of black and gold flew in between them. Bouchier swiped at it and in one swift movement squashed it flat on the table top. Lifting his hand away Bouchier laughed aloud but Jacques went silent as a ghost. With nothing more to be said Jacques left the room through the main door and out of the Chateau. He then walked across to the stables to fetch his horse. He missed Arc very much and the knowledge they both instinctively shared.

On entering, he acknowledged and thanked the stable boy and once he was in the saddle he quickly rode off to the local town of Morlaix and the Inn. He knew it was short notice but hoped they had a spare room for as long as it took for Bouchier to give word.

With Jacques gone, Bouchier felt heavy. He felt Jacques was passing his best and wondered whether he should replace him but, time wasn't on his side. So weighing it all up he sent word to the Inn at the port of Brest where the four selected young men were waiting and requested they come to the Chateau first thing in the morning for a team brief. He needed the day and night to himself to get this right.

Jacques made it to the Morlaix Inn and was in luck a room was free and was welcomed in. He had over the years of service frequented this place many times and very much enjoyed the brandy. The owners knew he liked his drink and more importantly knew he paid well.

Jacques was in a contemplative mood so once his horse was settled and his key to the room was in his pocket he sat at the furthest table away from the bar and settled himself in. The Cognac was beautiful and it feathered his throat delightfully. He sat back and relaxed and anticipated that it would be one or two days before Bouchier called.

He stretched his legs out and felt his mind and body give way from the emotions and tenseness of the situation he was in, regarding the Cornish assault. This is when he felt he could think and think he would. He then chuckled to himself when he thought back to the time when he was drinking a Cornishman in Penzance. The man told him how they should seriously go to war with Devon as those savages put jam on top of the cream with their scones and not cream on top of the jam.

He thought about the dagger hanging from inside his belt and the flintlock pistol tucked hidden away at his side and how heavy they feel. He also felt a slight unease that the mission was not going right and that something was niggling away but he couldn't for the life of him pinpoint what this niggling feeling of unease was saying. He then realised his eyes were closed, as they usually do when he thinks, and on opening them he slowly without notice to others surveyed the Inn and the people in it.

As a normal practice, he started weighing up who was who and then try to guess what each did as a way of life by their actions, tone and dress? It was a game he liked to play but also knew he was eyeing for any trouble, should it come.

This was his way of life and felt himself tense once again. He knew he was becoming paranoid and really everyone else was just enjoying themselves, or were they, he thought? He went for the jug and poured another large one and drank it slowly and smoothly back in one.

However, unbeknown to Jacques, sitting in the wings of the Inn was a middle aged non-descript male of average height, build and looks. He had been living and working in the area for many years and sold fruit and vegetables in the town. He owned a small cottage and had a wife. He never caused any trouble and lived his life simply.

He immediately spotted Jacques enter the Inn with his hard looking body, weathered good looks, black hair and those blue eyes of intelligence. 'So, he was back in the area,' he thought to himself. That means something is up. Jacques was, as with many others, bookmarked as 'of interest.' Therefore he would get a bonus this month from a grateful Kernow, once he got word to London through the safe channels they worked.

Bouchier's messenger got to the Inn in Brest late and gave word to the four new young team members to report to Bouchier first thing in the morning. This they gave a cheer and carried on drinking.

After a heavy night, the morning came all too soon. The four young men all with headaches from the evening's drinking got their horses ready and gave quick ride to the Chateau Morlaix. There they met Pierre Bouchier who was having breakfast and then asked them to join him. He had already made his mind up which two would stay the full course in England and which two would come straight back after the liquid was transported to Mr Ward the farmer at Sennon.

He would like to think his decision process was based on talent to get the job done. However, these young men would have to stay in the same house as Zoe. Therefore, he would bring back the best looking ones so Zoe would not be tempted by any of their young zest and dare. He convinced himself that the two who would remain were capable. He also threw into the mix that Jacques would have to manage them. Overall, the decision, somewhat tainted by emotion, was an average to good one and with that, he felt comfortable.

Once all seated, the four tucked into a hearty meal and listened with eagerness to the orders given by Bouchier.

He mentioned Philip Albret many times and the fact that our very own Prince of France believed in him. He felt this necessary to instil in the four men the importance of the task and how secret it is and that should they mess up in any way, their families will be shamed. This seemed to get the message across and once all were fully briefed he then asked for any questions. After answering a couple of their trivial thoughts he then advised all four they would report to a man called Jacques and all now were to go back to Brest and await further orders.

On reflection of the briefing, Bouchier noted their youth and thought that to send young men on a dangerous type of sleeper mission may seem to some irresponsible. But Jacques insisted he only needed the extra help to achieve the success of time and their main work would be limited to simple hard digging and carrying out non covert working, not front line risk. Bouchier felt relatively satisfied with this.

Bouchier now only needed to know the up to date situation of the Chemical Germ from the monks at Landerneau for the next phase to start. For this, he had to travel. So with that, he got up and told the stable grooms to prepare his horse.

The four young men went as they were told straight back to Brest. They discussed the situation and the two who had been chosen to remain in Cornwall felt very confident that their skills were better than the other two who were coming back to France, once the germ was delivered. But the two who were coming back couldn't quite make out or make sense of, why they were not picked, as their credentials were far better than the two who would stay. If only they knew. However, accepting the fact that it is, was it is, and knowing now what was expected of them, they decided to cheer, drink and be merry. They decided to let the day and evening pass with wine, women and song.

Two days later Pierre Bouchier eventually returned to the Chateau from the alchemists at the Abbey of Landerneau and was livid with those bloody nerds. They just did not understand the utter importance of time. Every time he challenged them they had an answer that mixing the chemicals together to achieve the results required was akin to making good wine and that the process couldn't be rushed. The distilling process was crucial and then out of the blue they mentioned, like it just wasn't important, that the final combination of fluid would be combustible and should be carried with care.

He had started to raise his voice to them but they wouldn't be moved. However, on seeing and hearing his frustrations they did relent on one thing in that they would fill and plug the false bottomed kegs on his behalf. But after that, it was up to Bouchier to move them out and away. After further heavy discussion Bouchier reluctantly accepted a finished product time line of ten days for pick up. He wasn't now too concerned about the possible combustion bit as after all, it wasn't he who going to pick up and move them, was it.

All the four men at Brest and Jacques at Morlaix were now informed to be at the Chateau for breakfast the next morning. Jacques was relieved as although he liked the drinking side, he was getting agitated about Zoe and the state he left things with her and Pascal. However, the four young men were quietly disappointed as they had all the girls they wanted with the money paid in advance from Bouchier and for lots more drinks.

The next morning all the young men were once again seated for breakfast with Bouchier at the head. They were introduced to Jacques who quizzed each of them on where they were from, their age, family and experience. Bouchier looked on saying nothing but as soon he had finished and things lay quiet Bouchier took over.

He briefed the four young ones in full, detailing when and where the Abbey of Landerneau is located for the picking up of the fluid and where the ship would be waiting to set sail and carry them to the waters off Sennon. In ten days it would be Friday week, which would mean that you must get the fluid on board and ready to sail by dusk. With average to good sail, you should reach the destination at midnight or before dawn the next morning being Saturday.

He then briefed Jacques by saying, "Jacques, a ship is waiting for you at Brest, sailing tomorrow and docking at Plymouth. Please could you prepare the Wards at Sennon and get the cottage prepared also for the extra two men." This was a lie but he wanted the four young men to believe that they and they alone would sail to England. However, he knew he couldn't afford them to go alone due to their immaturity but he liked deceit as it puts people off guard. Bouchier then instructed the four young men to go back to Brest, keep their heads down and behave themselves. They were to get back here very early Friday morning in ten days to pick up the carriage and be at the Abbey in Landerneau mid-morning.

Bouchier felt good the project was back on with time scales to match. Jacques was pleased he was going back into what he did best after his somewhat bold dash out of Mousehole. Yes, this move did break the sleeper's rule of silence, but on the other hand, had achieved the results he required. As for the four young men, you couldn't take the smiles off their faces.

As the four young men left, Bouchier pulled Jacques back into the breakfast to talk with him alone. "Jacques, I lied about you going back to Mousehole tomorrow. I'm sorry but I just cannot trust those four young idiots to pick up the barrels and get to Sennon without supervision. I have already discussed this with Albret and we have already sent a dispatch to the Wards at Sennon in preparation for your arrival early that Saturday morning. Also Jacques, Philip de Albret has awarded you for your work a handsome sum of fifty pounds to spend on some time off and, has also paid your lodgings at the Inn for the next ten days. So enjoy yourself and have a nice relaxing break but be back here Thursday evening for the final briefing." Jacque's hopes of seeing Zoe in a couple of days and looking after her were now dashed but, with a straight face and giving no outward sign of sadness and frustration, he nodded and accepted Bouchier's orders. He had no other choice.

Chapter 13

Little George hastily arrived at the Blue Anchor in Helston sweating and out of breath, as was Suzy his horse. He must find Mr Hosking quickly and tell him what has happened. He knew where to go and so dashed in and went to the rear of the Inn where his master's room was located. Knocking loudly and leaning fully forward, he spoke to the door, "Mr Hosking, Mr Hosking." He waited and then heard the sound of movement within.

Hosking's opened the door and saw Little George in a very agitated state and asked, "what is it Little George?' He explained what went on and how Rebecca is poorly and bleeding from being shot.

Henry thinks quickly and asks Little George to stay here, he will be back shortly. Henry quickly went off out of the Inn while Little George sat anxiously in a seat in Henry's room, waiting for his return.

It wasn't long before Henry and another man entered and startled Little George into an upright position. Henry introduced the other man as a friend and Physician and ask that he take him quickly to Rebecca and do not spare the horses. As both started to exit Henry took Little George's shoulder and said in a calm voice, "Well done my boy."

Galloping as fast they could Little George and the Doctor arrived at the cottage safely. As the front door to the cottage opened the cold air rushed in so Little George ran in quickly with the doctor by his side. It had taken a few tense hours but the sense of secrecy was paramount to their safety. Joshua knew it would take longer to use their own medical resource rather than use the local Physician but telling a locum Doctor a woman has been shot would be around Mousehole and Newlyn as quick as wild fire. No, he had to be wise and secretive so sending Little George to Henry Hosking for help was the only way.

The Physician introduced himself and informed Joshua that he has been sent on the orders of one Henry Hosking. Without pause, due to the urgency of the situation, he continued by asking where the patient lays.

Joshua showed him to the bedroom where Christine was sitting by the bedside ever so gently bathing Rebecca's head with cold water. Rebecca lay on top of the bed still fully clothed with a blanket over her. Joshua had tried to inspect the wound but the clothing had interfered and meshed around it. Also, to try and stop the bleeding Joshua had applied padding and pressure as best and as close to the wound as he could. He didn't know what else to do but had done this several times whilst in service with his mates who had been hit.

The Physician went straight to her side and started doing the basics in which doctors do. He asked for hot water and towelling. Joshua had already thought he would ask this and so had prepared things accordingly. Rebecca was still unconscious but her breathing seemed steady.

The Physician started cutting the material away from around the area of the wound which was over the right side of her right breast. The Physician then looked back over his shoulder and saw three pairs of eyes looking intently at what he was doing. He politely asked them all to leave and wait outside and will call if he needs assistance. Joshua, Little George and Christine reluctantly withdrew to the front room where the fire was roaring and closed the door behind them. Joshua wanted a drink but knew this was not the time as he had to have all his wits about him. So he took the hot water from the fire and made all of them a cup of tea. He also decided to have a pipe to steady his thoughts.

All were quiet until Little George got up and said he would go and tend to Suzy and put her down for the night and would also check on the Physician's horse and make her comfy too. Christine stayed close to Joshua and held his hand. Joshua started reflecting on what went wrong. The ruse about being Parish officials seemed to be a good one but he was not prepared or even thought about a shot being fired from inside an unopened door. 'Why?' he kept asking himself. Why, why could he not have seen this coming, but how could he?' Experience in the field is one thing but one thing it did show was his naivety or more to the point his inexperience in this type of urban conflict. He knew he was beating himself up but also knew he was analysing for the prevention of future incidents. He was learning, but at what cost.

It was getting late so Joshua advised a very sleepy Christine to go to her room and sleep a while and he would call her if anything occurred. Also, when Little George had finished his tasks was advised the same. Joshua would stay up and attend to the Physician if needed.

The cottage seemed very quiet with only the fire roaring its heat and crackle. Joshua dozed off and then before he knew it felt a hand on his shoulder shaking him awake. It was the Physician and once Joshua acknowledged him that he was awake and alert the Physician started to explain in a quiet voice that Rebecca was asleep and comfortable. The ball of shot it seems had indeed penetrated in the far upper right side of her body slicing some of the breast, but due to her wearing the protective garment, it had not penetrated deep enough to cut any main vessels and cause a life threatening wound. However, infection is a major concern, as is the trauma.

The ball and splinter had been removed and the hole cleaned and stitched up with the blood clotting well, as far as he could see. The physician then confirmed he would stay with Rebecca till morning and change the dressings accordingly. Joshua offered his sincere thanks and made tea for two with pipes to match.

The Physician took both tea and pipe in hand and sat down saying, "It is not for me to judge your doings as I have worked with Henry for some years, but what I will say it is thanks to the Lord you both were wearing your protective vests." He then asked if Joshua was injured in any way and he answered, "I don't think so." However, the physician got up and quickly checked him over and then accepting he was unhurt went into the other bedroom to check on Christine and Little George. Once completed and satisfied he went back to Rebecca and left the door ajar.

The night passed without any further ado and the cottage came awake early the next morning around seven thirty. The fire was on and Little George and Christine were cooking some bacon for all to have breakfast. It was not long after that the Physician came out and said they could all go in and see Rebecca if they wanted as she is now conscious but still weak. Joshua mentioned to him that we do not know your name. The Physician raised an eyebrow and replied simply, "How about you call me Doctor Smith." With that all just smiled with an understanding of thankfulness and went in to see Rebecca.

Rebecca was now fully in the bed and her clothes put on the floor by the window. Christine was first by her side and held her hand. Joshua and Little George then went in turn and kissed her on the cheek with a tender warmth of love. Rebecca was smiling and a tear left her eye which slid down over her cheek. The doctor then suggested that Christine be a nurse and to stay with her to wipe her forehead with cool water but as for Joshua and Little George, you should leave Rebecca in peace for a while.

Once back in the front room the doctor advised how and when to change the bandages and a little broth should be permitted with water on a regular basis. He said if Little George would accompany him back to Helston he would make up some medicine to give to Rebecca and some extra dressings to be applied every morning for a week. He would then come back and see the patient. But if anything seems wrong in the interim, to get word to Henry.

On seeing Little George and the Physician off, Joshua closed the front door and sat down by the fire. He was feeling at a loss on what to do and so decided to go back to basics and start washing everyone's clothes. He would also clean their weapons and importantly, take a look at the protective vest Rebecca was wearing. This kept him occupied physically but mentally he was arranging things on how to move forward and who shot Rebecca and how could he get this information and, once he got it, what to do with it.

One thing he did know is all of them were safe for now and that Rebecca would live, which pleased him but whoever is out there and whatever they intended to do were still out there. It was down to him to find them and so he needed to get a grip and grow up and take responsibility.

Later through the day the cottage once again started to become calm and peaceful with everything now cleaned and tidied up. Christine was with Rebecca and Joshua was resting in the front room, fire roaring with a lovely brew of tea and a pipe. He really needed to speak with Henry and find out what if any news he may have.

Not long after Joshua had sat down to rest, Little George came back with the medical supplies the so called 'Doctor Smith' had promised. There was also a note for Joshua from Henry Hosking suggesting the need for them to meet up early tomorrow morning at the Blue Anchor.

Rebecca, although still a little brain dozy, was starting to get an understanding of what was going on around her to the point that she now began suggesting things, albeit in a very quiet voice. 'It must be a woman thing,' Joshua thought. He made them all some broth and tea and they ate quietly with Rebecca in the bed and Christine feeding her. Whilst they ate they talked. Rebecca mostly listened but again whispered her thoughts and suggestions when needed.

Although George Kernow had mentioned the dangers of this task at the beginning they didn't realise the level of which this meant but, they certainly do now. So all in agreement they wanted to carry on with the mission but from now on, their safety and reducing risk levels must be a priority. The night was closing in and so Joshua set his bed up in the front room for an early night ready for a fresh start in the morning. Christine wanted to stay with Rebecca and was adamant that she would nurse her accordingly and change the dressings when required. Doctor Smith had showed her what to do and with a little nod and smile from Rebecca, it was agreed. For a young lady, she certainly had a tenacity and Joshua respected that.

The morning came with a new freshness and once Joshua had saddled Harry he was ready to go. The ride took him just over an hour reaching the Blue Anchor just after seven thirty. Even at this early hour, the Inn was moving with the early risers and the people running it. He found young Connor was waiting outside and when Joshua dismounted he took Harry to the side stables. Joshua thanked Connor and then went straight in and met Henry having an early breakfast in the front parlour by the fire. ''Good morning Joshua, please take a seat.''

They exchanged pleasantries and sat down together to share the food and discuss. Henry asked Joshua to explain in fine detail everything that had gone on. One thing Joshua has learnt when he is asked for fine detail, he means fine detail, as though he himself is visualising the moments in question. They got onto the subject of the house at No 4 and the subsequent disaster which followed and their indirect roundabout withdrawal to the cottage.

Henry listened intently adding nods and hmmm's along the way and stopping Joshua to elaborate on certain things. Henry liked debriefs to be methodical and slow to medium speed so he can take all the information in. Joshua also found that this slowness in speed helped him be more aware of what exactly happened or was happening when looking back at each event. Once his debrief was finished Henry took two pipes and offered Joshua one and then reached into the fire for a glow stick to light them. Both now smoking and Henry thinking things over in his head he leaned forward and said, "Well done Joshua and well done to Rebecca, Little George and Christine."

"Now let me tell you what's been happening behind the scene in west Cornwall whilst you and Rebecca have been away in the front line, so to speak." Henry went on to discuss all the information he had to tell of which one was Mr Rosevear the Landlord at the Turks Head in Penzance. Joshua had been thinking about him also. Rosevear had been taken in for questioning on the orders of Henry. He had been taken with the help of Bull and the gang from St Just, by covering it up with a fight that got out of hand. It had worked and as we speak Rosevear is on route to London for a discussion with George Kernow.

Henry then explained that the person who shot Rebecca through the door of No 4 was in fact a sailor of piracy who had absconded from ship and was lying low. He knew the authorities were searching for him for the murder of two ship mates and looting money from others. He has now been caught while trying to run from the house after the shooting incident and got as far as Mousehole Harbour.

He thought you were the authorities of the Royal Navy and had nothing to lose and knew if caught he will hang and, hang he will. Thank God Rebecca survived through your quick actions. "Thank you Henry but I wasn't that quick it was the protective vest that saved her life," Joshua replied. "Yes, they are good aren't they? Which reminds me, now that you are running with four persons I have here two new small lady pocket pistols which may I suggest you give to Little George and Christine for their protection. I have also had two extra protective vests made with extra material for them as well." "Yes, it seems that we are now four and thank you Henry."

Henry continued but with a more quiet voice, "now there is some information being fed down the line from London which arrived late last night. It seems that a certain person we know as 'Jack' has been seen in a place in France, close to certain people known not to me but to George Kernow.

This has raised suspicion and escalated things especially when this guy was presumably seen in Penzance not so long ago. This sighting prompted, among other things, why the traitor Rosevear of the Turks Head is now going straight into custody in London and not Bodmin. "What does this mean Henry?" "It means Joshua that something is coming or is being implemented." "What does this guy Jack look like?" Joshua asked""A little like you Joshua actually, but older and tanned, with a well-structured face. He is six foot tall plus, jet black hair and very knowing blue eyes, almost piercing with intelligence and calmness. In fact, we had an artist impression made of him." Henry then delved into his pocket and produced a small piece of paper with a sketched face of this man called Jacques and handed it to Joshua.

Whilst Henry was carrying on describing him, Joshua was looking at the sketch in hand and his mind immediately flicked back to the Fisherman's Inn in Penzance the night he took young Christine from Rosevear's clutches and where Little George broke the window to help their escape. He recalled that when he was surveying the Inn on his entrance he saw this guy in the corner and thought then that of all the people in the Inn he would be the most problematic but, somehow knew this man would not interfere. It was the strength in his manner and the calmness in his eyes.

"Henry, 'I have seen this man before," Joshua said, "in the Fisherman's Inn when I snatched Christine away from Rosevear." Henry nodded then said, "so it is confirmed then. Joshua, I must ask that you double your efforts and move quickly. If this guy has been seen in France in an area of interest to ourselves, we would surmise that he has taken further orders."

Joshua asked, "do you know anything more of this man Henry and please tell me all you know." Henry said what he could and nearing the end he mentioned "this man Jack or Jacques has one vice or possible weak link and that my friend is drink, specifically French Brandy. But Joshua do not under estimate him ever, even if he is or hasn't been drinking, he is very experienced."

With the meeting finished both said their farewells. Joshua left the building with his mind bubbling with activity. He needed to think and get this right. Simply knocking on doors like a simpleton Council worker produced nothing but overt attention and life threatening outcomes.

Joshua walked to the stables, picked up Harry and strode out into the open. Gunwalloe he thought, that's where he needed to go. So with that thought in mind, Joshua leapt on Harry and rode off at a gallop.

Whilst on route he decided to divert to Cury and pick up Queenie and Cecil at Mrs Stephens. They were pleased to see him and couldn't stop wagging their tails. He thanked Mrs Stephens for her kindness and offered some money but she would have none of it. So with both dogs on his lap upon Harry, who accepted these little mites lovingly, they headed for his cottage at Gunwalloe.

The cottage was dusty and felt lonely without him being there but it seemed to wake up when he kindled the fire. The afternoon was mild and fresh and so he sat in front of the hearth with the fire roaring and windows open. He made himself a nice cup of tea with fresh milk which Mrs Stephens had supplied. He then lit a pipe and sat back looking at the ceiling with Queenie and Cecil snuggled up by his feet.

It wasn't long before Joshua decided to head to the beach. Leaving both dogs by the fire he walked gently down the slope to the rocks. Apart from a couple of people, the beach was empty. It was now late afternoon early evening. He got to his usual place, sat down and thought.

After an hour of pure freshness and being alone his brain got it. He decided discipline and planning in a step by step approach was the way. Planning long term stuff didn't work. It sounded good but doesn't work on the ground.

201

He needed intelligence and knowledge. He also needed to know his strengths and weaknesses which there were many and use these strengths to his advantage.

So he thought, we have two young adults both girl and boy who are extremely loyal and tenacious and can be trusted no matter what. One experienced lady of the world who again had brains and loyalty. And he himself, experienced in life, not in love. He chuckled at that, but he was very determined and again loyal. Yes, he must now take steps to have more up to date team talks regularly and not just ad hoc when they felt like it.

He would use the instruments given to him such as pistols, vests, optical and garments to the best they could bring. He also knew that pride was sometimes getting in the way of things and must remember if he needed, he had heavy back up from Bull and his gang at St Just. They seemed very capable but as for their loyalty, he yet couldn't give reason. With all this going through his mind and a determination to succeed he knew that the overall word which kept coming back over and over was patience. However, he also knew that good planning was a form of patience and he felt happy with that.

It was getting late and he wanted now to get back to west Newlyn to be with Rebecca and the two young ones before the night was out. But then noting that no one was on the beach Joshua's inquisitiveness lent him to look over the sand at the entrance to the cave with the so called tunnel at the back. The one Rebecca said she took to get to his cottage. He was intrigued to use it just so he knew in his mind it was there and also see if he could orientate himself through it. Yes, he would do it.

On entering the cave, he went direct to the back marker and pushed hard, as Rebecca had told him, and the door moved. Joshua couldn't quite believe that after all these years he never actually believed these things existed. But now he was using one, it seemed somehow quite a normal thing to do in the field he was playing.

Without further ado, he boldly went in and touching the side walls for balance he walked forward and upwards. As Rebecca had said the tunnel route was a simple straight line ending in his back garden with the exit covered by gorse. Unbelievably simple but very effective, he thought. Going back into the cottage the fire had gone out. So he closed everything up, got Queenie and Cecil, and with Harry in good stead, moved on to Newlyn at pace. Joshua started feeling more confident with himself and felt he was getting somewhere anticipating his new more structured approach, would produce better results.

It was nearing midnight before Joshua eventually arrived at their cottage. The light was dim and as he entered saw the fire, although alight was almost out. Little George was asleep on the soft chair but started rousing to the noise of the door closing. Joshua suggested he go to bed and would discuss things bright and early in the morning.

Joshua went in to see Rebecca who was fast asleep as was Christine lying next to her. He quietly left the room with the door ajar. He tended to his horse Harry and went back into the cottage to make up his bed in the front room where he too would sleep soundly. As though understanding the situation by being quiet Queenie and Cecil, after sniffing around like rats, lay down with him.

The morning came all too quickly and Joshua rose with new vigour to get the job done with the new structure he had devised. So Joshua with the help of Little George and Christine got the cottage alive and warm with breakfast being made ready. Queenie and Cecil couldn't believe their luck with all the attention they were getting and running around the new place like demons.

Rebecca was awake and wanted to get up for the first time since the incident. So aided by little Christine and holding on to the wall for more support, she walked out of the bedroom and said "Good morning." Joshua along with Little George looked up in surprise, got up and helped her to the soft chair in front of the fire. Queenie and Cecil quickly raced around her as they wanted in on the act. A smile came over Rebecca which brightened them all.

"So Joshua, tell me what has happened and what are your plans?" With everyone now in attendance, Joshua explained in full what Henry and he had discussed. He went into all details and specifically focused on this person called Jacques or Jack. He passed the sketch around so all were familiar. Everyone listened carefully without any questions being asked.

Joshua then handed out the new small lady pistols to Little George and Christine saying that this afternoon they will go back to his cottage at Gunwalloe and practice as he did with Rebecca. He was expecting Rebecca to stop him there and protest at bringing the children into this web further but she did not, only nodded her approval. It seemed that for the first time they had all together now understood that they are in this together no matter what.

Joshua outlined from tomorrow how the new structure would start. Little George and Christine as brother and sister were to enter Newlyn and Mousehole during the day and mingle and play. However, while doing this they must keep their ears and eyes open and note particular things outside the norm. They must remember everything from names, places and people's actions. However, they must never ever be alone from each other. They must also report back to Rebecca every day. They were in complete acceptance and Rebecca again stressed the importance that they must stay together at all times and in no circumstance were they to separate, which they both understood.

With the non existence of any new information apart from the Jacks thing, Joshua was working out their next moves. Apart from Little George and Christine working the streets during day he would work the pubs at night. He had also identified and earmarked three full night observation sites which, if no information is gained beforehand, would start next Thursday. One is the Mousehole Harbour, the second being the main crossroads again and the third, is Sennon Woods. He explained his reasoning for the three targets and Rebecca nodded.

Mousehole Harbour he felt could only be safely completed at sea looking inwards watching the close activity in the harbour. Sennon was the place where a landing at sea was extremely attractive and the shortest distance overland to Mousehole. These places were briefly mentioned by Henry and George Kernow in the same breaths as the traitor Rosevear and so his assumptions were, that they needed attention.

Rebecca asked what her role would be. Joshua delicately said that due to her injuries and convalescence as advised by Doctor Smith she would need to hold the fort, make feed, nurture and give constant warmth of place to come back to. He repeated that they hold a meeting every night for all to input their thoughts and doubts. Queenie and Cecil will stay with Rebecca for company and support.

With that, Rebecca asked Christine to fetch their new vests of protection and also her sewing gear as she would adjust them now. Joshua made another pot of tea for all and suggested he tend to the horses and get them ready for Christine's and Little George's firearms training session at Gunwalloe. Christine looked at Rebecca with excitement and Rebecca nodded that yes she could use her horse Lilly.

Joshua went into the outhouse to prepare all the firearms and holsters for each of them and to clean and prepare his optical instruments for the day and nights ahead.

Whilst Christine was being fitted with the new protective vest, Rebecca went over again the importance that she must act mature beyond her young age. Christine was adamant that she was nearly thirteen and understood what she was doing and she was proud to be part of the 'family,' as she called it. Rebecca gave her a big hug and carried on with the fitting process.

Once Christine's vest was done it was Little George's turn. Christine, with her under protective vest now on, felt very grown up and turned her attention to making the tea for all. When Little George was done and tea finished, they all went into the outhouse to understand the use of a pistol.

As the new pistols were the new lady type they were small enough to fit into a pocket but Rebecca didn't like that idea and wanted them strapped to their bodies under their outer garments without the least possibility of them falling out and also, could only be used should either had to. So straps and holsters were made to fit them both. Once they were comfortable they were then taught on how a pistol is made up and then stripped them down and put them back together several times. Joshua then went over the ball and shot cartridges so they would understand what happened when the flint ignites the powder. They were as near to the end of their training when Rebecca hailed them all into the front room by the fire for an early lunch before their afternoon live firing training.

With the horses fresh and everything stashed in the side bags they said farewell to Rebecca who asked that on their way back could they check in on her cottage at Marazion. With Queenie and Cecil by her side, she waved them off.

The journey was carried out at a canter with no rush while keeping Christine in between Joshua and Little George. She was a little natural and Lilly liked her ease of gentle control. Once they were at Joshua's cottage they dismounted and got things ready for the firing. Joshua's land to the back was full of trees and high shrubbery and the cottage being very isolated was a great place to practise without any prying eyes.

They set up the targets and Joshua asked them to get ready but not to load. He then went over once again the importance of what they were doing and that safety with these deadly pieces of arms was paramount. Once all the safety checks were done he showed them how to load and watch him fire first. His aim was true and the ball entered the centre.

Joshua asked them both to aim and fire when ready. Looking at them both he felt so very proud that these young ones were doing all this with pride and with a sense of feeling of helping Rebecca and him. Little George's pistol went off first followed quickly by Christine, they both missed. They went over the reload and they aimed again. This time they waited for his order to fire which he did and they both missed.

On organising them closer to the target, Joshua got behind Little George to see what he was seeing and how he was aiming. On slight readjustments of both arm and sight, Little George pulled the trigger and made a hit. Now he could adjust future shots with eye and sight. He then did the same with Christine. However, he noticed that her right hand seemed to continually shake and so when she pulled the trigger she missed. Christine was getting a little upset as she was trying her very hardest and the target wasn't exactly that far off. For some reason Joshua instinctively suggested she change her holding hand to the left and use her right to steady underneath. She reloaded, steadied and fired just hitting the top of the target marker. Nevertheless, it was a hit and she shouted a thrill of delight. "Christine, my dear, you are left handed just like Rebecca." With that, she threw another delighted thrill and reloaded. They carried on for another hour or so with constant adjustments being done as required but the lesson was being learnt and they were learning well. They were now becoming familiar with the weapon as a tool to help them as was the lessening fear of using them.

With a good run of hits, Joshua decided that was enough for the day and should dismantle, clean and put them back in their holster straps. With all pistols fully stripped and put back together correctly they practised taking them out and putting them back. This part of the process had to be smooth and familiar and to their credit, they practised and practised until it was.

Asked if they felt happy with their new vests and pistols Joshua again stated that for their protection they must be worn at all times, even when going to the loo. They both laughed aloud and Christine went a little red in the face but said yes they understood and would wear them at all times.

With that, Joshua was happy that the day had been a success and suggested they do this as a routine every two months. With everything packed and ready they quickly went into Joshua's cottage to give it a little check over and once happy headed to Rebecca's cottage in Marazion.

Time was moving on and when they arrived the light was fading. Joshua asked Little George and Christine to stay back while he dismounted and went in alone. They were getting the message that caution no matter how clear and easy things look, was a priority.

Joshua peeped through the window and seeing nothing unusual went to the door and unlocked it. On entering things felt damp and cold but all seemed to be in place and nothing out of the ordinary and so called out to Little George and Christine. He asked Christine to get some extra clothing for Rebecca while he went into the cellar in the scrub area to replenish extra ammunition and anything else that could be useful. Little George tendered the horses.

Looking around the place and feeling happy that they had everything they needed, Joshua locked up and they went on their way.

Joshua felt good in getting home to their cottage in Newlyn with Little George and Christine. On entering, they smelt a lovely rabbit stew. Rebecca was up and the fire was aglow. What a lovely feeling Joshua thought. Rebecca asked how things had gone and he explained it all and how successful it had been.

Christine quickly and proudly said, "I am left handed just like you Rebecca." "That means you are both special," Joshua said. Rebecca gave him a roll of the eyes and gave Christine a hug and again mentioned that pistols are very dangerous and must be used very wisely. "Yes I know Rebecca," she replied.

When Little George came in after tending the horses, the stew was ready and they all sat by the fire with a hearty meal to eat, and they were starving. They chatted further into the early evening and Rebecca allowed Joshua to look at her wound. The Doctor had done a good job. The aggression had gone and the skin tissue was pink and healthy.

With that, Rebecca wanted to retire and asked Christine if she would change her dressing. Little George completed the plates and cutlery washing and so Joshua decided to drag Queenie and Cecil away from Rebecca and take them for a little refreshing walk. He couldn't work out, whether that pleased them or not.

Chapter 14

Pascal was in the tunnel totally jarred off. He was meant to be digging but found himself sitting with his back against the wall and legs pulled up to his chest with his arms wrapped around. He was a scientist or alchemist as some like to think, not a bloody miner. His hands and arms hurt and his back was no better. What was he doing here?

He thought back to the time in the laboratory near Morlaix where he was a budding scholar nearing his finishing with a lovely master of the arts who trained him daily. He was seen as something special and was introduced to the Count of Morlaix, a Mr Philip Albret.

It was when his studies had finished that he was invited to the Chateau and from then on his life had changed from being a young person with intelligence and no money to whatever he wanted and money no problem. He had fun and women whenever he wanted and lived in a lovely house in Morlaix free of charge.

It was quite a few months ago he was asked to help out with a project he was told so secret that the invitation had come directly from the King and to protect our beautiful France from the bullies of the English. The rewards and prestige of a successful mission would allow him a very privileged life style thereafter. Being young and seeing the advantages of such a life was the inspiration he needed in saying yes. His Mother and Father had fallen on bad times and weren't seen as anything important so if he could do this mission and get the money and the house with the small holding that Albret and Bouchier had promised, how good would that be. He started feeling better but his job was mine direction and chemical agent supervisor using his brain, not a bloody shovel and pick.

Pascal drew the candle nearer and took out his instruments and started measuring angles and distances. Then scratching pencil marks here and there on his parchment and doing his calculations, he concluded the tunnel was on course and that he was only seventy seven feet from the X zone. However, the tunnel direction needed to change and have a different angle of the lineage. He took the chalk out of his pocket and marked the new elevation accordingly on the tunnel wall as he had done previously.

Then once the tunnel was directly over the X zone they would dig a holding area of around three meters wide and one metre deep to pour the germ in and then let the natural earth and its elements take over. If correct the earth will drink the liquid at such an angle and volume it would then carry it naturally to the towns supply well through the water veins below.

Once he had finished his new conclusions and was happy, he then made up his mind that he would have it out with Jacques on his return and get this sorted out one way or the other.

He wasn't a shovel worker, he was an intellect and should be shown respect. However, one thing he did know was that Zoe wanted him, he was sure. She had changed and her warmer affections towards him were clear as ever since that bully Jacques wasn't around. With that, he took the candle and went back up the tunnel to the cottage.

Zoe was at the table with a brandy in hand. She also liked a pipe. She was thinking of the situation and trying to come up with logical reasoning and conclusions. Pascal was in the tunnel supposedly digging, 'bloody idiot' she thought. Then there was Jacques. Jacques, 'what about him she thought?' She loved someone else and it wasn't Jacques or bloody Bouchier. But she knew also that she had to be very careful.

These men don't just lie down and say I understand my love, that's quite alright my dear, they have vengeance and she cannot afford for them to use any of that once this task is finished. They will find her and destroy her unless of course, she could get to them first.

She knew the man she really loved and he had pledged his love to her forever and was hopefully still waiting for her. He wasn't a man of stature but this didn't matter anymore. He was her childhood sweetheart from the sticks of south western France in a small village of Cognac. He was a farmer's boy working in a small vineyard owned by his Father. She started thinking of the beautiful days they had together and the sun and warmth of their love. How she got into this position was beyond her and how now she wished she had never met Philip Albret and the promises he gave her parents, which all came to nothing.

She needed to think clearly and work this position to her advantage one way or the other. Jacques had been away now just over a week and should be heading back in the next couple of days or thereabouts. She wondered what news he would bring.

Zoe started going over the plan, as explained in detail by Pierre Bouchier. The point is that this particular task at Mousehole was a prelude to the main mission designated for Penzance with a larger populace of destruction. This main mission was to be made before a French navy invasion set for the summer or latest early autumn. He wanted her for both missions but she also knew he wanted her for his wife once the Penzance mission was done.

He also went over very discretely about the poison he had given her and that the other persons being used for this initial mission were not necessarily earmarked for the main one. She should use it before the task was ended and if no one came back other than herself, nothing would be said and anything that she had done would be washed under the carpet, so to speak. She would be safe. She went over this again and again and came to the same conclusion that Bouchier only wanted her back alive. The others would be killed in some way either from her hands or by other means leaving no traces as to jeopardise in any way shape or form the main mission.

With her mind deep in thought and the pipe being smoked lavishly through slow long inhales she heard Pascal come out of the tunnel. She took a large gulp of the brandy and quickly refilled her glass. What was she to do with this one? Jacques suggested she kill him before he got back but she hadn't got any further with the coordinates or how to decipher his writing. She knew he liked her and she had made every effort to forge an allusion that she fancied him. She actually hated people like Pascal who thought the world owed them a living due to their knowledge or position.

Maybe it was her upbringing in the lower middle class system that gave her this way of thinking. Whatever it was, she didn't like these people types which included Bouchier and Albret. Jacques, she thought, was different in this as he was from the working class like her. Funny that she thought that's the first time she had separated her thought process isolating Jacques away from the others.

Pascal came and sat down next to Zoe and rubbed her shoulder while taking the seat. "How are you?" He asked. "Very well thank you Pascal, how are you?" "I am tired and worn out but have completed my latest calculations and chalked the tunnel with directions and angles for the next push." "How far to go?" "Around seventy-seven feet," he replied. Zoe made him a cup of tea in a way that wives do for their husbands as if it is of no consequence.

"You're very clever Pascal, well done and you keep all this in your head, you must be very intelligent." Pascal patted his breast pocket and said, "I have to work things out and sometimes need pencil and parchment to scribble to get the sum right. If people could see my workings they wouldn't have a clue as I was advised very early on that I have to code everything effectively for me to understand, but for a foreigner not to. I also have my little instruments given to me by my master which help a great deal in giving me measurements of accuracy to complete my calculations." "Wow and I'm just a farmer's daughter."

Leaning back in the chair Pascal responded, "Don't beat yourself up Zoe, it takes all kinds to fill the world." Zoe smiled nicely and thought you are so far up your own arse. Then she said lovingly, "more tea Pascal?" He nodded his acceptance by pushing his cup towards her.

Whilst filling his cup she looked at him with a smile, thinking, what a prat and felt like poisoning him there and then.

Zoe suggested he go upstairs and lie down as he has worked very hard. This he accepted and with tea in hand, he got up and pecked her on the cheek. She again smiled and said, "Sleep well, you deserve it."

When Pascal was gone she pushed herself back into the chair, took a deep breath and blew out a long sigh and took a gulp of the brandy. It had never occurred to her that his calculations were coded. Bloody coded! How lucky she had been that she didn't kill him that very first night as suggested by Jacques. If she had, she would have been worthless and the mission would have had to be abandoned or at the very least delayed until a replacement was found. She realised she was a lucky girl and so would pass the decision to kill him to Jacques on his return whenever that be. In the meantime, she would carry on and play the blushing girl who fancies him.

She then had one last thought about going up to Pascal to have sex with him. With her guile and coercion, she would gain the code to decode the calculations once and for all. However, could she be certain they would be correct or true and lasting? She weighed things up and taking another long breath she accepted the realisation that they would not. Therefore, she had to talk with Jacques. You are a very lucky girl Zoe she thought to herself. She then changed her mind about carrying on playing the blushing bride to that tosser upstairs. She needed to look after herself and find a way out from here safely but knew she was in deep and therefore would need to use all her patience and guile.

So Zoe drank the last of the brandy and headed upstairs to bed. Once in her room, she bolted the door from the inside which she hadn't done since Jacques had gone to France.

Chapter 15

The two masted light Galleon with no insignia silently left the docks at London and sailed up the Thames heading east to a secret location, prepared earlier from the instructions of Kernow. It was dark and getting late. George Kernow had boarded only ten minutes before as he trusted no one and this meeting was vital to the agenda on what he wanted for the plan to succeed.

The Captain was a very capable man and gave up his own cabin for Kernow to do what he wanted. What he wanted at the moment was a drink of lovely Claret, which was duly given. When on these types of secret rendezvous George took only two escorts, whose sole job was to guard and protect him and stay out of sight.

The journey would take a couple of hours outbound and hopefully the same back once the meeting was finished. He hoped to be back in Whitehall by daybreak at the latest with the information to formulate his decisions.

George sat back drinking the Claret and started twisting one end of his moustache in thought about Hosking's and his resolute to be successful. He had many operatives but liked the Cornish for some unknown reason, possibly their sense of humour. But that apart he knew they were a soft belly for a French Naval landing. Also, most of his armour and defence were in London and the French knew this. He also started analysing Rebecca and Joshua and the reports he had had so far impressed him. Mistakes had been made, he knew that, but he also knew this was their first mission and subject to the outcome he knew he could use their skills and aptitude later. Hosking's he thought had been good in the field, especially when working with Rebecca's Mother, Jeanne, and Joshua's Father, John. However, working in a more leader type role behind the scenes, he was yet to be convinced. George was old enough and experienced to know that good people in the front line don't necessarily mean they would be good handlers. However, in the present situation, Henry Hosking was an important part of the plan and given the limited and cropped information he has to work with, was doing a pretty good job.

Kernow closed his eyes and rested his thoughts. This was the way he worked his information, wait, information, wait and then when he believes the timing to be right and with that information completely deciphered and analysed again and again, strike the plan into operation. This rendezvous was the last piece in the puzzle and activation had to be done by the morrow. The timing was tight but he had no choice, he needed to catch the mouse to get the cat.

The ship was making good steady speed as the Captain had promised and George wasn't minded at all with the sway and tilt. He was accustomed to this from his early career in the Navy until he was taken aside and advised to work undercover for his beloved Queen. With good service under his belt, he then took over the reins from his mentor upon his passing. Always better with whom you know and not hearsay on what others may say or portray.

Then came a knock on the cabin door, and with a "Come in" from Kernow the Captain entered. He reported that the other ship has been sighted and had displayed the correct torch code and will be aside in ten minutes. "Thank you Captain, please escort my friend to me on his boarding." They were now in the middle of the sea ten miles off shore directly due east from Ghent. Both ships would not drop anchor but will hold firm together as best they could, just in case they need to separate and get away fast. Cannons were also at the ready.

Although these meeting places have always been different, the procedure is the same until such time as Kernow orders otherwise. Kernow then felt the ships bang together.

Kernow got himself ready and made a pipe for his friend as well as a nice brandy. The door opened and in walked an average built man about fifty years of age, appearing like a vagabond dirty sailor sporting a red woollen hat with its end flapping down one side with a bobble on the end touching his right ear. Immediately they went to each other and boldly shook hands with total respect. "George," he said, "it's been quite a while, how goes you?" "Fine" George replied, "it's good to see you too old friend, take a seat, I have made you a pipe and drink as you like it." "Thank you George, I need it."

George was very pleased to see him and aching to get the information. However, he knew he needed to give each of them time to explain to one another what they knew and what they didn't know which, is just as important. The dirty looking sailor man did not say his name, nor did George say it either throughout their whole time together. However, this unassuming dirty scoundrel now in George's presence was his equivalent in France and had been for years.

After discussing side issues such as weather, health and family, George was the first to take directional charge of topics which had to be discussed in depth and without error. Knowledge, pure knowledge is what is wanted and this man would oblige without hesitation in a very clear and sometimes brutal manner of honesty.

"Is there an antidote?" "All the signs gathered since the time of Jeanne, John and Henry's French operation indicate that there is one," the sailor replied. "What makes you think that?" "The alchemists at the Abbey of Landerneau, as you know, were a subject that Jeanne had to gather information on."

The sailor continued, "as you know Jeanne got close to a particular alchemist who we found had a weakness for the opposite sex and was a womaniser. We therefore allowed Jeanne to exploit that weakness even though he was a married man and getting on in years."

"It appears that this man had been noticed on numerous occasions travelling to the Count of Morlaix to one Philip Albret and stopping over at the local Inn. He hasn't been seen for a month, vanished. His wife however has been seen in the town of Landerneau and hasn't stopped talking about her suspicions of him being killed by someone near to the King. It was also suggested after gaining her trust with low level chatting that her alchemist husband was a good man. He had also said to her many times that whatever they ask me to do I will do but as a true alchemist I must also have the knowledge to undo and, if it is in the nature of hurt, I must unhurt."

'This language mirrors the information gathered from our agent Jeanne, who had found out how and where. As I thought this information to be critical I did not meet her face to face but suggested she go directly to England and impart her information only to you. However, somehow they were caught in a trap and according to Henry Hosking she is dead, both her and John. Therefore, Yes George, I believe that with adding Jeanne's information is true and constant from that of the alchemist's wife and that there is an antidote. Moreover, the only person who can give us this information is Jeanne.'

George listened with intent silence and when the sailor too fell silent leaned back and slowly pinched and twisted the end of his long moustache in deep thought. "And what of the rumours?" "Rumours about what George?" "About Jeanne." "Yes they are true, she is alive." "My God man, tell me."

After a slurp of the brandy the Sailor continued, "Firstly let me say that I have checked and double checked Henry Hosking's version of events on that fateful day and I believe them to be true. If I was where Henry was at that time, my briefing to you would be the same as his. To all intent and purposes she should be dead." George butted in and said, "I also have checked his version and monitored him more than others and probably more than I should and conclude he is good. But, I always get suspicious when a party of three are in escape mode and only one makes it. Sorry, please continue."

"It appears that our Galleon waiting to carry them away did get a little damaged from the French gun salvo. Hence Hosking's close shave but safe return. However, as in his story, Jeanne and John were still in the rowing boat that was blasted into the water. The Frenchies we know retrieved the bodies that were still afloat. However my friend, it wasn't just Jeanne but John too who survived. But, as both were very near to death they were simply of no use to the French authorities. However, one Philip Albret had watched the action and had them taken without notice to anyone to the Chateaux and put in the deepest dungeon in the hope they may survive. He wanted human bodies for his trialling of new herbs and remedies gained from the alchemists and had nothing to lose. If they died they died but if they survived they could also be valuable assets in some way or another."

"Unfortunately, John passed away, his injuries too severe. But Jeanne started to improve and over a long period of being nursed came out of being near death and critical to surviving. It's ironic to think that maybe the very person treating her with these new herbs and remedies was the same alchemist she was told to befriend, who has himself now vanished, presumed dead. We know all this as after two years of working, we have at last got a person on the inside, albeit at a very low level working in the kitchens. So, the information is somewhat weak and sparse and made generally through gossip and things. However, what we do know is he had to deliver food to her jailer in the lowliest dirtiest part of the building and says he has seen her and his description confirms to us that it is Jeanne."

George understood very well that information is supplied through people putting their very lives at risk. Also, people like Philip Albret, accountable to the French King, do what he himself would do in England and that is monitor the monitors without them ever knowing. Information is never straight forward and nothing can be assumed, only after detailed consideration of risk and counter risk can you then plan from the information given. Both he and the sailor knew this.

George replenished the drinks and relit the pipes. He then spoke about what he knew so far on the English side of things, especially the threat of a germ type warfare scenario. He also thought to tell his sailor friend that Jeanne and John's children namely Rebecca and Joshua, were working for him under Henry Hosking's in Cornwall. The sailor knew this already but didn't say anything and nodded approval. He had worked in the field as long as George albeit in France.

George had one more directional question which, if true, would confirm the plan he would use. "Is it also true that Jeanne had an affair or some liaison with a person known as Jacques?" "Yes this is true, we encouraged it." George didn't respond to that but said, "And is it true that he fell in love with her." "I think George, they fell in love with each other. Jeanne was fully aware of what might happen and to her credit told us everything." "Does Jacques know of her still being alive?" "I believe he does not. Jacques, we understand is the type of person who is determined and if he knew, we would have heard things. It's only through our suspicions and years of determination to find out for sure whether or not she was alive or dead. Now we have eventually found the truth about her being alive. Let's not forget that Albret is very secretive in his actions and kills people without any conscious. Therefore, as we now know that she is alive then my boy in his service is probably also at risk as we talk."

The sailor moved forward and filled both his and George's drinks. George was thinking. The sailor then said, "Let me ask you a question George, have you heard anyone mention a Spring Tide?" "No I haven't, why has this anything to do with this so called germ thing?" "I am not sure but when Jeanne was working the alchemist the words 'Spring Tide' was mentioned twice as I reported. However, Jacques also mentioned it once to her whom she put in her report to me but I never put the two together until I went over the copies last week. It may be something or nothing." George got up from his chair and asked the guard outside the door to fetch the Captain.

On entering, George asked the Captain about spring tides. The Captain said that reports have come in that an unusual spring or very high tide is due in the South, South West of England in two weeks." "Is this common knowledge?" George asked. "Yes, most people in the knowledge of ebbs and tides would be aware." "Thank you Captain, we will be finished here in a short while, please prepare for the off, we both need to get back."

"What do you make of it?" asked the sailor. "Not sure, but something inside has stirred and if this is something then we have only two weeks to find out."

"One thing my friend, do you know where Jacques is?" "No" the sailor replied. "Can you get a message to your man at the Morlaix Chateau?" "Yes, but he is not a man, he is a young fourteen-year-old boy and so getting a message to him without raising any alarms to anyone is only once a week, when he visits the town market, every Thursday."

With that last piece, George instinctively knew what must be done. However, he needed his friends with their observations to secretly discuss what he had in mind. It was audacious but feasible if, he could move the players accordingly in the time given.

Both George and the Sailor knew the meeting was finished and that the information had flowed freely, both ways without hesitation to each, as both men liked. Both had to get back under the darkness and reach their destinations before daylight. They shook hands and said their farewells with respect for each other, both knowing the difficulties each will face in the decisions that had soon to be made.

George knew he had been takings things pretty much defensively but he had no other option to play it different with the limited information he had and knew it was right. However, with this new information, things would change. That means it was time to move from the slowly, slowly, behind the scenes approach of working to attack. With new orders given to the Captain, the ship changed course to Falmouth, at best speed.

Chapter 16

Rebecca felt better and better as each day passed and with that an increase in the sense of urgency of the task that lay before them all. Joshua also started improving his activities in this new covert and overt way of working. Little George and Christine too were fitting in very well and so everyone was working together better as a team.

"Rebecca," Joshua said, "Tomorrow we start our new three day observation, are you happy with things especially Little George and Christine's involvement?" "I am happy Joshua and hope you keep them as safe as you possibly can, they are as eager as you to get on with it." Joshua responded, "I understand, their safety gear and equipment have been done to the best of my ability and they have learnt well from both of us to keep themselves quiet and resourceful." With an approving nod of the head, Rebecca got up to retire for the night. Christine was already in bed and at last Little George came in after tending Harry.

Joshua said good night and allowed Rebecca some time to get herself ready and into bed. Little George also said his goodnights. Joshua finished off another brandy and as Rebecca was feeling much better from both wound and mind, Joshua was now allowed back into the bedroom in the large comfy double bed. However, the large wooden bed divider was still there.

The new day arrived and the first part of Joshua's plan was now to begin. Everybody was up and getting into their respective tasks. Rebecca's was the food and clothing. Little George and Christine were the horses and Joshua's were the weapons and gear. The idea was to get into a kind of routine, which he had explained to both Kernow and Hosking.

Although locations of observation may change, the basic plan had been agreed upon. The last thing to do was pass the sketch of Jacques around again so the image was clear in everyone's minds and a gentle reminder that their job was intelligence gathering. That means not to be seen, but to get information back as quickly as possible.

When all things were ready, Joshua got on his horse Harry and rode off towards Penzance. His job was to scout by easy riding, mixed with various Inn stops throughout the local area including the towns of Mousehole, Newlyn and Penzance. Joshua and his Harry were feeling fresh and the morning air was bracing. He was to be back by two o'clock for food and drink and then sleep till the late evening when he would go out again into the first of his night observation posts.

Next were Little George and Christine. Their job was to mindfully play in all streets of Mousehole with special attention to the port area and the blind alleys in the town. Again, they had to be back at two o clock for food and drink and report any findings.

Once all were gone from the cottage, Rebecca began to clean up and prepare things for their return. Although she was physically and mentally better from the shooting she knew she wasn't ready for the outside work and accepted her more rear echelon role.

The morning soon went by and all returned as suggested at the correct time with no hints of anything untoward. All were safe and the reporting went well. Joshua was really proud of the young ones.

Once fed and refreshed from Rebecca's cooking, it was now Christine's turn to tend the horses used through the day whilst Joshua and Little George went to their beds.

Around ten o'clock they were woken by Rebecca. It was a dark night and very cold so Joshua prepared his and Little George's equipment, especially the warm weather clothing. Joshua went out and noted how clear the night was and the crystal view he had of the stars. He repeated to himself that this was going to be a cold one.

Their first post for this night's observation would be the main crossroads. Their horses, Harry and Suzy, had been prepared by Christine before she turned in earlier that evening. Joshua had already done an in depth reconnaissance of the area noting the best places to lie tonight and the next two nights. He had also worked out both entry and exit points.

As with all night posts, Joshua and Little George will firstly circle the target area and then come in from the opposite direction. The position of this night's post location was just inside the forest overlooking the crossroads. Enough cover in not being seen and a good exit should they be. They would enter the post around the half hour past midnight.

After arriving and circling they got to the post location site on schedule. They then made cover by scrapping a shell hole out of the earth for them both to lie down. Little George completed the camouflage on top before squeezing in next to Joshua underneath. Harry and Lilly were reined about one hundred yards back with good feed to keep them quiet. Funny thing Joshua thought about how one feels when the silence of the earth takes over, as you become one with the woods and the dark of the night. They would stay there until four o clock, until such time as Rebecca would ride by. If she saw a spark from Joshua's flint, she knew all was well and would gallop back to the cottage. If she did not see the flint, she would go directly to Hosking's and report.

The idea was for Joshua to use his scopes and lenses and for young Little George to hold the loaded pistols with flint in and ready but not cocked. They would lay quiet, watch and wait.

Although the night was dark, Joshua's telescope and other new lenses could hone in on a face and give better evidence of identification other than just the eye. Not perfect but important. The hours passed away quite quickly without a murmur, bar a few riders and a carriage of no importance. It was now getting to the time for Rebecca to appear, in which riding Lilly she dutifully did and Joshua sparked the flint. With a gesture of her arm, she acknowledged the flint spark and turned herself about. Joshua and Little George then decamped and went to find Harry and Suzy waiting for the return journey.

A nice hot cup of tea for Little George and a large brandy for Joshua were waiting for them on their return which was gratefully drunk. It had been an interesting day and night for all. It would all start again in a few hours, being now early Thursday morning.

Time rushed by as the routine started again. The only difference was the location and this time Joshua and Little George would be undercover in a rowing boat out on the sea tied to rocks off to the left of the port. Although the location was different being in a little boat bobbing up and down in the water the routine remained the same. Apart from the lights and sounds and the occasional shouting from the town and the movement of a few drunken sailors going back to their anchored ships nothing unusual was happening. Rebecca again came at four o'clock and the sign was given so Joshua gave the order to decamp. He looked at Little George and saw the boy had been sick and thrown up all over himself. He hadn't said a word.

Again the tea and brandy were on hand after their safe return to the cottage. The only thing different from yesterday was a note had been delivered by young Connor from Henry Hosking.

R & J.
Closer contact - Emergency purposes.
= J. Trevenan – The Bull Inn - Newlyn.
A Colleague

Rebecca and Joshua understood and told Little George and Christine that should anything happen to them someone must get to this person.

That night for some reason Joshua couldn't sleep well and was tossing and turning and so, in the end, gave up and got up before anyone else. Making a pot of tea, he made a pipe and after lighting it from the made up fire, went outside. Again, it was chilly but the morning was coming alive with birds singing. He noticed a couple of glowing type moths fly about his head so looking inquisitively upwards towards them and into the clearing dark sky above. He then felt the hairs on his neck stand up and a shudder went through his body. Strange, he thought. It was Friday morning.

Once all were up, Joshua spoke to Rebecca about Christine and suggested that she was looking tired and maybe should stay indoors and help Rebecca today. Little George had got over his sea sickness and couldn't wait to get about the town and mingle. Joshua set off on Harry and whilst roaming decided to find the location of The Bull Inn in Newlyn, just in case.

Again, the day went to plan with nothing untoward and it wasn't long before Joshua and Little George returned to the cottage at the said time. Once again after eating and sleeping we're now getting their selves ready for the night observation at Sennon. As before Joshua had previously sighted where the location would be. The only difference between this and the others was the distance and being a little too way out of their comfort zone around Mousehole. However, it had been agreed that they must cover all angles as best they could with the resources they have. Nearing ten thirty they went to Harry and Suzy and once they were mounted, were off.

On entering the Sennon high woods from the opposite side they silently walked the horses close to the post site and tethered them quietly leaving them ample fodder to enjoy. They then crept forward to the edge of the wood and made their scrape as they have practised many times before. Joshua got in first and placed the scopes and lenses on the earth's frontal ledge which allowed minimum movement for him to use things should he need to. He checked his vision range and started noting the main landmarks of interest.

The farm was some way down in the valley with open pasture to the left. To the right was the main inlet to the sea. He noted how dark and vast the sea was at this time of night and how threatening and all powerful it lay. All was quiet.

Little George was still walking about quietly covering the ground sheet above the scrape with leaves and twigs till it mingled nicely with the other foliage around. Once happy he then joined Joshua by getting his body on the ground and then slithering himself like a snake under the sheet. Joshua gave him the pistols and with thumbs up between them, they lay silent. It was Saturday morning.

Both Joshua and Little George had been still now for nearly two hours and the animals and birds had now accepted them as no threat and were once again scuffling about their nightly movements as if they were not there. The night air was crisp and a clear night of stars and moon was above.

It was not long after that a faint noise was heard from the farm area which first alerted Joshua. With his ears now pricked and eyes in alert mode, he saw the glow of a small light. Joshua immediately touched Little George's shoulder and, when their eyes met, Joshua slowly moved his right index finger to his lips and produced a very faint shhhhh.

Joshua then very, very gently moved his head to the scope which was screwed onto a miniature tripod for stability and already aligned on the farm. On getting his eye to the optic he started to slowly twist the scopes focus dial in the hope of getting a clearer visual. He wanted to see what and who was down there and what he or she was doing at this time in the morning. He identified the person as a man of good build holding a lantern looking outwards to the sea. Joshua ever so gently moved the scope out onto the ocean where he saw a three masted galleon moving left to right. What the...

Chapter 17

Jacques was bored stiff. He didn't like taking this time out during a mission especially when time wasn't on his side. He had felt this type of inner anxiety before when working undercover in his native France, let alone this worse situation in trying to move around a foreign country like some kind of ghost in bloody Cornwall. However, it did give him time to enjoy his drink whenever he wished. He was also a loner and that was just as well as he needed to be in his line of work and so having and enjoying other people's company was out of the question.

Next Thursday week for the arranged meeting with Bouchier and the four young recruits seemed to drag slowly along and he couldn't wait to be active again. But, true to his word, Albret the Count of Morlaix had paid for all his food and lodgings, which he appreciated on one hand but didn't on the other, as this guy was the richest and most powerful person around this place. He was also openly ruthless to the point that no one dared to do anything against his wishes. Just a rich brute out for his own gain he thought to himself and Bouchier wasn't much better.

The meeting was set for early evening and when that day eventually arrived, Jacques made sure he ate well and more importantly didn't touch the drink, well not too much. He needed all his wits about him when he meets Bouchier later.

The ride from the Morlaix Inn to the Chateau didn't take that long. He missed riding his own horse Arc but knew he would be in Cornwall in a couple of days and so mentally looked forward to riding his trusted friend again soon. As always on his arrival at the Chateau, he had to use the tradesmen entrance and then told to wait in the anti-room while Bouchier was fetched.

Pierre Bouchier and Albret the Count of Morlaix were in the next room drinking brandy whilst sitting in two comfy arm chairs opposite a glowing fire. An usher advised them that Jacques had arrived and Albret said, "Thank you, we will get to him in a while". "Well Pierre, the time has come to implement the last phase of the mission. You have done well my friend, now tell me what you want and you shall have it". "I want Zoe, you know that," he replied. Albret started chuckling which riled Bouchier. "Oh yes, Zoe, of course, the love of your life." Bouchier stayed quiet. Then Albret changed his all smiling face and leaned forward with a grimace, saying, "You finish this with a resounding success and I promise you she is all yours." "Thank you Philip." "However, Pierre, I too want something." "What would that be my Prince?"

"When we have the finished formula in our hands and the mission successful, I want all tracks and traces to ourselves, including the people involved to be wiped, as though it had never happened. I want it done secretly and utterly without any trace. This is what I want and my liege King authorises it to comply with his wishes for total secrecy." "What about Jacques," Bouchier replied. "That means everyone Pierre, everyone except of course your young Zoe, who I will allow through the net for your loyalty to me and your pleasure to her but, only her." Bouchier got it, his own ruthlessness made him smirk with dishonesty and inner enjoyment of his method of deceiving people. He understood.

Bouchier opened the ante room door and walked in saying boldly as he meant it but really couldn't give a hoot, "Hi Jacques, don't get up, how was your time off, relaxing I hope." Bouchier poured each of them a drink, sat down opposite and started the briefing.

"Things have slightly changed Jacques. I want you now and the four young ones to meet at the Abbey of Landerneau earlier at midnight tonight. They have also been informed. You are to collect the hundred barrels from the monks and then supervise the loading onto four large coaches pulled by four horses each. The coaches are already there with the drivers awaiting your arrival. Once loaded and you are satisfied, you are not to go to Brest but head due south from Landerneau to the secluded Daoulas Cove where a three masted galleon will be waiting for you as close to the shore as it can. The Captain has been briefed and knows what to do.

You will be heading around the Lizard peninsular hugging the quiet inner waters of west Cornwall and anchor off Sennon. Once anchored you are to off load to the Wards Farm and then my friend it is once again completely over to you. But don't forget that two of the four young men will come back with the Galleon and two will remain in your charge. You know which ones I have chosen to stay and the ones which must come back and for reasons above my position this cannot change.

You must be at Daoulas Cove by no later than the break of day tomorrow which gives you seven hours from the moment you get to the Abbey at midnight tonight. The ship will sail directly once you have reloaded the barrels." Jacques got it and understood. He also knew Bouchier and the twists and turns he gives to put people off balance. "Understood," he replied.

"One other thing Jacques, when the germ has been laid, you and Zoe are to make your way directly back here and report all, is that clear." "Understood," Jacques replied and knew this may happen. "What about the other two young ones and Pascal the budding Alchemist?" he asked. "Unfortunately, for reasons and purposes above my control and for the King's glory of future use of success you are to eliminate them." Bouchier then waited for a response. Jacques had seen something like this coming as this germ type warfare wasn't exactly killing the enemy with chivalry as the French like to tell the world but he was older and wiser now to argue otherwise. He also had himself to think about and had a gut feeling that Bouchier had some other orders that he wasn't telling him. "Absolutely understood," he responded with surety. But Jacques didn't feel sure at all.

With the meeting finished, Jacques then headed back to the Inn at Morlaix to pack his things as quickly as he could. He would have one last brandy and then set off for the Abbey. On his arrival, he tethered his horse at the front of the Inn and on jumping off dashed into the entrance crashing straight into a little old lady coming out. With her begging hands filled with a few coppers, she went flying into the wall and the money went all over the floor. Jacques said sorry and couldn't have been more apologetic but as she looked up through her black netted veil into his eyes she hissed with a shrilling low hum like a snake, "Beware you, think you are strong than any other, the pup of its master will take you without you even knowing."

Jacques went silent and took a step back while she bent down picking up her pennies.

Jacques couldn't think of anything to respond except that he was again sorry. She dismissed his claim of apology with a hiss and picking up her last coin shuffled away as quickly as she could. Jacques was stunned by her outburst of venom and couldn't get out of his head what she had said. 'The pup, the pup,' he kept thinking all the way to his room.

With everything packed and ready he reached the Abbey at Landerneau around half an hour early and as mentioned by Bouchier, the horses, carriages and their drivers were there waiting but not the four young men. He acquainted himself with the drivers and then went off to see the main alchemist monk.All was ready, one hundred barrels. Then he heard them gallop up to the Abbey and watched them dismount laughing and full of young vigour.

He went to them directly and briefed them that twenty five barrels a piece needed to be put on each carriage as with their belongings and to leave their horses with the Monks. The barrels were not that big but were heavy enough that only one could be carried at a time.

He was supervising, so told them to get on with it and be quiet. Each one did as told and acted the feat like it was a game in that the first one to finish was the winner. Jacques felt the zest of youth in them and shuddered at the thought that at least two, or maybe all, would not see the fruits of their labour and grow old to tell the story. Jacques laughed at himself for being soppy and realised that he himself was older now and that youth was a thing to be enjoyed. He tried again to laugh it off but it didn't work as it had in the past. Jacques took a large nip of brandy from his flask and when everything was loaded and everyone accounted for, jumped on his mount. He then led them from the front, due south to Daoulas Cove, as instructed.

It was a silent road with forest on the left and open plains on the right. The carriages were cumbersome and slow and Jacques had to rein his nag back into a slight trot being not much faster than a walk. However, this slower pace gave time for Jacques to think about what really is going on here and how exactly was he going to manage this last phase.

It wasn't long, although it seemed to take forever, Daoulas Cove was sighted and the descent of the carriages started. The place was perfect for such a mission. With the coaches now at a halt, men from small boats already ashore, came to meet them with the Captain introducing himself. Jacques immediately got the understanding of what was about and started supervising the unloading, then the loading and the reloading on board the ship. The men aboard the ship helped out which made things easier for all and reduced the time it would have taken. Jacques was pleased that so far they were making good time.

When all was done Jacques went to the Captain who didn't say much to anybody. The sailors seemed to know him well and so just got on with things. However, what was asked was answered and Jacques was happy with that. A young sailor then showed them to their cabins and others helped with their belongings, which wasn't much. Jacques wanted to stay on deck and so was given a seat at the stern. Once again, the Captain didn't say anything, just got on with his ship and crew and let Jacques be. Once they were away Jacques went down to see the four young bucks. He opened their cabin and saw they were all nipping their brandy from their flasks and joking and laughing. Jacques didn't say anything except, "We should be on this ship till midnight tonight or at the very latest very early Saturday morning so I suggest you stop the drinking and get some sleep, you will be woken before we anchor."

With that, he closed the cabin door behind him and went back up on deck. However, just after closing the cabin door to walk away, he overheard one of them inside start talking using a mother's mimicking type voice. He leaned back and put his ear to the door and heard the one mimicking say, "Now, all of you be good little boys and go to sleep or Mummy will be very angry." They all laughed and Jacques himself couldn't help but laugh too and then carried on up the steps.

Back in his seat on the deck and watching the men heave ho, he started to relax a little and focus on what to do. He drew out his hip flask and took a long slow gulp of the liquid inside and, with a pulling together of the teeth combined with a facial squint and a closing of the eyes, swallowed the liquid down with inner satisfaction.

Jacques was enjoying the inner peace of being on board a ship with nothing to do but watch and wait. After an hour or so the Captain came across and mentioned that the wind was fair and they were making good progress and the timing set to reach drop off point should be alright. "However," he continued, "what we will find when we turn the cape of Lands End, I do not know." Jacques liked this man's no nonsense approach and so thanked him and with a tap of his hand to his head, the Captain withdrew.

The easy rhythmic movement of the ship and the ebb and flow of the sea allowed Jacques to relax and contemplate his position? He thought back to Bouchier's words of 'No trace of this mission.' Jacques knew he was getting on in life and that younger men were entering the field he had been in for twenty years. He also knew that Bouchier couldn't be trusted. Jacques knew he was still physically capable and felt good enough to carry on his work but mentally he was broken. His mind was exhausted and he craved some inner peace. What he needed was some time in his life to enjoy the fruits of his labour without harm or injury to anyone.

Jacques stretched and looked up. He had been sitting there for hours as the sun turned itself into the moon. The night stars were shining like little crystals against the black sky and the air was briskly clean. With the nipping of brandy and the fresh spray of the sea all around him, he knew that his time had come. He would finish this mission and retire and move right away from the world. Maybe he would buy a little farm stead from the money he had saved and get that inner peace he so craved. He could move away from France to somewhere like Scotland and even use a different name but, would Bouchier allow that? Why tell him, he could just disappear.

If he was Bouchier would he just accept the fact that he had disappeared without a trace? With first hand knowledge of his ruthless streak of treating humans like useless animals, he thought not. He would try and track me down. But why did Bouchier order him and Zoe to report in person directly to him at the Chateau on the mission's completion? This has never happened before. They knew where to find him if they wanted to talk. His reports have been always on time, so why? The old lady he bumped into sprung into his head and he started laughing to himself as a silly superstitious twit but quickly stopped and considered her words.

Then Jacques heard the deck door throw open and out ran one of the four young men spewing his guts as soon as he hit the railings. Luckily the wind and spray drew the vomit away from the ship. At least he got the right side, Jacques chuckled to himself.

With that Jacques decided to get some sleep and went down into his cabin located next to the four young ones. He lay down with his arms behind his head and looked at the ceiling. He heard the young one who had been sick on deck come back into the cabin and overheard the other three taking the Mickey out of him.

With his eyes closed his thoughts repeated on him and then he cried. The one thought he tried to always keep in the dark and locked away came forward. He would always love her, how he missed her and how so lonely his heart was without her.

It didn't seem that long before the knock on his cabin door woke him up. The Captain showed himself in and said, "Excuse me Sir, but we have turned the Cornish Cape and the wind has dropped. I anticipate drop zone around two or three o'clock or thereabouts." "Thank you, Captain," Jacques replied and with that started to get himself and his things ready. Jacques went on deck to get his bearings and his thoughts together. He had been away from the Cornish mainland for only a few weeks but it seemed ages ago. He decided to go back down and get the four young ones up and ready for the task ahead. They were all asleep but Jacques didn't pull his punches and told them with a strong voice to get up and ready. All were to be on deck within ten minutes for briefing, no excuses. He slammed the door shut and chuckled.

Jacques then went up and waited on deck and soon enough the young ones came to him. As the team leader, Jacques wanted to overrule Bouchier's choice and reselect who stays and who goes back with the ship once the unloading of the barrels at the Wards farm was completed. They all stood before him at attention knowing he may countermand the orders of persons to stay. Jacques looked at all four men standing in front of him in a line and then thought about why Bouchier had chosen the two weakest ones to stay in Cornwall. Yes, he would change that decision now as was his right and pick the other two who were more capable, more physical and more adapted for this type of mission.

However, he then thought no, he would need to play the game. Yet something was wrong but he couldn't put his finger on it and knew he needed time to solve the logic behind it. After a quiet minute or two, he then told them that the decision Pierre Bouchier had made back in France would remain in place and so prepare accordingly. The two stronger lads dipped their heads in shame as they couldn't work out why they hadn't got the mission on and above the other two scrawny dim witted ones. Maybe, they thought, they had been chosen to go back for a more dangerous mission and with that manly thought in their brains, preened their ego into the acceptance of the decision. With that, the Captain came across to give Jacques the news that they would be dropping anchor at the drop zone just off Sennon Cove in one hour.

Last minute details needed organising so Jacques set about managing things. Jacques soon realised his mistake in that Galleons do not carry extra boats for ferrying heavy barrels. However, to Jacque's happy surprise the Captain after being briefed on the job at hand had made provision for this. So four extra small boats were ordered and brought to the ship before sail. Two were being dragged at the stern and two roped down at the ship's sides and all available for Jacque's disposal.

The whole crew started to come alive and rushed about like flies. All the ships' guns were loaded and prepared and all hatches not important were closed. Jacques realised the small boats were not large enough to take fifty kegs each and so accepted that the landing of them had to be done in two journeys back and forth, the last trip would be manned by the two young ones going back to France with the ship.

All was in place and now the wait started. The ship was moving gently like a ghost across the water inching its way to the drop zone. Everyone was silent and in place. Jacques moved to where the Captain stood on the starboard side scanning his eyes across the Cornish headland for the sign he was waiting for. Jacques too did the same and thought about how rugged the Cornish coast was. Then out of nowhere, it came. Both the Captain and Jacques saw it at once.

The Captain then started counting to himself. Out of the pure darkness came one ten seconds of flickering light, then darkness. Jacques looked at the Captain who then spoke as quietly as he could in Jacques's ear, "We must wait five minutes and if the light shines the same as before, for the same length of time and in the same place, we anchor and set to." Jacques could feel his heart beating faster and started to get that tense feeling before a battle. His inner senses were also coming alert and knew his body was getting ready for some action. Then it came, the light mirroring the last signal. The Captain moved his head to the old sailor at the bow, who acknowledged and then reached down into a covered box and picked up a lantern. With its light glowing, he swung it in both directions twice and then as quickly as before lowered it back into its cover case to give pure darkness once again.

Jacques checked his pistols and blade and moved in behind some crewmen, laddering themselves down to one of the side boats chosen to be the first to shore.

The Captain manoeuvred the ship where he felt it best to lay anchor, as close as he could, considering exit and safety rules of engagement and also turning the ship about before he did so. Happy with the ship's final position he ordered the anchoring. The four young men came round Jacques who gave them orders to start preparing the first half of the kegs for offloading and do as the Captain orders but, await his signal before they cast off for the shoreline. They all nodded in complete acceptance.
The small rowing boat with Jacques now aboard pushed off and the sailors rowed strongly towards the shore.

All went well and once the small boat reached the beach Jacques jumped out and started looking around. He knew the farm from previous visits and so straight away started walking towards it. Two of the crew followed and both armed with muskets. About twenty metres from the farm's edge Ashley Ward came into view and approached them. "You are late Jacques." "We were doing well until we turned the cape then things slowed, is everything ready Mr Ward?" "Yes, we are ready." With that Jacques went with Mr Ward into the farm to see for himself what had been organised. The two sailors followed.

Jacques was acquainted with Mrs Ward and tea and cake were offered. Jacques took the cake but asked for brandy instead of the tea. Mr Ward started informing Jacques that only one medium gig pulled by two horses was favourable for transporting whatever he was transporting. Mr Ward then explained his reasoning that as Mousehole is a village, anything larger like heavy noisy coaches will get noticed. Jacques accepted the argument which made good sense. They may need to do more trips but safety and integration were needed. Mr Ward continued and explained that all things were quiet and nothing unusual has come across his eyes or ears since Jacques was last here. Jacques let Mr Ward babble on as he wanted this time to adjust his thoughts and get a feel for things around him before he gave the signal.

Once Jacques was satisfied and feeling as comfortable as he could in that all was well and no compromise of the mission was apparent, he asked where the cargo was to be stored. "You have two options;" Mr Ward replied, "you can have the secret underground cell within the walls of this cottage or it can go outside within the grounds in a locked barn close to the stables." "I would like to see both sites before I make a decision." The underground cell was large enough but a logistical nightmare with the man power at hand and so dismissed it. On seeing the outside barn he knew that it would be easier for the men to carry the kegs and quicker too so suggested to Mr Ward that this will do nicely. On walking back to the cottage they passed the stabling area when Mr Ward suggested he may want to see inside. With lanterns lighting the night Jacques went in as suggested and immediately spotted his favourite horse Arc. Jacques couldn't believe it and went straight to him. Both horse and owner were with joy in seeing each other again. "That's was very kind of you Mr Ward, Thank you." "It wasn't me, Zoe organised it." "Then I shall pass on my thanks to her."

Before re-entering the farm house Jacques, who was being shadowed by the armed sailors, suggested they both return to their mates on the shoreline and confirm that all was well and he will send the signal to the ship very shortly.

Sitting back down and feeling the time was now right he asked Mr Ward to signal the go ahead to the ship. Mr Ward acknowledged and said he would be back in ten minutes. Jacques sat back and waited.

The first two boats arrived on shore and Jacques was there to meet them. In each boat were two sailors and one young one of his team. He quickly gave orders to start carrying the goods to the barn where Mr Ward was waiting. Once completed the sailors rowed back to the ship. Two young ones of Jacque's team went into the farm house and introduced themselves to Mrs Ward. They were given refreshments, non-alcoholic, and then told to wait.

Jacques waited on the beach ready to receive the last two boats. He had watched the first small boats leave the shore and then saw them crossover but waiting for the last two to reach the shore seemed to take an eternity. He was deep in enemy territory which he did not take for granted and the sooner he was out of this exposed position the better. He felt vulnerable.

When at last the two boats reached the shore, Jacques with the sailors and the other two young ones, repeated the exercise of carrying the fifty kegs to the barn. Once all was completed Jacques went back to the boats and offered his thanks and goodwill. Jacques then turned and made for the farmhouse.

However, before he went inside he decided to stay out for a while to watch and listen. He quietly sat down in the shadows out of sight and let the night take over him. His eyes were nowhere but looking everywhere. The noise they had made during the unloading wasn't much that was true but now there was a real silence of the night and Jacques needed to hear what it had to say. He watched the ship silently drift away right to left out of sight, leaving the now empty sea ebb and flow as it does, as if the ship had never been there. The Captain had done well, Jacques thought.

Jacques carried on his silent watch and after a further ten minutes had passed took one last look across the sea, the fields and the forests above before his mind settled down in that all was well. He got up and walked briskly back to the farmhouse and into the warmth of the fire and a large Cognac, he deserved it.

With everyone now in the room together a sense of calm was taking over. Jacques was aware that dawn was fast approaching and so needed to act and make decisions. He asked Mrs Ward if the two young ones could stay in the farmhouse until at latest midnight tonight. They were each to take guard of the kegs on four hour watch periods. Jacques would then return and lead them to the cottage but he needed to get away now while it was still dark to prepare for the delivery. When all was agreed Jacques went off to saddle up Arc.

As he galloped away feeling the wind through his face and once again riding his old friend he felt a feeling of relief that the cargo was at last in Cornwall as planned. He rode as fast as he dares while remembering the old Cornish lanes and the pitfalls they give. Getting to the cross lanes he turned right into Mousehole and then before entering the town stopped and dismounted. He took the reins in his hand and led Arc away from the cottage location. Once far enough away he stopped, looked about and feeling he wasn't being followed jumped back on Arc and doubled back. These security measures may seem tedious but they save lives.

Leading himself through the yard he went to the back door. Waiting a few minutes in silence he then knocked on the door with the code, rat, a tat tat – pause – tat –pause, rat a tat tat. He waited, looked up at the night sky and noted that dawn was coming. A silent couple of minutes went past when he heard movement inside and the bolts being moved back. On the door opening, he saw Zoe and his smile was one of genuine thanks that she was alive and looking well. Zoe moved back allowing Jacques to come in. Once he had bolted the door behind him he turned around and faced her. Zoe too was thankful for his return and hugged him tightly with warmth and with relief that he was alive and knew he would help her get through this. She needed to talk.

Chapter 18

Joshua was still as the night and watched everything going on down at the farm and shore area. Little George lying beside him was getting a little anxious so Joshua calmed him down to be still and watch as he was doing. They lay silent under the camouflaged ground sheet and waited.

While the galleon lay dark and still out at sea Joshua saw the small rowing boat detach from the ship and head for the shore. Once landed, one man got out and walked directly to the first man who Joshua had seen an hour ago. Joshua knew who he was as watching through his magnifying lens he noticed the man's gait, shape and that inner confidence it gave off. Yes, Joshua was certain this was the French man they call Jacques.

Joshua wanted to dispatch Little George directly to Kernow or Hosking's to inform them of what was happening here but realised they would need more information to act in accordance with the threat. Was it a landing of battle, a reconnaissance mission or what? He had to be patient and watch and gather that intelligence.

He watched it all, the unloading and storing of the kegs and the number of men involved. After an hour or so Joshua knew this was no battle front but a secretive meeting of the landing of goods. He then watched the Galleon leave as it had arrived. Now was the time to act.

Joshua gave instructions to Little George to go directly to the Bull Inn at Newlyn and contact a Mr Trevenan. "Tell him everything I have told you and await his instructions.

I will carry on observing and await your return."With all his stealth and acting like a squirrel Little George slid out the back of the cover sheet above and crawled along the ground towards the horses reined half a mile back in the woods. Suzy and Harry were waiting as good horses do. Little George calmed them both with quiet whispering and gentle stroking. He then untied his own horse Suzy and walked her away with him. Getting to the lane at the back of the woods Little George then mounted Suzy and rode as quickly as he could to the Bull Inn.

Little George got to the crossroads and headed straight on thinking he would have normally turned right to where his sister and Rebecca were. However, riding a few more miles further he speared off slightly right heading to Newlyn a couple of miles away. He knew he needed to stay quiet through the town but also knew from Joshua the urgency of relaying the information as quickly as he could, therefore he galloped on.

He found The Bull Inn set away from the main hub of the town and standing quietly at the edge. Little George got off Suzy and was surprised to find that the front door was unlocked. He looked in through the windows and saw men still drinking and laughing. It must be three o'clock in the morning he thought.

Weighing things up, he decided to go around the back and find another way in. He was learning that the fewer people saw or knew the better. It was good that he saw no one but bad because the back door was locked. He now had no choice but to go back around the front and go in that way. He would be bold and ignore everyone so with a deep last breath of confidence he walked in heading for the bar and then realised that everyone ignored him. He waited by the side of the bar until a man came up and asked what he wanted. "I want to see Mr Trevenan." "And what is your name young man?" "My name is Little George."

Within a couple of minutes, a young lady escorted Little George through the back labyrinth of the Inn and on knocking on a door walked into a large room. She addressed a man by the name of "Mr Trevenan," then introduced Little George. The young lady then left the room without saying another word. Little George noticed the man had been in bed asleep as he was dressed in his night clothes with a silky light robe wrapped around him. Little George also noticed that the man had a large sword dangling from his waist belt holding the robe together.

What he didn't understand was that he had seen this man before in the Blue Anchor in Helston many times with his once Master Henry Hosking and he was definitely not called Mr Trevenan. Little George didn't say anything but turned around and saw another man sitting in a chair behind the once opened door fully dressed with a pistol at his side. The man smiled.

Little George was offered some refreshment and asked to sit down. They both sat down at the table opposite each other when Mr Trevenan asked Little George to tell him all. Little George did as was told.

Trevenan paced the room after hearing what Little George had said. Little George drank more of his drink and was silent. Trevenan was also silent while walking back and forth in deep thought finishing up at the window where he then stopped and looked through at the night sky. Slowly leaning forward on the sill and bringing his face ever closer to the glass pane he knew decisions had to be made. It was his decision and his alone that would give success or failure of what happens next. His main aim was to get Jacques the Frenchman and he would use all his skills to achieve it.

After thinking things through over and over Trevenan then slapped the window sill hard with both hands then turned around and said, "You have done well Little George, now this is what I want you to do."

Little George was instructed to go to the cottage and inform Rebecca to prepare a visit this afternoon from himself and his men then go directly back to Joshua the same way you went in. Tell him to stand firm and, if necessary, let the enemy come through his position. We need information. "You my dear boy are to be the go between and report back to me at the cottage when darkness comes or earlier if Joshua thinks it's otherwise too urgent."

With that, the man calling himself Trevenan opened the door and shouted for the young lady. As she came in Little George was thanked and asked to get on his way with the orders given. On his way out Little George heard Trevenan giving the young lady instructions.

Little George found Suzy where he had left her tied at the front of the Inn. Trevenan, who had got himself quickly dressed was now organising the writing of letters to be dispatched forthwith with all haste and speed. The machine was at last grinding into action.

Rebecca was just getting up when Little George got to the cottage. Christine was fast asleep. He went over all that had happened and what Mr Trevenan wanted her to do. Rebecca started about the cottage by clearing things up and preparing food for many people. She was going to wake Christine but decided to leave her to lie in a little more. Little George knew that daylight would be soon approaching in an hour or so and needed to get back to Joshua. Rebecca quickly filled a bag with food adding a bottle of brandy. She kissed his cheek and said, "Be careful Little George." Then he was gone heading back to the woods at Sennon.

Christine was still fast asleep when she heard a scratching noise which gently woke her up. She looked around but saw nothing. Then from the window, the scratching started again. Once she had rubbed her sleepy eyes she saw a little red squirrel outside on the window ledge jumping up and down and sliding down the window glass with two black and gold butterflies around her. Christine started laughing with a sweetness of love for them. She then ran out of the bedroom and found Rebecca and told her what she had just seen. Rebecca didn't say anything but kissed her cheek with a knowing.

Joshua was still in the hide watching when he saw Jacques move away from the house and sit in the shadows to watch and listen and see if the night talked. He felt somehow a sense of admiration for him as that is exactly what he would have done. He then thought who was watching who here. Joshua didn't move and carried on looking through the lens quiet like a mouse. After a short while, he then saw Jacques get up and go back into the farm house. Joshua then heard a rustling behind his position and tensed up. Just as he done this, Little George whispered, "Joshua." Relaxing his tenseness, Little George slithered himself back under the sheet into the scrape. Handing over the bag Rebecca had made he went over things. When Joshua heard that he must, if necessary, let the enemy walk through his position, felt a sense of dread and realism. In effect, he would be killed or sacrificed, depending on which side you are on, should he be found by the enemy in superior numbers. If he had any ego, it was now gone completely.

It wasn't long after Little George had come back that Joshua saw Jacques go to a horse and ride away heading towards the main road. Joshua did nothing, he couldn't, he had to wait and be patient. He knew this was going to be a long day. He turned to Little George who looked worn out and suggested he put the shawl over him and get some sleep. Little George did as was told and then Joshua went to the bag that Rebecca had made up and smiled when he saw the brandy so took a well deserved mouthful. He would wake Little George up in a few hours and they would swap places so Joshua could also get some shut eye.

The hours passed without further drama and when it was time, Joshua woke Little George to take his watch. Joshua advised him to focus on the barn where the consignment was stocked and the cottage where the people were. He showed him how to swivel the lens on the horizontal plane and the mechanism to focus. It was broad daylight now so movement was now crucial to be as little as possible if any. Joshua didn't stay awake long and went off to sleep. Little George felt good and excited at using the telescope as it made him see things that he had never imagined. Both muskets were loaded and ready as with their pistols.

At the Mousehole cottage, Rebecca was happy in feeling the place was now acceptable for a visit. What sort of visit, she didn't know? Christine had earlier gone into town to get some groceries, meat and drink. All was ready. Around four o'clock three men appeared in the back yard entering the back gate. They had laid their horses out of site further behind in the field at the back of the lane which runs past the cottage back yard.

So from the front of the cottage people would have seen nothing untoward. The first person to enter the cottage was Kernow alias Trevenan followed by his two lifeguards.

After the introductions were over Kernow asked about her health and thanked Rebecca for her pending hospitality. He suggested that there may be some others coming during their stay which may take between four and seven days. Hopefully, it would be the lesser but we cannot rush this. This took Rebecca by surprise as she thought it was just for the afternoon so had to start thinking about sleeping quarters and everything else to host the extra people.

The main room of the cottage was to be taken over by Kernow with his maps and writing materials as the main operations room and, as suggested by Rebecca. Also, they could use her bedroom should they need to sleep. This was agreed so she moved her things out into Christine's room where she made an extra bed for herself and left Little George's bed vacant should he return. Then as the day grew into the night a familiar face entered the back door. It was Henry Hosking who politely doffed his hat to Rebecca and asked after her health.

With refreshment given he then went straight into a heavy discussion with Kernow. Kernow wanted to know exactly what Henry had organised. Henry moved around the open map laid on the table and duly explained what he had done. He pointed with his finger his men's positions and also explained when they would be in place. Kernow nodded his approval and then went on to discuss different scenarios and assumptions and what their responses would be should these things happen. His expectation, should things go to plan and with the latest information gained from Joshua, is that either tonight or the days after they will have the desired answers to implement the trap. With the fire stoked and lanterns lit, a steady rhythm of talk and silence fell upon the cottage's main room.

Joshua was still asleep in the scrape so it was Little George who noticed the extra movement of people at the barn and the horse and carriage being drawn up and being loaded with kegs from inside the barn. He decided to wake Joshua immediately. Joshua slid over and eyed into the scope. After only a few seconds he said, "Well done Little George, it would appear they are now preparing the way to move the consignment and not leave it there at the farm." Joshua considered things very carefully, should he dispatch Little George or wait. It was nearing nine o'clock and although the night was in the younger part of darkness the stars were out shining through. Joshua decided to wait a further thirty minutes and watch. After that extra time had lapsed and the loading was still in progress he was sure something was up and so it had to be reported. He told Little George of his considerations and to dispatch this to Trevenan. Little George once again went through the procedure of exiting silently by slithering back out of the scrape, fetching Suzy and riding away. This time when he got to the junction he turned right to Mousehole.

Entering the back yard, he went into the cottage. He wasn't expecting anybody to be up as it must now be nearing eleven o'clock. However, the candles were aglow and he met Rebecca who kissed him on the cheek and told him to go directly into the main room and speak to Mr Kernow. As he entered the room Henry smiled warmly at him as a Father would to his son. Little George was a little surprised as he was not expecting Henry Hosking to be there.

Kernow stood up and apologised for misleading him with the name of Trevenan and then asked what information he has. Little George smiled knowing why this man changes his name so often but then quickly informed him of what he and Joshua had seen with clarity and preciseness he had been taught. They listened carefully and once Little George had finished his story was told not to go back to Joshua tonight but to stay here and get a good night's rest. He was to set off very early in the morning with an emphasis on being with Joshua before the break of the day.

Kernow and Hosking had confirmed that what may happen this night was just too dangerous for Little George to get involved either by accident or any other way. Now armed with this new information from Little George they needed to slightly adjust the positions of Hosking's men. Henry got the message and so left the cottage to organise accordingly. Kernow poured himself a brandy and hoped he had got all the angles covered, as best he could.

Chapter 19

As it was nearing eleven o'clock Jacques realised that the time had come for him to go back to the farm at Sennon and get the first consignment of kegs away and back here inside the cottage, with the two young men. They were now into the final preparation stages before Pascal gives the go ahead for the kegs to be carried up the tunnel and the liquid germ released into the soil.

When Jacques had previously got back to the cottage that morning he and Zoe had talked openly and at length. It was blatantly apparent that she disliked Bouchier not only for his massive egotistical manner and his older age but for his obsession with her. Zoe and Jacques had now both decided that each would be as truthful as they could with each other. He in turn opened his thoughts on not trusting Bouchier either and that maybe he felt threatened by him.

Although they had shared the same bed it was different this time. For the first time, they started asking each other about their loved ones and their hopes and dreams for the future. Zoe explained how Philip Albret had bribed her away from her family leaving her young love back in the vineyard. Jacques couldn't speak as openly as Zoe, as his broken heart wouldn't let him but never the less he tried his best. Altogether they both realised that something had changed between them and rather than playing games they started to understand that neither was comfortable with what was happening and both felt an underlying feeling of dread at being thrown to wolves. Jacques also mentioned the old lady he had bumped into and what she said and how she had said it with hiss and venom.

They both agreed, for their own futures, that from now on they would talk plainly and openly as best they could and keep each other informed. Zoe, realising the fatal position she found herself decided to further open up. She told Jacques that although he had once said to her to kill Pascal for his total incompetence before he left for France, the fact was that Bouchier had earlier given her poison to kill him anyway. Jacques then responded by telling her that Bouchier had ordered him to kill the two young men and Pascal to leave no traces of the mission once the liquid germ was dispatched into the ground.

Jacques also pointed out that Bouchier had. ordered him and Zoe together to be at the Chateau directly after the mission is completed. This is wrong and should not happen as once a mission is completed it is always best for agents to vanish somewhere of their choice. Then when things have calmed down they are only contacted by a courier by the agreed route.

"Jacques I really don't feel good about any of this, what are we to do?" "I feel the same Zoe and don't know what to do either but I will find a way."After holding each other a little while longer, Jacques went out and got Arc ready and when midnight struck he was off to fetch the first of the consignment. He told Zoe he would return before dawn.

Joshua saw the horse and rider enter the farmyard and go straight to the barn where the rider dismounted and started a discussion with the two other men. He saw it was Jacques.

Joshua saw him check the carriage over and then disappear into the farm house. The two men then got on the carriage, clicked the horses forward steering and moved to the front of the house where they halted. Just a few minutes later Jacques reappeared and getting on his horse went by the carriage seemingly giving the two men more instructions. With that Jacques led his horse steadily away from the farm and the carriage followed behind him.

Joshua, observing everything, surmised that whatever cargo went into the barn and the length of time it took to put it there and, the very short time they spent taking the same things out, must mean that only a small part of that cargo is being taken away. Therefore this must also mean a high probability of them returning.

Jacques was riding Arc at a steady pace. He was aware that the carriage was loaded with twenty-five heavy barrels but it was still moving too slowly for his liking. Jacques had to keep checking Arc's pace to keep the carriage and horses together.

At the cross junction, they turned right and getting closer into the town Jacques realised he couldn't do his doubling back routine to confuse anyone looking. Instead, he chose to slow down to a halt in a darkened area close by some trees and wait ten minutes. When happy with the silence of the night Jacques dismounted and then walked the carriage forward heading to the rear of the cottage and its back yard.

He didn't like it as the carriage was making too much noise and also was very cumbersome but he had no choice in the matter how else was he to get the kegs from the farm.

When Zoe opened the back door of the cottage they all mucked as one to get the kegs inside and out of sight as quickly as possible, except for Pascal who was fast asleep upstairs. When they had finished the two young men were then introduced to Zoe who with utter politeness expressed her happiness in meeting them and offered them a brandy, which both accepted.

Jacques then suggested they both now get a couple of hours of sleep before being introduced to Pascal on his waking. He will then lead the instruction of them both and also help in the digging of the tunnel. He also went on to say that when they return to the Farm at midnight tonight to pick up the next twenty five kegs, he would not accompany them and they would be on their own. Jacques saw no reason to compromise himself any further and that they would now be handling and moving on their own initiatives. This they were happy to do and both felt an inner self confidence of getting the job done faster without an oldie getting in the way.

Jacques then discussed things with Zoe who advised him that she had prepared beds for the two young men in the third smaller upstairs bedroom. This use to be Jacques's bedroom whennot sleeping with Zoe. Jacques stayed for as long as he could but needed to get away and be on his own. His job there was done for the time being and he wanted to get away to his isolated digs in Penzance where he felt safer away from everyone. He could then have a good drink and sleep soundly.

He lastly advised the two young men that he would see them again on his return before the dawn tomorrow. He also reminded them of their courtesy towards a lady and their duty of work that the tunnel to be further on and the next batch of kegs to be here, no excuses. As he said his goodbyes Zoe ran out after him. As he turned towards her she said, "Jacques, you will not leave me will you?" He kissed her on the cheek and said, "Zoe, I am a man of my word, I will find a way for us both to live as we each desire, trust me." With that Jacques turned, saddled Arc and headed off to Penzance. Zoe turned and went back into the cottage being left with three young men to cope and feed.

Chapter 20

Henry had done his job well. On receipt of his first orders from Kernow that morning he had acted decisively and with help of his right hand Bull, dispatched and deployed twenty trusted and experienced men in strategic positions from the main road cross junction through to Mousehole, Newlyn and Penzance. They had all been paired up so communication runners can be sent immediately without losing the observations. Once deployment of the men was achieved Hosking galloped back.

Kernow and Hosking's were now in the cottage main room when the first of the observations men came in around four o'clock the following morning. A carriage had been seen entering Mousehole moving to the North east of the town, location unknown. There were two men on the carriage seats and another on a big bay horse leading them. The identification of the rider is unknown but fits the description of the man known as Jacques.

As time moved on the observations and reports steadily flowed in, allowing Kernow and Hosking to paint their picture of riposte. Every time the riders came and gave their information they awaited further orders and every time they were given the same, which was, to do nothing but observe and report and let the targets carry on their business without any interference whatsoever.

Rebecca was up cooking and working around the cottage. She was advised by Henry with the authority of Kernow that Little George should stay here until further notice and not at all go back to Joshua. Rebecca questioned Henry on how Joshua would be feeling about him being out so long and isolated. Kernow sensing her empathy and logic nodded in agreement saying, "he would send a relief for Joshua so he could come back." Rebecca thanked him and carried on her duties.

By ten o'clock that morning reports had come in that the carriage had been spotted in the back yard of a cottage north east of the town at the top of Enys Road near the northern most water well. Also, the man known as Jacques had been seen at approximately six this morning leaving that same cottage moving north out of Mousehole heading towards the cross junction.

With information being fluid Hosking again went out to meet Bull, his man in command of the observations, to discuss and tweak his men's positions accordingly. Bull was also asked to pick two men for when night begins to fall, they were to relieve Joshua who himself was to make his way directly back here. However, they were to visit the cottage first and talk with George Kernow to understand the exact location and entry directions. Happy with the new arrangements and Bull's suggestions to now widen the catch area, Hosking went back to the cottage.

Joshua was getting really tired and kept nodding off. He knew Little George couldn't come back in daylight but was concerned for him anyway. Nothing was happening in front of him but alert he stayed as best he could. As the long day light began to fall for night he heard the familiar rustling behind his position and a voice he didn't recognise whispering his name. So with pistol aimed at the ready, Joshua poked his head through the back of the cover sheet to see two bearded ugly faces staring back.

"Don't shoot Josh, we are to relieve you, orders from Hosking."

With the takeover completed, Joshua couldn't quite believe he was on the way back and being on Harry felt wonderfully free. When he arrived at the cottage he quickly realised that Kernow had taken over. However, he went straight to Rebecca and asked after her and sensed real warmth he hadn't felt for what seemed like ages. On hearing his voice Little George and Christine ran in with happiness to see him. With a fresh pipe in hand and a glass of brandy in the other, he went into the main room.

Kernow and Hosking stood up as he entered with Kernow first saying, "Hello Joshua, very well done my lad, by the way, you look terrible." "Thank you George," he replied. With pleasantries over they got down to business.

Without going through too much detail Kernow explained the up to date situation. "Why don't we take the cottage now and imprison them all?" Joshua asked. "That's not the way I work Joshua. That would simply stop an operation in motion and we'd have learnt nothing. We then also have exposed ourselves and that is not clever.

No, we need more information and as I mentioned before to you and Rebecca, we specifically want Jacques. In fact, to be more precise, I want Jacques isolated without any of his accomplices knowing. Therefore, I firmly believe we need more time observing to achieve that goal." "Can I ask why Jacques is so more important than not stopping their dirty mission in its tracks?" "Yes you can ask Joshua, and you have, so let's leave it at that for now shall we."

Joshua looked at Hosking for his support but didn't get it, more a simple shrug of the shoulders to maybe let things be. Joshua accepted this but felt that George Kernow knew something he and Henry didn't.

Kernow was silent in deep thought and slowly looking and waiting patiently for some pattern to emerge no matter how small. If there was one, he would act with more definition and less risk. If there wasn't one, he would act more blindly with increased risk. Joshua and Hosking were becoming more impatient but accepted George's experience and rank.

Early morning came a report that two men had been seen getting into the carriage heading north towards the cross junction. A woman was also seen but went back into the cottage on their leave. Kernow, Hosking and Joshua were now taking turns to sleep or rather cat nap where they sat or when available in the large bedroom for a lie down.

Then the report came in that Kernow was waiting for. It was eight o'clock the next morning. The man called Jacques had been seen coming from Penzance through the cross junction to the cottage at Mousehole at four o'clock this morning and seen again leaving the cottage at six o'clock, as yesterday. It was a repeat and so it was time to act.

With both the cottage at Mousehole and the farm at Sennon being covered, Joshua was asked to lead a small team into Penzance, find Jacques and take him captive. How he did this was up to his discretion but it had to be accomplished discreetly and he was not to hurt him in any way unless of course, he resists. Once Jacques was arrested he was to bring him directly to the Bull Inn at Newlyn, not here, not yet. A room was being prepared for his arrival and one of Kernow's men would be there to meet. Joshua accepted his new orders and was advised to take six men including their leader Bull and set the trap. With that, Joshua got himself ready. On hugging Rebecca and the children goodbye he jumped on Harry and rode off to meet Bull and his team.

After meeting Bull and his selected five members they rode quickly away. They got themselves to the edge of Penzance and went into the thick woods located on the direct road out. Joshua was discussing things with Bull and although he had seen this man on his travels with Hosking he had always thought of him as a brute of a man. However, now he was seeing a different side to him, a more understanding man with a diplomatic type inner manner. This pleased Joshua and so started warming to him. They both knew the position they were in and the responsibilities they were under to make this successful.

If the pattern emerged as correct then that would mean Jacques would be passing through this point of the road around three to three thirty, the next morning. He would then meet the cross junction to Mousehole a little later. Thereafter, he would be back through at around five thirty or thereabouts but, something was bothering Joshua. If Jacques was armed which Joshua assumed that he would be and suddenly became aware of being captured as he rode, his natural instinct would be to fight and flee as that is what Joshua would do. Joshua pondered.

They decided to set the trap at a bend with a slight angled dip in the road just further on out of Penzance. A rider with any sense of coming to meet the bend would have to slow up a little. So having ample time to prepare, they set the centre point up and put two cut off positions twenty yards out in either direction. Should he then fight or flee, no matter which, they were to shoot the horse down instantly.

As the evening started to fall, Joshua and Bull were talking in a more casual way allowing their inner thoughts to come out a little. Joshua had a hunch that knowing this man Jacques liked his drink maybe, just maybe, later in the evening and before he rides out, could be at the Fisherman's Arms where he last saw him sitting in the corner quietly and alone in deep thought. Bull and Joshua discussed the positives and negatives of this idea and realised they had nothing to lose in attempting to see if they were right. If he was there, so it was to be.

So an hour or so later and after leaving two of the men at the stand point, Joshua and the rest of the team went off to the Fishermans Inn in search of their prey. Once outside the Inn they split up and surrounded both exits and entrance with their pistols locked and ready. Joshua couldn't afford the risk for one or two of his men to go in first to check if he was in there as this man Jacques needed just the slightest feeling of unease and he would flee with pistols blazing. So standing just outside the front doorway of the Inn Joshua and Bull turned and looked at each other. Then with a deep understanding of the situation calmly but boldly walked in.

He was there in the same place on his own with his brandy in hand. His body and staring eyes didn't flinch at all when he saw Joshua walk straight up to him and sit himself down opposite. After looking at one another as man to man for a few quiet seconds Joshua said, "Good evening Jack or is it Jacques?" "Good evening Mr Pendragon," he confidently replied. Joshua couldn't believe that Jacques knew him and that took him by surprise so asked, "How do you know my name?" "I have a good mind for people and names. I especially remember you when you came in here around a month ago and took on that Rosevear and his bullies to relieve a very young lady of her duties, you did well Mr Pendragon." Jacques carried on, "I presume all exits are covered and that man over at the bar with a pistol in hand looking this way is with you." "You are correct." Jacque's mind was thinking fast yet he had to remain calm.

"How did you know I was here?" Joshua being calm also replied, "we didn't but looking at patterns and habits it was a chance worth taking." 'So you have been watching me Mr Pendragon?" "I didn't say that Jacques and it isn't for me to answer such questions."

"So what do you want with me Mr Pendragon?" Joshua was quickly realising that this man was experienced and his manner was one of calm yet precise as though working on a mathematical sum. "We would like to have a chat with you that is all and I promise, as a Cornishman and gentleman, no harm will be done to you while you are in my care." Jacques was going to make a quip about Cornishmen but hesitated and decided that respectful silence was best.

Jacques was also weighing the situation up looking at all angles. What do they know? What don't they know, how long have they been watching? Eventually, no matter how he looked at it and his own mistakes he accepted and understood the seriousness of this situation. He knew that if he made one false move he would be shot immediately. Jacques looked at Joshua and Joshua looked at Jacques. Silence reigned between them until Jacques relented, took a deep breath of acceptance of the situation and surrendered pistol and blade laying them quietly on the table. "Thankyou Jacques," Joshua said and then politely asked him, "Would you please come with us?" Jacques nodded, slung back the last of his brandy and went with them. Then walking between both Joshua and Bull and just before going outside, Joshua turned around and handcuffed him as Bull frisked him looking for more weapons. Jacques had to accept it all knowing that his fate now rested with this man called Pendragon.

One of the men went to find Jacque's horse and another dispatched to the Bull Inn at Newlyn. If Kernow wasn't there he should ride on to Mousehole to inform him that the man called Jacques was in their possession.

When all were securely mounted, Jacque's horse Arc was lashed to Bull's horse and away they went picking up on route the remaining men still at the trap point. The route to the Bull Inn at Newlyn was pretty much straight forward and it being later in the evening fewer people were about. They rode at a steady pace taking just over an hour to reach the Bull Inn.

While Bull and his men guarded Jacques, Joshua went in to find the room of Mr Trevenan and was directed to the back of the Inn by a young lady. Outside the door stood one of Kernow's guards who advised Joshua to wait while he went in. Kernow was in fact here. The guard came back out and suggested to Joshua that he bring the prisoner straight up and then for you and your team to wait by the bar area and refresh yourselves with Mr Kernow's compliments. Joshua did as was told and Jacques was subsequently handed over to the guard who then opened the door and all three men entered. Kernow now wasn't there but the other life guard was, "Thank you Joshua," the guard inside said, "we will come back to you downstairs in a little while." Now alone with just the two guards, Jacques was ordered to strip off. Jacques knew these guys were at another level and didn't hesitate. Once they had gone through and searched every little hem, curl and buckle of his complete attire and were happy that nothing could harm their master they allowed Jacques to redress himself. They were polite but firm.

Although there were no windows, the room itself was very sweet and delicate with drapes, lanterns, pretty ornaments and a lovely fire which was roaring warmth. At the centre of the room was a single square table with two upright chairs opposite each other. On the table was another pretty lantern, one bottle of brandy with two glasses and clay pipes. Asking Jacques to sit in one of the chairs the two guards then left. He wasn't bound, gagged or blind folded. He was free to move, look around, stretch or do anything. He looked at the brandy and was tempted.

The quiet seconds ticked by into minutes allowing Jacques to fully consider his position and let him think. Jacques did exactly this trying to fully understand his position and sort things in his head. Why they hadn't killed him was really playing with his mind. He was in deep trouble and he had to remain calm. His past life then started to filter into his thoughts from early childhood to particular events that had occurred which he was grateful for. He looked at the ring on his finger next to the little one on his left hand with its unusual shape of the letter 'J'. He smiled and was content.

Jacques then heard the key twist in the door and in walked a man of crisp appearance with an experienced looking face and, somehow Jacques thought, had an inner kindness. The man then without saying a word walked up to the table and sat down opposite Jacques. He then quietly looked around the room while twisting his groomed moustache in thought. "Lovely, absolutely lovely," the man said. All the while he still had not even looked at Jacques.

Then the man turned his head and looked Jacques straight in the eye and with calm politeness of manner said, "Good evening Jacques, my name is George Trevenan, have you killed any Cornishman or Englishman whilst you have been on this mission of yours?" Jacques looked at him to try and work him out but the question was one of absolute brutal truthfulness with a beautiful delivery of strength. Jacques knew this man in front of him, whoever he was, was good and held authority. "No, I have not Mr Trevenan." "That's good Jacques."

George continued, "yet from your cottage here in this town of Mousehole and being in collusion with the treacherous Mr Ward at Sennon, your mission is to ultimately kill the people of this good land?" Jacques thought very carefully about his response to this question and knew only the truth would keep him alive. "Yes." Trevenan then replied with calm, "I understand."

Trevenan again continued his calm clarity of questioning, "and may I ask how you are supposed to do that Jacques?" Jacques answered with clinical precision, "by poisoning the town's northern drinking well through the natural source of its feed." "And by what means do you intend to poison the water?" "By placing a chemical germ into its feed line about twenty metres from the well allowing two to three days for soak and with the help of the spring tide." "The spring tide you talk about, is it the one due this Saturday?" "Yes." "That's very good Jacques," Trevenan replied. Then he was silent allowing the quietness and mental strain to increase. After what must have seemed an eternity of silence between them and feeling the time was right Trevenan said it, "By the way Jacques before I forget, you do know Jeanne is alive."

Jacques was stunned, his mouth dropped and his heart pounded with utter fear of loss and found. His heart and mind were in total confusion. His heart had been destroyed the day he heard she had drowned. Every night and day since, he has struggled to get through without his lost love. He had somehow managed, through the very depth of despair, to slowly sew his heart piece by little piece back together. Now this person in front of him calmly says she is alive. He sunk in his chair unable to fight.

Trevenan let this news of Jeanne sink in and waited in silence, not moving a muscle. "Where is she, is she safe?" "She is in the deepest dungeon at the Chateau Morlaix under the strict authority of Count Philip de Albret and no, she is not safe."Jacques was in utter turmoil; he didn't know what to say or where any of this was going. "What do you want of me Mr Trevenan?" "I want you Jacques to carry on what you are doing and not endanger yourself. I want you not to kill any of my people and I want you to get Jeanne and bring her back home safe, that is what I want." "What about my compatriots at the cottage," Jacques asked. "That is up to you Jacques. What I will say is that if we can cooperate and agree on a way forward then no harm will come to them. Now I will leave you in peace to consider things."

Trevenan got up and walked to the door but as he was half way across the room Jacques spoke, "and what if I get Jeanne freed and back here safe, what of me then Mr Trevenan?" He turned around and said in a clear voice so there was no misunderstanding, "If you and I can achieve what I want then you and Jeanne are free to live the rest of your lives together, now I will leave you in peace."

As Trevenan left the room and the door relocked Jacques had time to think. 'Jeanne his beautiful love is alive, he wanted to shout. That bastard Albret and what of that man Bouchier he thought, he knows everything Albret is up to as he is his pup. He said it, he couldn't quite believe he had just said the word pup but knew he should have said the words vicious pup. He kept thinking about Jeanne, Jeanne is alive, how wonderful, how beautiful. How life isso joyous with love in its midst. He will save her, he will fight for her and he will love her again.

Kernow left his guards outside the room and went on down to the bar area where Joshua and his men were drinking ale and eating their hearts out, at his expense. Kernow's plan was taking shape but the next moves were more a risk and which he had weighed up and down over the last weeks. However, he could see no alternatives other than to keep them in the need to finish the job successfully. He located Joshua and took him aside asking how he was. Joshua replied, "am very well Mr Kernow." "That's Good Joshua," Kernow replied, "we need to talk, please take a seat while I talk with Bull a while."

Bull was to take himself and his men back to Hosking's at the cottage in Mousehole and once there inform him of what had gone on here. He was also to tell him that the observation teams must continue but redirect them to only the cottage at Mousehole and the Sennon Farm. They must do nothing but observe and send information.

With Bull and his men gone it was now only Kernow and Joshua in the bar area. With both men seated, it was down to Kernow to start. "Joshua, since we met a few months ago I have been watching you and I must say that I am pleased with the way you handle yourself and the tasks you have been given. You are a credit to your Father. By the way, how is your relationship with Rebecca, I mean is it one of intimacy?" "My relationship with Rebecca, Mr Kernow, is one of friendship and trust and no we are not intimate." "And may I ask what of the future?" Before Joshua had time to answer, Kernow continued. "Joshua, please believe me that we are at a critical stage in this mission to save the lives of hundreds of our good people and I would not ask these questions if they were not necessary."

Joshua understood the position Kernow was in and replied truthfully, "Although it may not be Rebecca's intentions I do hope that one day Rebecca and I may get closer and that I would ask her hand for marriage." Joshua thought to himself that he had never said anything like this to anyone, especially after his first wife passed to the Lord and whom he loved dearly and thought he would never love again. "Thank you Joshua for your honesty, this game we play isn't easy at times."

Joshua listened with intent as Kernow, now knowing that intimacy had not yet taken place between them, felt more confident and continued. "What I am about to disclose to you now will give me satisfaction that it will remain only to us both and no other shall hear." Joshua thought a while and gave his assurance of secrecy which Kernow responded by saying, "So be it."

"Joshua, as you now know by our earlier conversations that your Father John, Henry Hosking's and Rebecca's Mother Jeanne were on a mission a few years ago in France and that it didn't bode well in that your good Father and Rebecca's Mother lost their lives. It has come to our attention and belief that Jeanne, Rebecca's mother is in fact alive, and I want you with the help of Jacques who hopefully has considered his options well, to prepare for France and get her back safely to us." "And what of my Father may I ask?" "The reports that came in at the time of your Father's death by drowning have never been contradicted or contested and therefore we must presume that he did drown."

"Does Henry Hosking know of this." "No he does not, as I said, no one knows except Jacques upstairs, and he was informed for good reason." "Why was Jacques informed Mr Kernow?" "Because Joshua they were lovers in the deepest sense and I used this most upper of all human emotions as a fulcrum for him to cooperate with us."

Joshua was intrigued and felt inwardly excited about being given this type of secret information and was beginning to understand the mysterious and wonderful world in which Kernow moved. However, although grand and powerful, it seems it must be a very lonely life and knew that he was being drawn into it deeper and deeper, which he wanted.

After a small silence, Kernow asked, "would you like me to continue Joshua?" "Sorry George, I was thinking and trying to analyse the information you are telling me, please do." Kernow then went over a few more things of clarification and then suggested that when he goes back upstairs to see Jacques that Joshua comes with him and listen in to all that is said between them. Kernow also suggested that once they have finished with Jacques upstairs that Joshua not hurry off back to Rebecca but have a debrief between the two of them to thoroughly discuss responsibilities on what happens next and, this may take hours. "Are you happy with this Joshua?" 'Yes I am." "Good then let us have a drink and let Jacques stew for a little while longer. Patience and correct use of time are vital tools to get want we want to achieve Joshua." Joshua was learning.

With drinks finished Joshua and Kernow went up to see the prisoner. Once at the door Kernow suggested that Joshua wait outside a while until the time is right for him to come in. He explained that he didn't want Jacques to be diverted in any way shape or form with another person in the room until such time as he alone had voluntarily accepted his will to cooperate. If he does, then good, we can then invite you in to divulge our plans together. Kernow, Joshua thought was a wise thinker.

Jacques heard the door unlock and swing open and the man Trevenan walked in as calm in manner as before.

Jacques had indeed had time to consider all angles as best he could. He was not in a position to barter, he knew that but knew also that he may get some concessions or at least promises that will ease his conscience.

"Well Jacques, have you come to a decision?" "I believe I have Mr Trevenan but before I answer, I would like to ask two or three questions myself if that is permitted?" "Yes, of course, please ask," Trevenan replied. "Do you intend to harm or kill any of my party here in Cornwall?" 'No." "Do you want any secret information that I may have or not have as the case may be on and above this mission I and my team are on?" "No." "Do you want me to betray my nation?" 'No." "One last question if I may if we succeed in getting Jeanne to these shores safely and she doesn't want me, what of me?" "Then Jacques, we have concluded our business and you are free to go, but rest assured we would want you to retire. If we find you again messing in the lives of our good people of our good Queen Anne, we will kill you."

Jacques fell silent and let the answers flow into him to mitigate his judgement. "Mr Trevenan, I believe that in the best interest of my party's safety and my own, and that of my love for Jeanne with the fact that I will not betray my nation outside of this mission, I agree to cooperate, what are your suggestions?" "Thank you Jacques, I believe you have made the right choice for all concerned."

"As for suggestions Jacques, I would like to bring in Joshua Pendragon who I believe you already know. Also, now that the decision of cooperation has been made we can all have a drink and relax a little. Help yourself

Jacques, it's the best French brandy one can buy." Jacques cooperated.

With the three men now around the table they set about in heavy discussion. They all agreed the main emphasis was to let the French mission run naturally, it had to, as seen from their side. It was down to the intricacies of managing it that needed to be agreed between them.

Being open and as honest as one could there was no room for delicacies. Many issues were discussed and most were agreed but some couldn't be agreed upon and would therefore need further input. One point Jacques raised was the order he had been given by Bouchier to kill the three young men once the chemical had been dispensed. "How do feel about that Jacques," Trevenan asked. "I do not feel good about it at all Mr Trevenan, especially of the orders from one Pierre Bouchier who feels life is a trivial thing and he can wave his hand and have authority over God."

Trevenan responded to his observations that he also didn't agree with Bouchier's orders but, somehow understood the need for this brutal action as this mission of yours is dirty and extremely non chivalrous. It would look seriously bad on the French King trying to keep and promote good relations with neighbouring Countries and also the America's.

Jacques nodded to Kernow's open thoughts and then went on to say, "If he did not kill the three men then Albret and Bouchier would be suspicious and activate a search team." So together they discussed a plan to save the lives of the young three men. While they carried on talking, Trevenan sent for the young lady to fetch food and more drinks. The other main area of concern was the woman Zoe. This again was discussed at length with an agreement that it was up to Jacques to sort this out and to turn her support of loyalty by promising a life of freedom without Bouchier. Whatever he decides to achieve her loyalty he would need to put on an armband of yellow and black when he exits the cottage in the early morning. This will give us the sign that she has agreed to cooperate and that all is well for the plan to proceed as agreed. The only other factor was that the cottage was loaded with explosives and all doors and windows were filled with gunpowder and booby trapped in case of an attack. With one flick of a flint in the right place, it could bring the cottage to dust and all within her.

Tomorrow was Monday and the kegs of liquid germ had to be emptied into the ground by no later than Thursday to achieve its run and soak for Saturday into the Mousehole's Northern Water Well. That means Jacques and Zoe were to be expected in front of Bouchier no later than that weekend. No exit route had been planned for them, as the flexibility to escape their own path back was seen as crucial. However, what it did mean was that the three young men would need to be killed or seemed to be killed and breathe their last this Wednesday or possibly Thursday at the latest.

With time pushing on the meeting started coming to a close. Jacques needed some sleep, as did they all, but he had to be at the cottage before daylight. They all got up, shook hands and went to the door. The young lady was there and so Trevenan asked that she escort Jacques to his horse, Arc, and then report back. They also agreed that a message for Jacques would be at the Fisherman's Inn on where they were to meet next.

They had done well. Trevenan had worked on the fear of death and heavy emotion to achieve his goal. Jacques really had no options in trying to minimise his failure to save his life and also that of the others, especially Zoe. Joshua was in the middle thinking that it all sounded well but he would have taken hostages to acquire success.

With Jacques gone, Kernow and Joshua started to prepare their way back to Rebecca's cottage in Mousehole, as what needed to be done here was done. It was getting late and they all needed sleep. However, Kernow needed updating from Hosking's before he thought about sleeping. Fetching their horses Joshua rode with Kernow and his bodyguards.

When they got to the fields behind the cottage, Kernow and his men dismounted and allowed Joshua to carry on to the back yard as the normal procedure would have it. They would follow on foot shortly afterwards. On entering, Joshua was pleased to see all were up and went directly to Rebecca and pecked her on the cheek. He asked how she was and the children, who also quickly appeared and came to him. The atmosphere was one that Joshua relished and had missed for so long. He then went into the main room where Henry Hosking was busy around the map on the table and then soon afterwards Kernow came in. His guards were told to stay outside and keep alert.

Chapter 21

While seemingly free to ride back to his digs in the midst of Penzance, Jacques was confused, bewildered but somehow still alive. He just did not see this coming, bloody English. How was he to get out of this he thought? He could simply flee and leave them all to it but what of Jeanne and Zoe. He was in a bloody tight fix. However, where there is darkness there must be light somewhere and just maybe this might be a blessing in disguise. He must find that light. Reaching his place of refuge, he silently entered his room, reached for the brandy and lay back on the bed. All these years in control he thought with all the accolades it brought him and now, in the gutter struggling for survival. He must think very clear and straight for his very own existence. He felt eighty years old and was tired of this continual fighting.

The early hours soon came and Jacques was on Arc in the freezing darkness riding to Zoe at the cottage. He knew he was being watched and whoever they are were discreet and professional which funnily impressed him. Also, Trevenan was keeping his promise which gave him some comfort.

Zoe was waiting and as he entered she hugged him tightly and said, "Jacques I can't take much more." "Zoe, we need to talk, where is Pascal?" "Asleep upstairs." "Did the two young men leave on time for Sennon?" "Yes Jacques, they have worked hard and slept very little, while that Pascal has worked little and slept hard. They were going to beat him up for being so idle and rude to me so I had to step in and quiet things down." Jacques took Zoe upstairs into her bedroom and as he did she started to undress. "Zoe put your clothes back on, we need to talk."Zoe reluctantly, but then again pleased, did as she was told but knew instantly that something was wrong and asked, "Jacques, what is it, you have changed I can feel it." "Zoe, I think we have been compromised." "How do mean Jacques and please speak clear so I can understand." "We are being watched, all of us, even now the two young men are being observed." "How do know?' "I have seen them and I also know who they work for." Jacques continued in a fearful tone and finished by saying. "Zoe, we are in deep trouble." Jacques expected sheds of tears on hearing this but instead got a resourceful, "So what are we going to do about it?"

"Zoe, please tell me exactly and truthfully what you want to do with your life, assuming we get out of this alive?" "I want to go home and start my life again with the love I left behind." Jacques considered the position and asked. "Zoe, I believe I could make a deal with these people but I need your total support." "Jacques if you can give me the chance to meet my lost love again and let me live a life, you have my full support, now do what you have to do and keep us alive."

With timing just about right the two young ones appeared at the cottage with the kegs from the Sennon farm. Jacques started warming to their zest in getting the job done.

Jacques enquired after the tunnel and was surprised to hear what they had done. Pascal was asked to come down and explain exactly where they were with this tunnelling and when will it be finished. Pascal calmly acknowledged the request and said, "at the pace of these strong good men, the tunnel and the liquid hold will be ready in probably two more days, that would make it late Wednesday night."

"That's good Pascal," Jacques replied, "then all you three men be ready to leave before midnight Wednesday or at the very latest one o'clock Thursday morning, no excuses. Be ready or you will be left behind." "Where are we going," Pascal asked. "Back to France, where else." Jacque's mind then quickly thought back to the orders from Bouchier to eliminate all three and not leave any breathing. This was their lucky day, only they didn't know it.

Zoe made them all breakfast and started tidying the place up as best she could with all the piles of dirty rubble being brought up from the tunnel. Jacques quietly took Zoe aside and reassured her that he would be back again tomorrow. Being also satisfied that the tunnel was now being dug with a young man's gusto, Jacques went to the back door. Once outside he looked around and then felt in his pocket for the yellow and black armband that the young lady at the Bull Inn had given him after the meeting with Kernow and Pendragon. Once he had put it on his upper right arm he felt sure he was being observed and that this overt act of compliance would be relayed to Trevenan. Then as soon as he was on the back of his horse he rode fast to Penzance.

After a long tense day on his own Jacques went to the Inn for the comfort of brandy. While he was at the Fisherman's he was given a message requesting he be at the Harbour at nine o'clock. He smiled at the order but had an hour or so before to enjoy his drink. On arrival at said time and place, two of Trevenan's men came up and quietly took him into the shadows to search him. Once happy they escorted him to a small but well gunned schooner and as soon as he was on board he saw Trevenan and Joshua waiting for him.

Trevenan had indeed got the message of cooperation and handed Jacques another band for Zoe to wear on her leave from the cottage. "Well Jacques," Trevenan said, "Have you the time when your plan will start its operation?" "We will be ready to leave the cottage at midnight Wednesday or one hour past into the early Thursday morning." "That's good and what of Zoe?"

"Zoe is ready to leave as well and has pledged that she will trust me." "Very well Jacques and you will diffuse the booby traps and the gunpowder bombs on your leave, we don't want any accidents now do we?" The geographical areas were once again discussed as with timings and when all three were in agreement Trevenan went over the plan again. Jacques looked at Trevenan and although he was on the other side, so to speak, he respected his thoroughness and methodology.

Once Jacques had left the cabin, Kernow called one of his trusted runners to get messages to various people without delay. With the seed now laid, the plan of execution could start.

Chapter 22

The moon was full and the night dark with stars glittering in its background when Jacques entered the cottage around ten o'clock Wednesday night. The young lads had indeed worked well and were covered in dirt but full of laughs and zest as they boasted to Jacques that they had delivered the tunnel with good time to spare for a large brandy. Jacques congratulated them and let them have their drinks. His mind was on Pascal and Zoe and getting them all out.

"Where are the kegs Pascal?" "Where we said they would be," he replied cockily. "Good, then get yourself ready as you three are to leave in one hour." "And what of Zoe?" he asked. "Zoe and I will clean up the mess, pour the chemical into the ground and set the fuses then meet you in two to three hours." "Where are we to meet?" Jacques was tired of this young man's bravado and continual questions upon questions. "Pascal, get yourself ready and once all three of you are, then and only then will you be given instructions on the rendezvous point for getting back to our glorious homeland, understood?"

When the three men and their horses were ready Jacques asked them to come and see the map. With the lamps glowing Jacques pointed his finger at a place called Gunwalloe Cove also known as Church Cove. They all noticed it was quite a long way away but Jacques convinced them it was the best place as it was far enough away from Mousehole but the closest and safest place for extraction after such a successful and dangerous mission. They all looked a little hesitant but nodded their agreement.

Once there, they were to go into the Church by the rocks and wait there for pick up an hour before sunrise. Do not let yourselves be seen and keep the horses away from the Cove out of site. You will be going aboard a ship and there is no room for them, just yourselves and your belongings.

When the two young men and Pascal had left, Zoe and Jacques sat down at the table opposite each other and held hands. "Jacques, are we in trouble?" "Zoe I cannot tell you everything but I can assure you we are safe for now, now let's get things sorted here and get ourselves away from this place."

Jacques did as he promised. With the gunpowder defused he went into the tunnel. Counting the kegs to one hundred he was satisfied that all was in order. Whilst Zoe was sorting out her last things Jacques went outside and got his beloved Arc. He also got Zoe's horse ready with her gear. Going back in and taking one final look around upstairs and downstairs he was ready to go from this place. Zoe was also ready. Standing together just inside the doorway Jacques pulled Zoe's band out of his pocket and put it on over her arm, saying, "This is for good luck to us both," and then put his on as well. When both were ready they walked out into the fresh night air and rode to Newlyn to wait at the Bull Inn where they would be met by a young lady.

Bull and his small team saw them leave and stayed low in the shadows. Waiting half an hour he ordered one man to go forward and enter the cottage building through the main door that Jacques, Zoe and the three men had come out of. This was a brave thing to do and Bull knew it but the man he had picked he trusted and would reward him well. After a few long minutes had passed Bull's front man came back out of the cottage waving his hand high for them to come in. Bull broke his cover and moved forward leaving his other two men to cover him.

Bull was amazed at the wreckage to the inside of this small cottage and the mountain of earth that filled it, but he went on and did his duty. Finding the tunnel entry point he scampered himself down the walled ladder and crawled up along on his hand and knees. He found the kegs as described and counted them as to one hundred and then checked the seals for any tampering as best he could. The seals looked perfect and untouched and the liquid inside had not been emptied. He inspected the ground around him just to be sure and found the area dry. Taking one keg with him he scrambled his way back out. Now he had the information, Bull and his man went out of the cottage to their horses and rode the short distance across the town to the harbour and meet Kernow.

George Kernow and Joshua were on board the ship when Bull arrived with the information and the one keg. Kernow then asked Bull and his men to return to Rebecca's cottage and meet Hosking as he has further orders for them. Once Bull and his men were safely away, Kernow gave orders to the Captain to weigh anchor and head for Newlyn.

Joshua had the keg on the table and started breaking the seal. Whilst he was doing this Kernow gave him six small metal cylinders which Joshua started to fill with the germ. Each time one was filled Joshua handed it to Kernow who then screwed a cap on tight. Once all six little capsules were filled Kernow gave four back to Joshua and kept two.

When Bull and his men had reached Rebecca's cottage they were all given refreshments. After all had drunk the cider, Henry Hosking started to rearrange his men and the tasks they were next to do. Two men were dispatched back to the cottage and guard it from the inside until relieved. They could eat, drink and sleep but not light a fire or smoke due to the gunpowder being unknown. They were also to stay on high alert as the people who will take over them will be coming from London, probably in two to three days.

Back on the schooner both Kernow and Joshua, sitting in the Captain's cabin, relaxed a little for the plan had started well and so rewarded themselves with a small brandy. The ship had left Mousehole and was heading the small nautical distance to Newlyn. On entering Newlyn Harbour Kernow dispatched two men to go to the Bull Inn and to bring back Jacques and Zoe and being reminded to act with courtesy and respect.

When Jacques and Zoe had entered the Bull Inn earlier, the young lady was waiting and escorted both to the main fire place and then waited upon their needs. The conversation between Jacques and Zoe was mostly of silence with an air of nervousness. However, eating what they could and drinking neat brandy eased their tensions a little. After a while, the young lady politely informed them that they were both wanted outside in the back yard where their horses were stabled. Zoe looked at Jacques with dread. "Be strong Zoe, be strong, trust me," Jacques said.
Two men were waiting and politely asked Jacques for his weapons. Jacques did as asked but Zoe looked frightened.

Jacques saw this and quickly reassured her that all was fine and do not worry. The men looked at Jacques and nodded towards Zoe to do the same. Zoe did as was told but the men also needed to frisk her. However, they needed to act with dignity and respect, so went and asked the young lady of the tavern who worked for Kernow, to search her. This she did and found nothing untoward. "Thank you my lady," one of the men said to Zoe, "please now may we escort you to the ship." This kindness and courtesy had an effect on Zoe and calmed her a little.

Asked to leave their horses in the stables they walked the short distance and boarded the ship being greeted by the Captain. He welcomed them aboard and escorted them to separate cabins closest to his. Brandy, pipes and flints were put in their cabins on the table with lamp and bed for their comfort. The Captain suggested they get comfortable and someone will be along shortly.

Thirty minutes later they were asked to join their hosts in the Captain's Cabin. Trevenan and Joshua could not have been more courteous towards Zoe offering her a chair and then both not sitting until she had. Once all were seated Trevenan started, "Thank you for coming Jacques and thank you also Ms Zoe, my name is Mr Trevenan and this gentleman is Joshua Pendragon."

Zoe was confused, these were pure Englishmen, what had Jacques done, oh my God, what has he done? Trevenan saw the fear and bewilderment in her eyes and was prepared for this. "Ms Zoe, I don't know what Jacques has said or not said but would you like me to explain?" Zoe saw the brandy and replied, "If I may have a brandy first then I think that would be good Mr Trevenan."

With the first brandy drank and glass refilled Trevenan asked Jacques if he would now allow him to explain to Zoe what has happened and also what had been agreed. Jacques was quiet but gave the nod of approval so Trevenan explained as Zoe listened. He mentioned Jeanne being captive under Philip De Albret for his own use and also the man called Bouchier. The mention of these names made Jacques come over with sorrow and pain and his puppet Pierre Bouchier made Zoe shudder. He also mentioned that Jeanne was the Mother of a lady called Rebecca who Joshua Pendragon was deeply in love with and is asking for her hand in marriage. This made Joshua go red with embarrassment and made Jacques sit up a little as this was unknown to him.

He also mentioned that he didn't wish anything from them except their help in getting their beloved Jeanne back home to England. In exchange for that help, they would release them both and the three young men to their own freedom and liberty. He then gave again the opposite angle he had given Jacques in the same calm tone as before, that should she not agree to help and cooperate then she would be held in her cabin under arrest until they had achieved their goal. Then, as agreed with Jacques, she would be freed on French soil unhurt and at liberty to do what she pleases. However, if she was found on these shores again working against our gracious Queen Anne, she would be killed. Zoe understood the explanation and was agreeing on much of it but the last item startled her into a realisation that this was her life or death. Now she realised why Jacques had done this.

Trevenan suggested she may have many questions and that it would be a good idea for all to go back to our cabins to relax and consider things carefully before any decisions are made. They would be weighing anchor to Gunwalloe any minute now to pick up the three young men and maybe we should all meet back up in an hour or so. With all getting up from their seats Zoe and Jacques went to their cabins to do exactly what Trevenan suggested, escorted by two men.

When Jacques and Zoe were out of sight, Kernow looked at Joshua for his thoughts. Joshua wasn't convinced that Zoe was on board and Kernow agreed. This may have been a mistake on their part but they had discussed it thoroughly and thought it best to try and get her on side.

Zoe was lying on the bed when a light knock on the door came. It was Joshua and asked if he could come in and talk. Joshua suggested she hadn't heard the full story and asked he be permitted to tell all. He explained in detail how his father had been killed with Jeanne on their escape whilst working in France and how it had come about the hearing two years later that Jeanne was indeed still alive. Therefore she could, with careful planning be rescued, and we ask for nothing more. Zoe listened patiently. He then went on to explore and delve into her future plans and what she would do when set free. He also, under guidance from Kernow, was to mention the name Pierre Bouchier in his conversation with her.

Zoe started to calm herself down and talk more openly to this man. It was now Joshua's turn to listen patiently. He thanked her for her allowing him to talk and would now let her be so she could consider things. As he was leaving, Zoe said, "thank you Joshua, I believe your honesty."

After a few minutes of thought, Zoe went out of her cabin and crept into Jacques to question him and also thank him for now she understood. He could have just escaped and left them all to their death, at least now she had a fighting chance. She found him lying on the bed and so walked over and quietly lay down by his side. Both hadn't said a word to each other and also kept silent as they lay together looking up at the ceiling. With minutes passing slowly by and still no words spoken Zoe broke the silence and asked quietly, "Jacques do you know this lady Jeanne?" "Yes," he replied softly. "And is this the woman you have talked about in your heart?" "Yes."

Back in the Captain's cabin, Kernow asked, "How did she take it Joshua?" "I found her to be more encouraging than before and believe she may well make her decision to be a positive one." "Well done Joshua, either way, we will push forward no matter what. But thinking about it, maybe we should have used her as a hostage as you suggested."

In the Church at Gunwalloe, the three young men were getting anxious and nervy about when and who was going to pick them up. Pascal didn't seem bothered and had shown off somewhat as to be braver than the other two. He had also stopped off at the Halzephron Inn a mile or so before the cove and although it was late and closing he made them give him a drink and took away a large bottle of brandy. He offered it to the other two who refused.

It wasn't until just past four o clock when the Church door swung open and Bull and his seven men entered. The

298

three young men immediately stood up. Bull spoke politely saying, "the ship was ready to take them back to France and would they now please follow him." As each one went through the Church door they were asked if they were carrying any weapons and if they were, the Captain asks they be given to us now and will be handed back when they leave the ship. There is a no weapon policy on board, it's a sailor thing.'

All three looked at each other for support as this order to disarm took them by surprise. However, they accepted it as it made sense and could see no real reason not to, they were going home.

After getting into the rowing boat they were transported to the ship where Jacques and the Captain were there to greet them. Then three of the ship's crew with Jacques in tow took them and their belongings to a large cabin for them all to sleep. Once they were inside and the three helping sailors gone, Jacques asked if they were in good health and looking forward to getting back to France. Pascal couldn't help himself and blurted out aloud that this ship is English and crewed by bloody Englishmen. Jacques just wanted to strangle him but looked at him and said, "My young friend, all is not what it seems, the game we play is never straight forward. All will be well and we shall all feel the soft earth of our beautiful France under our feet tonight. Now relax, stay in the cabin, have a drink and congratulate yourselves on doing a fine thing for your King and Countrymen. Food and drink will be sent to you throughout the day and I will be back later this evening."

With two bunk beds on either side of the cabin, the two young men raced for both top beds. Pascal skulked to one of the bottom ones and started mumbling about Englishmen and how inferior to the French they are. Both men heard him rant aloud calling them bloody savages while gulping the neat alcohol from the brandy bottle.

The more Pascal thought about the English and the English ship he was on the more anxious he became. He wasn't happy as things didn't stack up and that made him annoyed. If two plus two doesn't make four, then there is a problem. He rationed that he could play their game acting stupid like the other two laughing and joking on their top bunks or, he could be bold. The ship also at this time could be no more than a good swim back to shore which was an option and, being still dark was a plus sign to that option. The only other option was to wait but then he would be in the middle of the sea and he would have no way of escape. Then the English could simply kill him and throw his body overboard. 'Never trust the English' Bouchier had said.

Taking another large swig of brandy he got up. Then going into his belongings found the little pistol he had not handed over at the Church. He had to do it. As a highly intelligent Frenchman, it was simply logical, he had to get away. The other two young men saw his movements and asked of his well-being. Hearing of what he was planning they tried to reason with him that Jacques could be trusted but Pascal would have none of it, his mind was made up. "If you two idiots believe that then you cannot be proud Frenchman or have no brains like the English." The two men looked at each other and knew they would stay with Jacques.

Finishing off the brandy Pascal walked over to the cabin door and once opened popped his head outside. Seeing no guards he stepped out and walked quietly away with pistol at the ready.

He made his way to the steps leading to the upper deck and with still no one in sight he quietly went up. Getting to the upper deck into the fresh air he again found he was alone. Looking around he saw the headland was behind him and as calculated was quite a long way off but doable. Once he had swum back he could then regroup and find his own way back to France. Bending down he crept to the side rail and started to climb over when he heard a loud shout, "Oi, you stop where you are." Pascal turned, drew his pistol and fired then jumped.

Two quick reaction marines on board heard the commotion and quickly rallied to the point of confusion. The sailor had been shot but shouted, "Get him, he has jumped overboard, shoot him." With muskets loaded they leaned over, aimed and fired. They missed and Pascal kept swimming as fast as he could. They reloaded, aimed and fired. This time their target in the water stopped and floated still on the sea. The Captain quickly ordered for a small boat to be launched and a small crew to fetch the body back.

The four of them were talking in the Captain's cabin when they heard the commotion. Kernow's guards were quick to react to protect them. After the chaos had quietened down the Captain entered the cabin to brief Kernow on what had happened. Kernow suggested that he speak openly to all present. Somewhat bemused by this the Captain replied, "Very well if you say," then turned to look at all of them.

"We believe the man known as Pascal," and then went on to explain all in a no nonsense way on what had happened.

After the Captain had finished, Jacques asked, "and what of the other two young men?" "I have no idea Sir, I thought it best to report the initial action and then be advised by your leave." "Thank you, Captain," said Trevenan, "please carry on with our voyage we will deal with the other two men." Trevenan looked at Jacques who got up and left the cabin.

Reaching the outside of the cabin where the young men were in Jacques quickly opened the door and saw the two men look at him in fear. "What the hell is going on here," Jacques shouted aloud. The two men then tried to explain what had happened. Jacques listened with utter despair and decided there and then to come clean. He informed them about the reality of the real world and what was really meant to happen to them on orders from Pierre Bouchier. Jacques had had enough of pussy footing around these young men and they needed to hear the truth and he was going to give it to them clearly so they bloody understood the seriousness of what is happening around them.

While Jacques was gone from the Captain's cabin, Kernow felt it was the right time to inform Zoe that she doesn't have to go along with the plan if she didn't want to, it was her choice. "Mr Trevenan, I have weighed things up, discussed matters with Jacques and listened to your good colleague Joshua and feel if you wish nothing more of me and that I am free to pursue my life thereafter, then I believe it is right to answer that I will cooperate." "Thank you Ms Zoe, we promise we wish nothing more and I am sorry about young Pascal." "Thank you but you do not need to apologise Mr Trevenan." Joshua listened to them speaking and tried to weigh her up thinking one minute she is hard as a man and the next she is soft as velvet and then, Rebecca sprang to mind which made him smile.

When Jacques re-entered the Captain's cabin, Trevenan suggested that all that could be done for now was done and that they should all retire to their cabins and try and get some rest. "We shall be on this ship until at least tomorrow night when at the hour of eight we will begin the approach phase."

Later that day and away over in the lovely town of Morlaix a middle aged non-descript man was at his stall selling his fruit and vegetables as he always did. The young boy from the Chateau was also about doing his weekly shopping trip to buy groceries and stores for the Philip Albret's household as he always did. While walking innocently up to the fresh grocery stand the young boy stopped and looked at the nice fresh produce on display. Then buying what the head chef had written down the middle aged man behind the stand quietly asked, "How are you my son?" "I am well Father, thank you." "Tomorrow night at midnight, leave the lower back scullery door unlocked and speak only to one named Joshua." "I understand Father." "Be careful my son and I will see you in England." With the groceries ordered and loaded on the cart, the young man of fourteen was gone.

Chapter 23

Going over last minute details Trevenan wished them good luck and the three of them went down the ladder into the boat. It was eight o'clock Friday night and the sky was moody dark with hardly a star to be seen and only a small moon. They would need to be back in ten hours' maximum or left behind. Once all were safely aboard and sitting down, the boat pushed off from the ship being rowed by two sailors and two armed marines. They were headed for the French mainland, to the small cove of Plougasnou about ten miles due north from Morlaix. Once away clear the Captain gave the order to swing the ship about and as it did the sails filled with wind and away she went.

The sailors had to row hard against the swell but delivered them safely to the tiny out of the way inlet. The two sailors stayed at the cove and quickly got themselves and the boat out of sight to await their return. As planned the horses were there waiting, reined and silent with one spare in which Joshua took control. Then when they were all in their saddles Joshua and Jacques nodded to each other and Zoe, with the two armed marines, galloped off at pace.

Once on the outskirts of Morlaix, they came to a halt and dismounted and went over the plan once again. Joshua asked Zoe if she was good and had any last questions and if so to ask them now. She shook her head and said, "I am ready Joshua." "Have you the letter?" "Yes," she replied. Joshua accepted her answers but like Kernow, he had doubts she may not go through with things. Hence the need of the two marines who had been briefed to take over should she not complete the task that only she could do. With that they split up, Zoe and the two marines headed for the Morlaix Inn and Joshua and Jacques headed for the Chateau.

Zoe and the marines entered the stable of the Inn and once handing over their horses they were welcomed and shown to their rooms at the back away from any noise. The two rooms were spacious with double beds in each and had an adjoining door. The marines stayed close to Zoe and never let her out of their sight on the orders of Kernow, not even to the toilet. Zoe accepted their precaution as she would have indeed done the same if the roles were reversed. They all stayed in Zoe's room and waited for the appointed time.

Joshua and Jacques saw the Chateau but kept a wide birth and detoured completely around it to get to the desired spot. They reined and tethered the three horses a little further back in the cover of the trees and then slowly and quietly edged their way forward to the front centre left of the Chateau. They were in sight of the scullery side walk with the steps leading down to the door but also, able to see the front of the large drive to the front of the house. Joshua noticed that to get to the scullery door they would have to walk twenty yards on gravel and that would create noise so they needed to be careful. Joshua quietly informed Jacques of this possible problem who nodded his agreement. They laid themselves down under a large tree with sweeping low branches that gave excellent cover and then got as comfortable as possible to watch and wait.

The hour passed with nothing and laying there silent within the acres and acres of land around them made the

Chateau feel almost ghostly. Then Joshua heard the sound of hooves coming down the drive heading towards the Chateau's main front door. Tapping Jacques on the shoulder he responded by giving the thumbs up sign.

Joshua slowly drew his telescope and zeroed in on the now dismounted rider. He saw it was one of the marines who spoke fluent French. Rapping the front door, the rider with the letter in one hand and holding his horse's reins in the other, waited anxiously. Nothing, so he rapped again. This time a flicker of light could be seen and getting brighter as it came closer to the inside of the door. When the door opened the marine handed the man the letter and said confidently in French, "Mr Pierre Bouchier, urgent." The man took the letter as a matter of business from an urchin and closed the door shut. The marine jumped on his horse and rode away quickly.

Bouchier and Albret were in the parlour playing dominoes drinking wine when the door was knocked. Albret turned his head while still stroking the young maid's hair who was kneeling like a lap dog by his side and said, with a couldn't be bothered attitude, "Enter." The butler walked in and apologised for disturbing them at this time of night but he had a letter for Mr Pierre Bouchier delivered just a while ago saying it was urgent. The butler then handed it directly to Philip Albret as it would have been bad mannered if he had given it straight to Bouchier. "Thank you, now please leave us in peace, I am getting a headache with all these interruptions," Albret said.

"So Pierre what have we here, a sealed letter for only your attention, I wonder who it is from, shall I open it for you?" Although Albret was seemingly coming across light hearted, underneath Bouchier knew he was deadly serious. If he said no, things could instantly turn nasty so had to play the game. "Please do my Lord Philip; I have nothing to hide as a loyal servant to the Count of Morlaix." "Then I will," he said, but before he did he viciously slapped the young maid on the head ordering her to pour more wine for both Pierre and himself and to quickly lay back down by his side so he could stroke her. This she did instantly without murmur.

Philip broke the seal and opened the letter. It read…

My Love Pierre,
I write in favour that the mission has been a success and praise yours and Count Morlaix planning.
I am in wait at the Inn at Morlaix with my passion being aroused for you and your strong hands touching me.
You may find this letter a little naughty but please come quickly and release me from these chains of wait.
Zoe. xxx

"Yippee, Yippee!" Albret shouted, "it's been a success, they are back. Excellent news my Pierre, excellent news, more wine, more wine," he ordered to the young girl.

With that, he passed the letter to Bouchier who sat back and read it. "Indeed my dear Count, excellent news and what would you have me do of the letter?" "What are you Pierre, are you not a Frenchman, can you not see the woman for the woman. Go and tell her that Count Philip Albret will reward her himself. Now go and let me alone." As he said these last words he put one of his hands down the front of the young girl's bodice and with the other gulped down the large glass of sherry. "As you wish my

Lord, thank you, we will see you tomorrow." "Yes, yes, now leave us in peace and mention to the butler on the way out that I am retiring to bed and wish not to be disturbed." Philip Albret was elated as not only was the mission a success but now he would be duly promoted up the line before his good King Louis.

Bouchier was also elated and now he would get his reward as she will, without fail, love him and want him more after he had finished with her tonight. He was convinced of this, his pride, position and ego knew no bounds especially now that his master Philip Albret would probably be knighted. He quickly went out and ordered the stable boy to get his horse ready and then went to the butler to tell him that the count has retired to his bed chambers and was not to be disturbed. He himself would be back tomorrow.

Joshua and Jacques saw a horse being led around the front of the Chateau by a young boy. Then they saw a man come out of the main front door, jump up in the saddle and whip the horse forward into a straight gallop. Jacques leaned into Joshua and whispered into his left ear one word, 'Bouchier.'

It was nearing eleven thirty but Joshua knew he had to wait a little more and be patient. Knowing it was still too early to move forward, he decided they would wait one more hour taking the time to twelve thirty, one o'clock. Joshua leaned over and whispered in Jacque's ear, "one hour." Jacques got it and nodded without any objection and laid his head back down watching. Joshua was impressed.

Back at the Inn, the two marines were now lying in wait in the adjoining room next to Zoe with the door between them locked with them having the key. Zoe was lying on the bed feeling nervous and very anxious. She had to do it, she had to, she kept saying to herself. Then she would hesitate and reconsider, what if she didn't, what if she didn't. She went to the brandy bottle and poured herself a drink. Lying back down, she knew this was only going to go one way. The consequences of her actions tonight would seal her fate for her lifetime. 'Oh Zoe,' she thought, what of the consequences. 'Oh Zoe, what are you to do.' She decided to have another drink. 'You got to do it Zoe, you got to.'

It was midnight before she heard the knock on the door. The time had come for her to get up and face life. She got up and slowly went to the door and on unlocking it she saw him. Zoe took a few steps back but Bouchier boldly pushed the door wide open and strutted in like a bull wanting what he wanted. Without saying anything he went straight up to her and putting his right arm around her waist pulled her whole body roughly into him taking her very breath away. He then kissed her passionately on the lips with his tongue going deep down her throat and his hand going up her skirt straight between her thighs. Zoe felt physically sick and repulsed, but she had to think, think girl, think.

She pulled away from his grasp in a heartfelt dizzy manner saying, "Oh Pierre, Pierre my saviour, thank you I couldn't have lasted another minute without you, let us bed together and be entwined as one." With that, he started to throw off his clothes laughing aloud and saying, "Zoe, you will have no other after tonight, you are mine forever." Zoe let him strip off as she went to the cabinet and poured the brandy, one for each of them. With her hands shaking she slowly reached for the small capsule and poured its contents into his glass. Turning around, she saw he was near undressed apart from his pants and how aroused he was.

"Pierre, I am so nervous on how I will manage your passion towards me this very night please let me have a small drink to help calm me. I have made one for you also so I am not alone," she then offered the glass. Bouchier took the drink like a man of no consequence and said, "of course my little sweet I can understand you being nervous. Here's to our new life together and then chinked his glass with hers and swallowed it all, Zoe did the same.

Bouchier threw his empty glass across the floor and then took his pants off. He then picked her straight up off the floor and took her to the bed. "I will undress you in here," he said boldly and once they were laid down side by side started to unlace her bodice. Zoe was paralysed with fear but knew she had to play for time but how much time she didn't know. "Pierre can we just kiss and hug for a while and let my body get ready for you." "No," he said, "when I am ready, I am ready, you will learn my ways my little sweet, do not worry you will love it."

Zoe laid back and could do nothing as he was too strong to fight. His hands were all over her like a leech and yet when she pulled them away he got more aggressive. So she went limp in body and looked up to the ceiling as if in a trance of surrender. Then, with nothing else to be done or to lose, she took a deep breath and screamed at the top of her voice.

On hearing the scream from the adjacent room the marines quickly unlocked the adjoining door and rushed in. They immediately went straight to Bouchier and wrestled him off the bed to the ground and then tied him up like a rag doll and gagged his mouth. Bouchier didn't see it coming and was taken by complete surprise, he then started to cough.

They then dragged him through the door into their room. One of the marines then came back and asked how she was. Zoe was shaking with dread at what had just happened as she had never ever done anything like this before. The marine asked in which glass she had poured the chemical as they were side by side on the cabinet. She said, she couldn't remember. "No matter," he replied and quickly picked up both and smashed them on the ground. "Where is the empty capsule?" Zoe pointed and the marine pocketed it. The marine then went and stood in front of her and said, "Zoe, listen to me, you have done nothing wrong here, get yourself calm. We must all leave this place within the hour, is there anything you want?" "Yes, she said, I want out of this bloody room and I want a bloody drink."

Bouchier was laid on the floor completely wrapped up with a blanket on the other side of the bed out of Zoe's sight. His convulsions had steadied and his body lay limp but life was still in it as they could hear his coarse breathing. But, as the minutes ticked by those breaths of life were becoming less and less. Although Zoe was now in the marine's room and had taken a few shots of brandy she was still coming to terms with what she had done. However, she was getting there as the marines kept up their talking to her.

At the Chateau the hour had moved on and Joshua knew it was now or never. So, giving Jacques a nudge they checked their weapons and ran quickly to the side steps that led down to the scullery door of the Chateau. Although they ran as lightly as they could the gravel still seemed to crunch loudly under their feet but as the air was fresh and the night silent it probably seemed louder than it was.

Getting to the scullery door they went straight for the latch and found to their relief it unlocked and with a slight push the door opened. Before entering Joshua stood and waited a while with Jacques closely behind him.

Jacques was now beginning to understand the way Joshua's brain worked, wait then move, wait then move. With everything silent, they both quietly stepped inside. Then again waiting in silence for a minute or so they heard a young voice break the eerie silence, "Joshua?' Joshua whispered back, "Yes, I am he." With that, the young man came forward away from the dark corner where he had been crouching and waiting. "I didn't think you were coming," the young boy said. "You are a very brave young man and yes we are a little late, we had to be sure the timing was right." Joshua then talked with the young boy for quite a while asking him many questions as he needed to gain the knowledge of what was before them. On the answers given Joshua weighed things up and asked the young boy to firstly lead them to the captive Jeanne.

Quietly they followed the boy through many quiet dark corridors of the Chateau. They then started to go down some deep steps which seemed to go on forever. The young man was carrying a jug of water giving a credible reason for him to be there should he be seen. Joshua and Jacques stayed back quite a distance giving the young boy plenty of room to work with. Joshua thought they must already be thirty feet below ground yet still the boy continued.

As the boy turned a sharp corner they heard someone speak aloud and so stealthily, keeping out of sight, closed the gap between them and the young boy. "What do you want here boy at this time of night." "Sorry Sir I was ordered by my master to give water to the lady." "Well, you have, now leave it there and piss off." "But my master will punish me if I do not give it to her directly." "And my master will cut my head off if you do, now piss off before I whack your arse." Just as the young man was turning back up the steps he put one finger in the air meaning one guard. Joshua and Jacques dashed around him taking the guard by complete surprise and without any hesitation knocked him out cold. He just didn't see it coming.

The keys were quickly taken and once the cell was unlocked they pulled the door open but it was difficult. It appeared the door hadn't been opened in quite a while but the little hatch at the bottom of the door was swinging easily. After pulling and pushing the door hard with both their weights the door eventually gave way and opened in full. They took the guard's lantern and went in and on raising the light, saw Jeanne and Jacques simply couldn't help but rush to her.

Jeanne was not well and seemed to be emaciated with lice all over her body. Jacques bent down, put his hand ever so gently on the side of her face and whispered lovingly and very tenderly her name, "Jeanne." It was meant for Joshua to have been the first to get to her on specific orders from Kernow but somehow felt that Jacques should be there first, especially on what he was seeing, so remained at the door.

Jacques tried again but spoke a little louder. This time her eyes flickered open and straightaway said to him ever so tenderly, "Jacques, the love of my life, I knew you would come," and then her eyes closed. Jacques started to weep seeing his true love in the state she was and so bent down and kissed her gently on the forehead. He then wrapped the worm eaten blanket around her and with his strong arms picked her up like a new born baby. Holding her safely in his arms he looked up and swore that Philip Albret will pay with his life for treating his beautiful love of his life like a dog.

On leaving the cell Joshua dragged the unconscious guard back inside the cell and locked the door. He then threw the keys on the floor beside him. With the young boy leading they started to make their way back to the scullery the way they had come. Once there Joshua allowed Jacques to take Jeanne away to where the horses were tied and wait there for him.

When Jacques had left with Jeanne in his arms, Joshua then asked the young boy if he was ready, who responded with a confident, "Yes." With that, they found two empty jugs and filled one with fresh red wine and one with naturally sourced spring water. Joshua then got out two capsules and poured the chemical into both of them.

While Joshua was pouring the germ the young lad fetched two small and freshly washed linen towels. Then once Joshua had finished pouring the germ laid them neatly on top of each jug. This was a sign that both wine and water inside has been freshly replenished. Joshua said, "now be careful, be calm and strong, I will be here to wait for your return." The young boy picked up the jugs and went out of the scullery heading to Philip Albret's bedroom door.

Directly outside Albret's bedroom door in the vast corridor and against the back wall was a beautiful mahogany bureau laden with freshly cut flowers, glasses and ornaments. The young boy quietly replaced the two half empty jugs on the silver tray with the two freshly filled ones and once done he quickly came back down. Joshua was waiting for him and said, "well done young man, now we have one more task to complete and then we are off so please wait here in the scullery until I come back. I will be as quick as I can."

Joshua darted out of the side door to where the horses were reined. Jacques was there and already in the saddle with Jeanne held strongly in his front arms. Joshua said, "Jacques, we must wait for the others, it is too early to go back." "Joshua, I have trusted you and understand your meaning but I am afraid. Jeanne is very weak and if I don't make a start back to the rendezvous point now at a slow pace then the fast ride later will most probably kill her. Joshua, I have trusted you with my life and so I ask that you trust me now." Joshua understood the logic of what

Jacques had said and so agreed for him to make haste. He would now have to wait on his own.

Joshua waited nearly thirty minutes before he heard the rider come up behind him. He stayed crouched down and waited just in case. Seeing it was one of the marines he stood up and as the marine saw Joshua, moved in closer. Joshua saw it was only one of the team and asked, "Where are the other two?" The marine explained that the poisoning of Bouchier, pointing to a body lying across the front of his saddle, took its toll. Zoe didn't want to be near him or this place ever again and so she is being guarded by the other marine and both have gone to the rendezvous point. "Apologies Joshua, but it took us quite a while to sort things out with both the lifeless Bouchier and Zoe."

Joshua sighed but knew through his own experience things don't always go as planned no matter how well you have organised. They got Bouchier's body down off the horse and carried him back into the scullery in the Chateau. The young boy then led them through the back stairway to Bouchier's bedroom. When they were in they stripped him naked and put him to bed and tucked him up. "That's it," Joshua said, "now let us all get the bloody hell out of here while we are still alive." Being led back to the scullery the three of them dashed out the side door to where the horses were. The extra horse was meant for Jeanne but now that Jacques had got her, the young lad can ride him. Time was now nearing three o'clock. They had better get a move on.

Chapter 24

George Kernow was in the Captain's chair deep in thought. Although the pickup point is at five o'clock in the morning at the small cove at Plougasnou he felt agitated. He had got this far by being tactful and unpredictable. He decided to wait a while to see if his feelings would change. He took the brandy and drew the pipe as the ship rolled idly with the waves awaiting his decision.

He thought to himself that two years ago he was at the very same point in his mission when they were surprised by a French galleon and was lucky then to get away with his life. Jeanne and John were not that lucky. How did the French know, was it coincidence? He had time to change. He waited and considered his options then reconsidered. He then shouted for the guard outside the cabin door. When the guard came in George said, "Fetch me the Captain."

The Captain duly arrived and was asked to sit down and have a brandy. The Captain refused the drink but readily took the pipe. George went over his thoughts of concern and asked the Captain's advice for an alternative pick up point. Both of them went to the table and leaning over the table assessed the large map. Although George was nervous about the present pick up point the Captain also had doubts about the ship's safety going to an alternative point at short notice to a similar secluded cove in enemy territory without any reconnaissance. "So what would be your solution then Captain?" Looking closer at the map he started running his fingers up and down giving himself further thought? After several minutes went by he then tapped the map with his large finger at a place called

Roc'h Loue't Point, one mile North West of the present pick up point at Plougasnou. The Captain suggested that to overcome his concern a more open type peninsular of land was needed with the open sea all around so no enemy ship could sneak up unnoticed within cannon distance. This would also alleviate George's fears that if unknown people were aware of Plougasnou then this new manoeuvre would counter act that danger.

George smiled, made himself and the Captain another pipe and drew a deep puff. He then lifted his brandy glass and said, "Roc'h Loue't Point it is Captain, make ready and send the messengers, we have little time."

George was taking no chances with this extraction. Last time it was covert but catastrophic. This time he would go overt on land and sea for meaningful purposes. He ordered a full platoon of heavily armed marines to land and secure the new rendezvous point in readiness to receive our fellow escapees and repulse any attack should it come. The ship also would be at full alert with extra cannon at the ready. It was also agreed that once our people are in the boats the ship would dare to move closer to them to speed up this most dangerous and vulnerable part of the exit strategy.

Riding fast from the Morlaix Inn and the first to arrive at the initial rendezvous point were Zoe and the marine. Zoe's hands were bound together and her horse was tied to the marine's saddle. Although she was in fair spirits the soldier was taking no chances with this lady. They were stopped by a small rear guard of marines who after explaining the situation directed them to the new pick up point one mile further up the coast.

Next to arrive was Jacques who was still holding Jeanne's frail body close to his chest. Although surprised by the rear guard's orders of the new pick up point he wasn't daunted as he knew this was a vital time in the operation and would probably have done the same himself. Jacques asked if they had any water and when they handed him the water bottle he poured what he could into Jeanne's mouth and then with his lips ever so gently kissed it closed. The guards looked at each other but Jacques didn't care.

Not long after Jacques had ridden away Joshua came with the marine and the young boy. They had galloped at full speed without let up from the Chateaux and were getting exhausted. However, when they were informed about the change in plan, without a blink said their thanks and pushed on at pace. With the last of the escapees being accounted for their job was now done so the rear guard fell in behind.

With all now present at the new pickup point the marine commander was satisfied and so signalled the outlying ship to move closer. After Joshua and his team had scrambled into the two rowing boats the oarsmen pulled hard and strained the boats out into deeper waters while the outlying ship turned to meet them and close the gap. This was a critical moment in the escape phase and so the marines on land became ultra alert. Their orders were to defend the point until such time as the two boats had reached the ship and off loaded its precious cargo. Once this first phase had been achieved and the ship had signalled accordingly they were then to withdraw from the point and hide. Another vessel would return at midnight to make their escape. The marine commander accepted this stay behind tactic as just another day in a soldier's life. He would have preferred to be off this French soil now but orders were orders.

On board the ship George was being kept up to date minute by minute. Hearing that the signal from the land had been received he felt the ship turn its bow towards the little boats rowing out to them. George sitting in darkness in the Captain's cabin could do nothing now but wait in silence.

After waiting on what seemed an eternity a loud knocking came on the Captain's door which made Kernow jump into life. "Come in," he said. It was the Captain who entered reporting that all persons are safely aboard and the ship is at full sail heading home. A feeling of glad relief came over Kernow and then asked if all persons were well. "Everyone except for the lady named Jeanne, she is with the medical officer as we speak." "Thank you Captain, thank you. You and your crew have done well, please could you ask Joshua that I wish to see him."

When the Captain turned and left the cabin George got his already made pipe and large brandy out. He then sat back and after taking a deep gulp of the brandy and large puff on the pipe, let out a big sigh of relief.

Feeling tired but proud that the mission had been a success, Joshua sat opposite George Kernow and explained in detail their actions upon leaving the ship. George was not one to be messed with and only precise detail would do whether it is good or bad. "So you allowed Jacques to get to Jeanne first, even though you had strict instructions that you should be first." Joshua was unaware of the importance of why he needed to be first as Kernow never explained it further. "This is true George, I did allow it but the circumstances at the time and the feeling inside me allowed it to be." Joshua then went on to explain the circumstances. "That's fine Joshua but did you hear Jeanne say anything?" "No, she was too weak and covered in lice and what I could see seemed to be dying." Kernow was silent, he needed to speak to her urgently.

Joshua went on with his debrief with Kernow interrupting where he thought necessary. "You also allowed Jacques to ride with Jeanne alone?" "Yes I did," and again Joshua defended his actions of integrity. Kernow, although giving Joshua the third degree was inwardly impressed with the man in front of him thinking he was very much like his Father. "Joshua, I know you are tired and have explained things well but I need to know from your own lips, is Philip Albret the Count of Morlaix dead?" "I cannot answer that question yes or no as we couldn't get to him directly. Other things took precedent in the time we had, such as Zoe's indifferent actions of killing Pierre Bouchier and Jeanne's extremely poor condition."

Kernow knew these were tough questions but he needed answers. "So Joshua, would you say your mission was one of success?" "I would George, we achieved ninety per cent of the desired results with no casualties which in my book is good." "I agree, however, you may have forgotten our brave platoon of marines who are still on French soil at the rendezvous point." Joshua kept silent and didn't respond to that remark. "For the record Joshua, I believe you have done well and thank you for your excellent debriefing. I suggest you go and get some well earned rest and we will meet here again later this day. However, before you take to your bed, could you inform Jacques I want to see him."

Jacques was in the medical quarters next to Jeanne holding her hand when Joshua found him. He informed him that Trevenan wanted to see him as soon as possible. The doctor on board quickly realised after he had taken Jeanne as his patient that this man Jacques would not leave her side for a moment. However, after hearing that he was now wanted elsewhere, came over and assured him that she would be in good safe hands until he returns. As Jacques gently kissed her forehead goodbye Jeanne roused a little and with her eyes still closed raised a shaking hand to the left side of her lower neck line. Jacques watched in silence but didn't know what she meant.

She then started to fumble the top of her blouse. Jacques touched his hand to hers and felt something in the hem line. With both hands, he started to unfold whatever was in there when finally he pulled out a gold ring marked with a 'J'. "Oh Jeanne, my darling, you are the love of my life, I will love you forever," he said with tenderness. He took hold of her shrivelled left hand and gently slipped the ring on her finger as he had done before many years ago. However, her fingers were so bony it slipped off. He ripped a small piece of cloth from his shirt and wrapped it around inside the ring and tried again, this time it stayed on. With her eyes remaining closed Jacques saw a loving tear slide down her cheek. As Jacques kissed the tear drop Jeanne fell back into unconsciousness.

"Thank you for coming Jacques, would you like a brandy?" George said. Without hesitation, Jacques said,

"No thank you." George Kernow looked at him in utter amazement but said nothing.

Getting over the fact that Jacques had just refused a drink George went on to thank him for his integrity and for keeping his word. He also asked if Jeanne had said anything to him, to which Jacques replied, "She has not, she is so very ill." "Yes I have heard, and Jacques, we know you love her very much and like you, we will keep our promises. But I must ask you to leave the doctors and medical staff to do their job without hindrance and give Jeanne the best chance to pull through." "I understand, I will do my best but I have one question." "Please, speak freely Jacques." Then in a serious tone, Jacques asked, "Is Philip Albret dead or alive?" "When we left him he was alive as to whether he is now, we do not know." Jacques was a little confused by the answer but then knowing how the plan was to work understood and nodded acceptance of it.

"Now Jacques, I want you to please talk with Zoe and the two young men to find out what their wishes are and we will do our best to accommodate. Once you have done this may I suggest you all get some well deserved sleep and we will all meet again later this evening refreshed."

When Jacques left and closed the door behind him George drank a large brandy and put his arms behind his head. He then stretched his head back and looked up at the ceiling thinking, what was he to do? He had to make big decisions for the safety of his people but also knew he had to play the long game. He could renege on his deal with the French captives and kill Jacques and his compatriots and live with the belief that the inner security of his beloved Country was kept. Or not kill them and keep the integrity he had made which would also keep open the possible use of their skills for further incursions. He was very tired and needed some rest but knew he needed a last crucial piece of information before the meeting tonight. But before he did anything he called one of his guards to wake him in two hours. He then leaned back in the chair and closed his eyes.

When the hours of rest were up he was awoken as ordered. The time was now early evening and now that he had the sleep he urgently needed he was thankful and felt better. He got himself up to wash and dress and when all done walked to the cabin door.

When Kernow got to the medical room he simply opened the door and walked straight in. He then stood still and looked around spotting in the end bed the gaunt face of the woman he wanted to talk to. A young orderly saw Kernow come in so left what he was doing to ask what this stranger wanted. Kernow told him told to be quiet and carried on walking up to Jeanne's bed. The young orderly then ran out to seek help. Sitting next to her he couldn't believe this was the beautiful Jeanne he once knew. He touched her hair but she didn't move. He whispered her name but again she didn't respond.

He pulled back the blankets and was shocked at the sight of just skin and bone before him. My God he thought. Just then the head medical officer rushed in and without any nonsense went straight to Kernow and told him to leave this minute. Kernow turned around and told him like he had told the young orderly to be quiet. However, with the medical officer came the Captain and two armed marines who would have none of it. Kernow was once again asked politely to leave and leave now. Kernow realised he had pushed his authority too far as the Captain held full jurisdiction on ship.

Kernow realising his mistake got up and did as was told. It seemed that whatever was driving Kernow's mind to talk with Jeanne this reality check brought him back into real life. Once Kernow was outside he asked if he could speak in private to the Captain and Medical officer together.

When the three were alone Kernow said, "I apologise most sincerely gentlemen for my doings but I need most urgently to talk with Jeanne." The Medical Officer replied instantly, "She will not hear you, she has been given sleep remedies." Both men could see Kernow's anxiety build but kept silent to await his response. "Gentlemen, I will say this again I need to talk with her in the highest matter for the defence of our realm and our good Queen Anne and I need to do it now." "It may kill her if you startle her into wakefulness before her body has time to come alive naturally," the medical officer replied.

The Captain intervened, "Looking at this from both sides and the importance of it, how long do you need to talk to her for?" "I need only to ask one question now, the rest can wait, if and when she pulls through." The Captain turned to the Officer and said, "can you help Mr Kernow achieve this?" The officer was quiet for a while then said, "Given time I can gently reverse the sedative solution but I assure you her mind and body will not take any pressure questioning at all and we may lose her if you did so." "I wish only to ask her one question and one question only."

Kernow and the Captain kept silent awaiting the response from the Medical Officer. "Very well then, I will start the reversing process but on one proviso that I stay in the room near to you but not close enough to hear." Kernow agreed and was asked to come back in two hours at seven bells.

Back in the Captain's cabin Kernow tried to relax with pipe and brandy but being so close now to the information he had wanted all along his nerves were becoming frayed. Another brandy should do it he thought. As the minutes ticked by he decided to send word to Joshua and Jacques to be in his cabin at eight o'clock sharp. He then made up his mind that once he knew the answer from Jeanne before at seven bells he would then know what to do with their fates. He closed his eyes and breathed slowly but it was no good he needed to move and decided to go up on deck and speak with the Captain.

"Are you alright?" "Yes, fine thank you Captain," Kernow replied, "I am just a little edgy after all that has gone on and I do need to speak with Jeanne." "Well you won't have to wait much longer it will be seven bells shortly." They then went on to discuss routes, destinations and time frames for the voyage back to England. If all went well it would be Plymouth and not Falmouth for their preferred port due to better medical facilities for the patient Jeanne. However, due to the French persons being on board and information needed in London they had to be flexible so things could change. The Captain didn't pry into anything further as he understood Kernow's position and situation. Not long after the bells then tolled seven times. "It is time Captain for me to leave you, thank you for your time and understanding."

On entering the medical quarters, he stopped and talked to the Chief Medical Officer. Kernow asked how the patient was and if she was ready. "The patient is ready for you Mr Kernow but please don't be fooled by her alert appearance. She has been given things to make her be this way but it will last only five to ten minutes and after that, we will then put her body and mind to sleep once again. I must tell you she remains seriously ill." "Thank you," Kernow replied.

Walking over to her bed he saw Jeanne sitting up and then turning her head towards him as he neared. As he sat down she smiled at him but didn't say a word.

Now he could see her more closely he could not help notice her deathly gaunt appearance which made Kernow sad and lost for words. Taking a deep breath and getting his pencil and notebook ready he looked directly at her and in a calm and precise manner asked, "Jeanne, thank God you are alive, where is the antidote?" Without emotion of any kind Jeanne replied, "There isn't one." George thought she had misheard him so asked again. "Sorry Jeanne, I missed that, where is the antidote?"

Jeanne looked at him in amusement. She had never done this before but time, deadly experiences and lost loves, had shown her what is important in a person's life. So playing Kernow's games as she had done in the past was not part of her anymore. She would tell him the truth but she was finished, done.

It was then that her mind tracked itself back to the first days of her imprisonment in the wet, cold dank cell of the

French Count. Feeling absolutely terrified and abandoned she then remembered how she had whispered aloud, "O Zelahnor of the Cornish, please save me?" She then started to giggle aloud at the thought but then stopped and turned her full attention back to Kernow.

"Mr Kernow, I tell you the truth, the alchemist I befriended was also the person who saved my life in the dungeon. If it wasn't for him I would not be here. He confided in me as he hated Philip de Albret and what he stood for. The virus or germ he devised was too virulent and aggressive for the supposed antidote to work. Every time he tried to calm the germ down it then took too long to kill, in the time frame Philip Albret required. The germ also became volatile with combustible tendencies. More importantly, he wanted it to stay in the blood stream but for the life of him, he couldn't work out why it kept seeping up into the wind pipe and lungs. This I tell you is the truth from the alchemist's own lips". Kernow was dumbstruck and couldn't quite believe what he had just heard. All his actions, experience and dedication have come to nothing. He looked at Jeanne in stunned silence taking in what she had just said. Also, the way she said it needed no response. Nothing could be gained from more questioning. Jeanne was looking directly at him without a trace of emotion. It was then the Medical Officer came over and touched him on the shoulder.

Kernow then knew he had somehow misjudged something or someone along the line but realised his time was up. He got up, touched Jeanne on the hand and left the room. The Officer and his young team immediately got to work.

Jacques was in Zoe's cabin finding out her intentions now that things were completed as promised. She had taken the Bouchier death badly as it were an act of treason.

Jacques did not see it that way and tried to reason with her that it was a matter of life or their death and he and others would have done the same. He also said that Bouchier had no right to bully or coerce her into a lifetime of imprisonment especially when she hated him and loved another. "Zoe, please do not feel this way. It was your bravery that saved me and the others. We owe you immense gratitude for our lives ahead and I for one am proud of you." "Thank you Jacques, that means a lot to me. Maybe given a little time I will come to see things your way." "You will Zoe and if you need help no matter where or when I will be there for you." With that, they hugged each other warmly.

On releasing each other from the hug Zoe stood back and asked with sincerity, "how is the love of your life?" "The doctor on board is extremely worried for her, as am I. He has put her to sleep to rest the body and mind and with good medical attention he is hopeful she will pull together and get better." "I am pleased for you both Jacques." "And what of your future Zoe, what do you wish." "I wish to go home away from this life of deceit and be with my young true love and live together happily." "Then so be it Zoe, I will ask Trevenan and am sure it will be done." They hugged each other again and then Jacques left to visit the two young men. Zoe laid herself down on her bed and felt much better talking with Jacques whom she well trusted.

"So what do you want?" Kernow asked both men. Joshua went first and said, "Now that the mission is finished he would like to go back home to his cottage at Gunwalloe to rest up and visit Rebecca." Jacques went next explaining the wishes of Zoe and the two young French men. "That's fine Jacques, but what of you?" "I wish as promised when we first met to be with Jeanne and I believe that to be her wishes also." They waited in patient silence for Kernow to respond to their requests but before he did this he took a drink of his brandy and scanned his mind over the mission and the objectives he had set versus the overall outcome. Yes, he had successfully saved Jeanne. He had also found the sleepers, stopped massive civilian casualties and they have the barrels of the chemical germ. What he didn't have was the categorical proof that Philip de Albret was dead. Yes, this was disappointing but you can't have it all. He also didn't have the antidote. However, he reasoned the alchemists in London will have to work a little harder and find it through reverse engineering. He smiled inwardly and chuckled aloud. Joshua and Jacques saw him laugh at himself and looked at each other in bewilderment. Kernow then stopped and looked at them both and in a serious tone said, "Agreed on all counts."

Earlier that morning at about seven thirty in the Chateau at Morlaix the young girl felt Philip de Albret stirring awake. She quickly got out of the bed and ran around to the bottom end, knelt down and started gently massaging his feet.

He liked this to be done every time he awakens. If she did not, he would soundly thrash her and the bruises from last night were a reminder of how powerful he was. Her

Mother and Father were poor and the little money he gave her allowed them to buy minimal food to live. She took what he dished out and said nothing back but 'thank you,' as he liked her to say.

She thought and prayed that one day if given the chance and knowing where Philip Albret kept his money, she would take it and run away with her Mother and Father far away, never to be seen again and live a better life.

Then out of the blue, she felt the pain as he kicked her in the head and she went flying backwards on her bottom. "It is a beautiful morning" he shouted. "Go fetch me a fresh glass of my best wine and be quick about it wench, I have a little headache." She got up immediately knowing what he was like if she didn't do things he wanted. He then said, "Stop, before you get the wine go over to the cabinet and open the large jewellery box." This she did and when the box was opened he said, "what is in there?" "A crown my Prince." "You are right, now fetch it here then get the wine, quickly now."

As he held the crown he smiled and said to himself, 'now I will be a Prince.' He then sat up and gently placed the crown on his head acting like a king being coroneted. After filling the large glass full of fresh red wine the young girl hurried back into the bedroom and on handing the glass to Albret was told to kneel and bow her head.

With wine in one hand and a steadying of the crown with the other hand, he loftily shouted aloud, "to the new Prince of France." He then drank the whole glass of wine down in one go. With total arrogance, he then threw the empty glass across the room and ordered the young pauper girl to kiss his feet and get back into bed. Again, she did as was told.

With his crown still on his head and the young terrified girl lying beside him, Philip de Albret started to cough.

The End

Appreciation & Dedication

My sincere thanks to Roger Bolton for his knowledge and guidance, and love to my Mum & Dad